HIDE OR SEEK

THE SUPERPOWER PROTECTION PROGRAM

DAN DIDIO

WITH ANTHONY MARANVILLE AND CHRIS SILVESTRI

A PERMUTED PRESS BOOK
ISBN: 978-1-63758-701-0
ISBN (eBook): 978-1-63758-702-7

Hide or Seek:
The Superpower Protection Program

This book is a work of fiction. People, places, events, and situations are the product of the author's imagination. Any resemblance to actual persons, living or dead, or historical events, is purely coincidental.

Permuted Press, LLC
New York • Nashville
permutedpress.com

Published in the United States of America
1 2 3 4 5 6 7 8 9 10

HIDE OR SEEK

THE SUPERPOWER PROTECTION PROGRAM

DAN DIDIO

WITH ANTHONY MARANVILLE AND CHRIS SILVESTRI

A PERMUTED PRESS BOOK
ISBN: 978-1-63758-701-0
ISBN (eBook): 978-1-63758-702-7

Hide or Seek:
The Superpower Protection Program

This book is a work of fiction. People, places, events, and situations are the product of the author's imagination. Any resemblance to actual persons, living or dead, or historical events, is purely coincidental.

Permuted Press, LLC
New York • Nashville
permutedpress.com

Published in the United States of America
1 2 3 4 5 6 7 8 9 10

To my wife Leilani, who never stopped believing.

PROLOGUE

Paul Pappas wiped the sweat off his brow, evidence of the gut-turning carnival ride he was experiencing as a passenger in his own vehicle, "Ease up on the gas, kiddo. This isn't a racetrack."

Behind the wheel sat his tense son, sixteen-year-old Nick Pappas. He was a slightly smaller yet spitting image of his father, right down to the deep black, wavy hair and muscular build—but they were nothing alike. Paul was a stickler for the rules and aggressive in his seriousness toward every task, big or small (he once had the neighbor kid's parents' background checked before agreeing to a playdate). On the other hand, Nick had adopted a more relaxed approach to life, only tensing up around his old man.

Nick eased his foot off the gas, barking back at his father, "That's not how they taught me in driver's ed! I know what I'm doing!"

Paul sighed, remembering how tough it was being a teenager. He let it go and took a breath, searching for a measured tone, "I'm on your side, buddy. I'm here for support—"

"I don't want your support. Just let me drive."

"Stop the car."

The family's Chevy Tahoe screeched to a halt, jerking them both forward.

Nick knew he messed up. His dad had little tolerance for angry outbursts, ironic since that was precisely what he was known for. Nick also knew whiplash wasn't going to help his cause. He wondered if he lost his shot at driving again anytime soon. There had been an undercurrent of tension all day, but now it was palpable. Nick and his dad sat in silence. Nick fidgeted his fingers on the wheel, knowing he had gone too far.

He waited for his dad's lecture, watching the heat waves rise off the asphalt in the pristine, recently paved parking lot. It was mid-August, and the Brookfield High parking lot was empty of all cars, which, according to his dad, made it the perfect place to learn how to drive.

They had been at this for a while, hours maybe. Just the two of them, practicing a string of endless hand-over-hand turns. All the time, Nick was dreaming that one of these parking spaces would soon be his in the upcoming school year.

His driver's test was two weeks away, and all he knew was he had to pass. The last thing he wanted was to end up like Thom Riley, the kid who had to walk to school his entire junior year and lost his girlfriend in the process.

Nick didn't want to live that fate. Instead, he saw driving himself to school as the first step toward independence. It wasn't that his life completely sucked as it was—he was still doing better than Thom Riley—but with an overprotective mom and a hypercritical dad who was gone on business most of the year, it made him long for a place in the world to call his own. Some way, he would escape and finally feel some true freedom.

Lost in thought, Nick now realized they'd been sitting there for a long time. He looked over and clocked his dad on his phone, not paying attention. The only sound came from the radio, which Nick forgot was left on. Finally, annoyed, he let out, "I wish Mom was here."

The words left his lips before he could catch himself. His father was in sales, a job that required a great deal of travel. The products he sold and the cities he visited were a mystery to Nick. For all he knew, his dad sold shower curtain rings and had a second family in Secaucus. In short, Paul was rarely around, and Nick wondered why he picked today to show up—a root canal would have been better than this driving lesson.

Nick spent most of his time with his mother, so when he'd finally got his learner's permit, he just assumed she would be the one to take him out for a test drive. Like she had taken him to his first day of T-ball, or Tae Kwon Do classes, it was usually just the two of them, and Nick, for one, had gotten used to that dynamic. But Mom being Mom, she'd decided to step aside so her two "boys" could have some quality time together.

Paul knew all of this, of course. He looked away, knowing he had earned some of his son's ire at this moment. "I'm afraid you're stuck with me, buddy."

Nick felt the guilt sinking in. "I'm sorry . . . It's just that I've been practicing for months and Mom . . . ."

Paul's hand went up, cutting his son short. "Stop. Just hold it."

Nick sank, thinking his father was dismissing him, but then he realized he was focused on something else entirely—the car radio.

Until this moment, the radio was just providing background noise to the drama playing out. But now, it rang with a breaking news report. Nick and his family lived in a world filled with real-life superheroes and villains. They were rarely seen, but it was a significant news event when they were. Now was one of those times. And Paul Pappas was engrossed in the story on the airwaves.

Taking a cue from his dad, Nick tried to follow along with the newscaster's panicked and rushed report: *"The local police held their own against a band of Enhanced thugs that wreaked havoc in the city's financial district. But, since Odysseus's disappearance, the responsibility to stop events like this has fallen on the local authorities . . . ."*

"More EH sightings?" asked Nick.

Paul cranked the knob, nearly maxing out the volume.

Nick couldn't help but think of his best friend, Dante, who idolized the lifestyles of these so-called "Enhanced Humans," much like how his mother fawned over aging rock stars from New Jersey. For centuries they had roamed Earth in the shadows, operating on the fringes of society. Some reported having extrasensory powers, and others were said to possess heightened strength and intelligence. But it was getting hard to separate fact from fiction. As the years went by, sighting one of these individuals in the wild had become an increasingly rare event—so much so that when they were in the news, it was a big deal, and it was usually for some high-profile robbery or cataclysmic event.

Perhaps the most famous EH in the world was Odysseus. Depending on who you believed, he had the strength of an army and the ability to absorb and direct pure energy, or he had a genius-level intellect and could freeze an object with his touch. Either way, he spent his time helping the authorities fight crime and other powerful EHs who used their gifts for evil—or, at least, he used to. Unfortunately, nobody had seen him in over a month.

Dante took Odysseus's disappearance hard. "He's either dead or retired," Dante theorized, "Either way, without him . . . we're all screwed."

Most of New York and parts of the United States agreed with Nick's friend; the loss of Odysseus had left a deep void. He had been mysterious and aloof, but he also dominated the land and skies as the most powerful EH ever known . . . and for decades, he'd made the world a much safer place. Now, with him gone, everything felt just a bit less certain, especially with the wave of Enhanced criminals that had been returning to the city. Nick rarely paid much attention to EH activities and cared even less. That's why he was a little surprised his father now seemed to give so much of his concentration on the news report.

He'd never seemed to show any EH interest before.

As the newscaster continued to drone on, Nick watched his father, waiting for the other shoe to drop and for his temper to reveal itself, but it never did.

With a flick of the radio knob, silence dropped back into the car's cab, and Paul stared off into the middle distance. Then, after a long while, he turned to his son and smiled. A true smile. A loving smile. Whatever demons he was wrestling with had been put aside.

"Let's get something to eat."

Relieved, Nick unbuckled his seatbelt and reached for the door to change seats with his dad, but before he could exit the car, his father stopped him and said, "You drive. I'll pay. Sound good?"

Nick brightened at that, his first easy breath of the day. Those simple words had more emotional impact than a two-hour Hallmark movie or a heartstring-pulling credit card commercial. Nick beamed as he shifted his car into drive.

This was the first time he felt his father saw him as an adult. Little did he know any vestiges of childhood were about to die, along with his father, in less than two weeks.

CHAPTER 1

Nick pressed the barrel in between his eyebrows and squeezed the trigger. A display in the handle lit up with a green ninety-nine. He sighed and let the thermometer gun fall to the floor.

Being sick was the one time he liked having his dad around. The old man possessed a comprehensive knowledge of home remedies, passed down from generations—he claimed he could cure virtually any ailment. They'd all be billionaires if he could ever be bothered to write it down. But, once again, his dad was traveling for business. He'd missed their final parking lot driver's lesson nearly a week ago and wasn't even bothered enough to apologize by text.

"What's the verdict, Snotrocket?" yelled a muffled voice.

Lost in self-diagnosis, Nick completely forgot he was on the phone. Kicking off his sheets, he frisked his bed, searching for the device that had somehow ended up inside his pillowcase. He turned his camera on to mime an obscene gesture, but Dante wasn't looking. He never was. All that was visible was the back of Dante's big head covered in a battered Mets ballcap. And his stupid pet cockatoo, Steve, who he let perch on his shoulder. Steve stared into the camera at Nick, side-eyed, making him certain humans weren't the only self-aware beings on the planet.

Since the fifth grade, Dante and Nick had been inseparable. When they weren't together in person, they kept an open FaceTime going, even when there wasn't much to say.

Dante yelled louder, "Yo, Nick! You there? Is the fever gone or what?"

"You don't need to shout," said Nick. "The mic picks up everything."

Nick had spent the past three days in bed, and it looked like today would make it four. While ninety-nine degrees was a mild fever at best, his driver's test was tomorrow morning, and he wanted to be well-rested.

"Oh, heck no. I'm gonna smoke these fools!!" shouted Dante.

Pops of gunfire and screeching tires followed. Steve, the cockatoo, screamed. Nick was well aware of Dante's short attention span and incessant need to multitask. During their calls, he was known to juggle several devices, constantly interrupting Nick to reference a viral video or generic piece of trivia he'd stumbled across. Today it was video games.

Nick rolled out of bed to inspect his art wall. After the remodel, his parents had given him one wall in his bedroom behind his dresser (not visible from the hall) to hang whatever he wanted. With Dante's help, Nick had slowly curated what he considered the perfect collage of photos from friends and family, capturing every memorable moment of his life. There weren't many pictures with his father but those he had were placed front and center. There weren't many pictures with his mother either, but that's because she was usually the one with the camera and had no desire for selfies. There were also articles of school awards and New York Mets memorabilia, but something seemed off to Nick. It didn't take long to identify the problem: Someone had placed his old teddy bear on the dresser in front of his masterpiece. It was messing up the whole aesthetic.

"What in the freak . . .? Dude, you gotta see this!"

"I'm not playing your *Thug Run* game, Dante."

"No. Dude, get on your social. This is bad . . . ."

Nick swiped open his feed and felt the blood quickly drain from his face. Images of a massive fireball swallowing a Midtown office tower took over his timeline—the explosion shattered windows as far down as Chelsea and as far up as 85th Street. Soot and debris had blacked out the sun. Not since 9/11 had the city seen carnage at this scale.

"What am I looking at? Is this for real?"

For the first time in their relationship, Dante hung up first, leaving Nick alone with his thoughts on the horror show on his phone. Then, a piercing scream cut through the stillness, jumpstarting Nick's adrenaline. It was coming from downstairs.

"MOM!"

Nick took the steps, two at a time, racing to the living room, where he found his mother on her knees in tears, her outstretched hand pressed against the TV. The images were pixilated where her wedding ring touched the screen.

"Mom, are you okay?"

But she was too distraught to answer. On the screen, a distraught newsreader was clearly in shock, updating viewers, *"We have just gotten word that beloved EH soldier, known only to the public as Odysseus, has been killed in this horrific attack. Details are still coming in, but authorities advise people to avoid the city center . . . ."*

Nick reached out his hand to help his mother, confused by her grief. Nobody who knew Constance would ever accuse her of being the emotional type. She was known for being level-headed and in control—she once stopped a gas station robbery by calmly shaming the assailant for scaring people. And while the events unfolding in Midtown were tragic, it was hardly like her to get caught up in moments like this.

"C'mon, Mom, you're freaking me out. Get up."

Just then, her phone chimed with a text. A glance at her screen changed her mood as if flipping a switch. Then, with steely determination, she got to her feet and grabbed Nick by his shoulders, locking eyes with him. In a tone that chilled him to his core, she told him, "Get whatever you can carry. We must be out of this house in the next sixty seconds."

Nick froze with confusion, a white-hot panic rising from within. It was as if he was suddenly watching himself from outside his body. His mom wasted no time; charging to the front closet, she tore the winter coats off the rack and tossed them to the floor to access two pre-packed suitcases. She screamed at Nick, "Move your ass! Now!"

Her unusually crass prompt slammed Nick back into his body, and he bolted to his room, looking for things to grab. He picked up his phone and smartwatch and headed toward his dresser at the base of his art-wall shrine. His attention was drawn to an old photo of Odysseus. Dante must've put it there because Nick didn't remember seeing it before. The iconic superhuman hero lifted a tank over his head in the middle of a riot.

"Thirty seconds, Nick! Hurry!" yelled his mom from downstairs.

Nick opened his dresser drawers with such force that it sent his teddy bear flying across the room. He stared at his clothes, overwhelmed with choices. How many days should he pack for? Where were they going? What the hell was happening right now?!

"Fifteen seconds! Where are you? We gotta go!"

Waves of panic washed over him. No time to decide. He slammed the drawers shut and grabbed his teddy bear off the floor, but instead of putting it back on the dresser, he held onto it. As he stood there for a moment, hazy memories clipped through his mind: He was five years old, with his parents at a traveling fair. Mom and Dad were happier then, more affectionate. His dad won the bear, shooting water into a clown's mouth—or maybe it was throwing rings onto bottles. It was a long time ago. He recalled getting food poisoning from the cotton candy that night. The rest of it was all blurry.

Constance grabbed Nick's arm, pulling him out of his reverie and forcibly escorting him out of his room. "We have to go. Where's your bag?"

Nick held up his teddy, causing her to raise an eyebrow, "That's all you're taking?"

Nick shrugged. Constance just offered back a sad smile to her son.

Downstairs, Nick braced himself for something big to happen as his mom checked her watch, and he wasn't disappointed. Right at sixty seconds, the front door exploded open and half a dozen soldiers, clad in all-black tactical gear, burst into the house. Nick and his mother were swarmed with red dots from laser-guided weapons.

Two soldiers stayed with them while the others stormed the house, tossing furniture and poking potential hiding spots. They met up with another group of soldiers descending the stairs, who had apparently entered from the roof—close to a dozen in all.

There was one man among the soldiers who truly stood out. He wore a three-piece suit and had a well-groomed salt-and-pepper beard that matched his slicked hair. He walked over to Nick and his mom with a silver-tipped cane that clicked along the floor.

Constance gave him a knowing look and uttered only two words: "We're ready."

The man allowed a gentle smile and slight nod. "Very good."

The man gestured for the soldiers to lower their weapons, turned, and walked out at pace. The soldiers followed, exiting almost as fast as they entered. Constance tried to reassure her son with a squeeze of his shoulder. "It's okay. Follow them."

A blacked-out SUV waited for them in the driveway, one of eight surrounding the house. Each was decked out in armor plating, bulletproof windows, and run-flat tires. Neighbors stopped and watched as the soldiers ushered Nick and his mom into the SUV. The door slammed shut behind them as Nick just looked at them with confusion.

The man with the silver-tipped cane—who Nick would come to think of as "Mr. Handler"—got into the back of another SUV and motioned it was time to go as he shut his door.

As his SUV raced off like it was the start of the Grand Prix, the other SUVs followed suit. The entire deployment from door to door took no more than thirty seconds. The normally busy suburban street was wide open, thanks to the convoy blocking off traffic at intersections ahead of them. Everything about this was precise and efficient.

Nick stared out the window of the speeding SUV, gripping his teddy bear tight as he looked back at his house one last time. He wondered if he would ever see it again.

Then, suddenly—an energy bolt dropped from the sky and vaporized the only home he had ever known in a massive blast.

Question answered, no more house to see.

CHAPTER 2

The vehicle tremored as its tires howled across turnpike rumble strips. They were doing close to ninety in the emergency lane near the Palisades in a joy ride from hell. Nick held his phone to his ear, desperately trying to reach his dad. His mom hadn't said two words since they left the house, too busy firing off a steady stream of emails and texts to what seemed like her entire address book, and he needed answers.

"You've reached Paul. Please leave a message."

"Dad, where are you? It's an emergency—!"

An ominous tone assaulted Nick's ear. The call had been dropped.

"Damn it!"

Since the explosion in Midtown, cell networks had been flooded with people trying to reach loved ones. This was only the second time Nick had gotten through to his father in twenty tries, but that only fueled his determination. He immediately hit redial.

Traffic had been thick getting out of the city, but it wasn't gridlocked yet. They managed to get ahead of the masses who would inevitably try to flee with their families for fear of another attack. It helped that they were being escorted by an armored SUV battalion, who made it their business to clear a path.

Hidden emergency lights pulsated from their grills, and ear-piercing sirens pushed commuters out of the way. Even though the SUVs looked official, they lacked identification. There were no agency logos, no official seal, and there wasn't even an exempt plate among the lot. Nick wasn't sure if they were part of an official government agency, private security, or something more sinister.

Every so often, a clearing in the bluff offered a straight shot of the entire Manhattan skyline—premium seats to the carnage unfolding. Helicopters swarmed around an impossibly tall high-rise. It was being swallowed whole by insatiable flames that bled a toxic plume of smoke into the stratosphere. From this vantage, Nick thought that Manhattan resembled an old ocean liner with billowing smokestacks.

Another sharp tone rattled his eardrum. Another dropped call. Another round of frustration. Nick slammed his phone into the seat. He felt the sting of his tear ducts swelling, the body's natural antidote to stress, but he steeled himself.

His mother took his hand and grasped it tightly, "Breathe, honey."

"Who are you texting?"

Constance worked for a nonprofit that helped find and vet candidates for leadership positions in other nonprofits. This role gave her access to every important social event New York had to offer, from the Met Gala to the Central Park Conservancy Luncheon.

Every time Nick tried to talk to her, she silenced him with platitudes and yoga slogans. *How could she prioritize work at a moment like this?* he thought; aside from his dad, *Who could she possibly need to talk to right now?*

He pleaded with his mother, "What is going on!? Our house was blown up, and the city was under attack. I can't get ahold of dad—"

"I know—"

"And you won't say anything. You're just on your phone." Nick gestured to the SUVs in the convoy. "Who are these people? Where are they taking us?"

Constance squeezed his hand even tighter. "I know this isn't easy. But, as soon as I have answers, I promise you'll be the first to know."

"Answers to what?" he asked.

But it was a pointless question. Even if Constance wasn't buried in her phone again, he knew she wouldn't give him a satisfactory response. Despite his age, she treated him like a little kid, always sugarcoating everything—but he was nearly a man.

Nick eyed the soldier behind the wheel stealing glances at him and his mom, apparently expecting to be shot, stabbed, or burned with all the body armor he had on. Not to mention the two inches of level four bullet-resistant acrylic glass separating the front from the rear of the cab. Nick also noticed oxygen tanks along the baseboards of the interior, so that the cabin was sealed off from the outside world.

If his mother wouldn't answer his questions, he'd figure it out on his own. Like every teenager with a pulse, Nick turned to the internet for information. He went to his favorite aggregate site that showed trending headlines from the most popular news outlets worldwide, but the data network was jammed, and nothing loaded.

His jaw clenched with frustration as he tried to focus—there had to be a way to find out what was happening. Then, it occurred to him that his mother was somehow getting a signal. In the past, whenever he tried to join her hotspot, he had been met with opposition; it throttled her signal, she said, so he figured now he didn't stand a chance.

He'd have to improvise.

He went into his network settings, and when he asked to join his mother's network, he grabbed his mom and yelled, "Look!"

Constance jerked her head up, "What happened?"

Nick shook his head and said, "Nothing. Sorry, I thought I saw something outside . . . ."

In that split second of distraction, his hotspot request had popped up on his mom's phone, and he touched her screen to grant himself permission. She was none the wiser.

"Please don't scream, Nick. I'm dealing with a lot," his mother said, back to scrolling.

Nick apologized as he watched his newsfeed load, proud of his low-rent con. Headlines began populating his screen, each one exclaiming a version of the same thing: The beloved hero Odysseus's true identity had finally been revealed.

It was Queens native . . . Paul Pappas.

Nick stared at the screen in disbelief. He must've reread each headline five times—they had to be referring to a different Paul Pappas. There's no way his dad, the anal-retentive traveling salesman, was the world-famous Odysseus. The Enhanced Human who had taken on entire armies and saved countless lives. Nick would've noticed that, *right?*

He clicked on a link that directed him to a side-by-side comparison of Odysseus and Paul Pappas that had been independently verified by the Pentagon and the Bellagio Casino's proprietary facial recognition software. There were no two ways about it, Paul and Odysseus were the same person. It appeared the entire world learned that the planet's most powerful superhero, Odysseus, was Nick's father before Nick did.

In movies, people cry and scream upon learning their parent died, but no tears or rage took hold of Nick. He held up his phone to his mother, his hands trembling so badly he could barely hold onto it. Her calm façade immediately melted beneath a flood of tears. She pulled her son close to her. "I'm so sorry. I didn't want you to find out like this. I was trying to get confirmation . . . ."

Inside Nick, a flicker of hope burst into a bright flame. "So it might not be true? He might be alive?"

She pulled Nick in tighter. "I'm so sorry."

At that moment, he understood he'd never see his dad again. He felt his mother's tears on his cheek and thought it odd how other people's tears feel cold to the touch but warm when they fall from your own eyes. Gone was the tiger mom protecting her cub. What was left was a woman grieving the loss of her husband, packed into a speeding SUV going God-knows-where, scared out of her mind.

"Did you know he was Odysseus?" Nick asked.

Before she could answer, the SUV rapidly decelerated and turned into the chain-link and barbwire back entrance of an executive airstrip. They parked in front of an eggshell white Gulfstream Six with no call signs.

Constance wiped her eyes and smoothed her blouse as their driver opened her door. As she exited the vehicle, she told Nick, "Don't say anything about your father to anybody on that plane. Do you understand me?"

Nick's brain hurt trying to process his new paradigm. In under an hour, everything he knew about his life had been redefined, and now he was being asked by his mother to lie about his dead father—who was apparently a superhero—to a bunch of mercenary soldiers on a private plane, on his way to places unknown.

"I'm not getting on that plane," said Nick.

With a calm resignation his mother said, "We don't have a choice."

Nick watched his mom move toward the boarding stairs. At the top, at the entrance, was Mr. Handler. He raised his silver-tipped cane in welcome. Constance handed him her phone when she got to his level. The whole exchange churned Nick's stomach.

Maybe it was self-preservation kicking in, habit, or both, but Nick felt an overwhelming need to text Dante.

His thumbs moved fast, *"I think I'm being kidnapped. I'm at an airport somewhere in Jersey. This is not a joke."*

As he went to press send, a gloved hand reached over and snatched his phone.

"You need help with your teddy bear, Mr. Pappas?" asked a polished voice with a slight British accent. Nick looked up to see Mr. Handler standing over him, flanked by two soldiers with machine guns at the ready.

Mr. Handler allowed a gentle smile to bend his lips and said, "I'll show you to your seat."

CHAPTER 3

The hydraulic whir of landing gear deploying jostled Nick awake. He felt the blood in his head squeeze through constricted veins as he moved his tongue around the sand dunes of his mouth. He hadn't remembered falling asleep or even being tired, but now he struggled to raise an eyelid.

Somewhere in the cabin, a man and a woman were arguing in hushed tones. Nick strained to make out the conversation as he wiped the grogginess from his eyes.

"This is the protocol, Constance—"

"I'm just trying to wrap my head around it."

As Nick's world came into view, he saw his mom talking to Mr. Handler under the wet glare of the cabin lights. The sky was black now; when they'd left Jersey, it wasn't even noon. How long had he been out?

The argument ended when Constance noticed Nick's eyes were open. "Hi, honey. Did you get some rest?"

Mr. Handler cast a side-eyed glance at Nick as he returned to his seat for landing. Nick rubbed his face, trying to clear the cobwebs. His voice cracked as he asked, "Can I have some water, please?"

Nick had no experience with drugs or alcohol, other than his grandfather giving him a few sips of whiskey at his Aunt Nancy's wedding last year, but he imagined this is what it might feel like to be hungover. He tried to retrace his steps after he'd boarded the plane. He took his seat, drank some orange juice, and then . . . nothing.

His mother handed him a bottle of water, and he chugged it while trying to get his bearings.

He got little insight staring into the abyss outside his window and decided to change his approach.

"Where are we?"

"We're going someplace safe," his mother assured him.

His hand stuck to the armrest when he put his water down in his cupholder. He leaned in closer and discovered the unmistakable pulpy remnants of spilled orange juice. His mind reeled as he let himself entertain the impossible: Maybe, just maybe, he had been drugged, and maybe his mom had been the one to drug him.

Sensing his wayward thinking, his mom sat across from him and pushed the hair from his face. "How are you feeling?"

At that moment, his conspiracy theories vanished, and the pain of reality came rushing back—that sickening realization that accompanies waking up the day after losing a loved one when you remember they're dead.

"I had a dream about Dad," he said as his voice broke with emotion. "I had to tell him . . . that he was gone."

Nick's expression grew heavy with the thought that from this day forward, he would have to face the world without his dad. His stomach churned as he and his mom shared a look of grief. "Better get buckled and sit up. We're landing . . . ."

Nick's eyes were glued to the window as the plane touched down, but the entire descent was a black void. Upon landing on the tarmac, there were no lights. No buildings. No people. Just a lone Town Car waiting for them.

Soldiers opened the door as the boarding stairs lowered. Mr. Handler nodded to Constance as Nick stepped out of the plane toward the car. Nick had a million questions but lacked the energy to ask. His knees wobbled as his mom helped him to a stand. Not caring about the fact that he was too old for it, he grabbed his teddy bear and headed to the exit with the sense that he had entered an eerie new existence.

✖

The Town Car glided along a rural highway. Its glossy black finish stood out against the moonlit backroads they traveled. Wherever they were, Nick had never experienced terrain like this before. Even though it was dark, he could make out jags of mountain crest and tangled forest shadows. It reminded him of an angry German Expressionist version of the Bitterroot Mountains in Montana. They had been planning a family vacation last summer to Yellowstone, but it all fell apart after something came up with Paul's work. Now, that trip would never happen.

As they rounded a bend, the landscape began to sparkle. A constellation of halogen balloon lights floating over the road ahead bounced off the mica in the mountain rock, making it look like a disco ball.

It was the first sign of any other humans since they'd departed the plane.

And as the car slowed, Nick could see a clutch of people under the light balloons—soldiers standing sentry at a guard gate blocking access to a private road. Like the soldiers that escorted them, these people also lacked insignia and identification.

Mr. Handler got out and spoke to the soldier in charge, flashing some sort of credentials that changed the woman's posture. The soldier looked over to the Town Car, shining her flashlight on Nick and his mom. Constance assured her son, "It's okay, honey. They're not going to hurt us."

The soldier nodded to some unseen figure in the dark, and the heavy gate rattled open.

Mr. Handler walked back to the Town Car with a smug grin and got back into the seat, "Shouldn't be much longer."

On the other side of the gate, the road turned into gravel. Even the Town Car, with its superior shock system and emphasis on passenger comfort, had difficulty negotiating this backwater outpost's potholes and dirt moguls. Prone to motion sickness, Nick opened his window in an effort to avoid vomiting. As the crisp mountain air kissed his skin, a flash of light streaked across the forest. It happened so fast; Nick wasn't sure he actually even saw it. It was like a shooting star *inside* the woods.

He was prepared to dismiss the whole incident as a trick of the mind until he saw it again—a strange shimmer, like the kaleidoscopic tail of a comet, dancing alongside them in the forest. It was unlike anything Nick had seen before.

He grabbed his mom's arm. "What the hell is that light!?"

But when she looked, the light was gone. Constance patted Nick's hand in a patronizing maternal pity that pushed all of Nick's buttons. "Try and get some more rest, honey."

"I know what I saw! There was some sort of quicksilver shimmery thing happening—"

"You would be wise not to go out into those woods, Mr. Pappas," Mr. Handler warned.

The cryptic authority his intonation commanded left Nick with an unsettling pit in his stomach, but that seemed to be par for the course with that guy.

The rest of the car ride was silent.

After what seemed like an hour of crunching over loose gravel, the Town Car found a paved road and began winding down the mountain. It wasn't long after that Nick found himself cruising down the main street of a sleepy slice of Americana straight out of *Friday Night Lights.* Constance patted Nick's leg in anticipation. "We're almost there."

The streets of the town were perfectly paved and intentionally laid out. Main Street was lined with Mom & Pop shops that led to an actual town square with a courthouse and high school overlooking it. As they moved through the neighborhoods, the lawns of every house were green and manicured, the sidewalks free of cracks or tree roots pushing them into a gnarled mess.

There was a strange energy to this place that felt both familiar and foreign simultaneously.

As they passed a water tower, they slowed enough to turn into the driveway of a large tract house, the kind of nondescript two-story job you could find in Anywhere, America. Every house on the block had that feeling. At least the yards were big.

As the car's engine stopped, Mr. Handler stepped into the driveway. He took a deep breath of the fresh air and tapped his silver-tipped cane on the ground.

Before he could shut the door, Nick called out, "Can I have my phone back now?"

Mr. Handler just smiled and tapped his cane on the driveway again. "Ah, but you won't find any use for that sort of thing here."

Nick looked to his mom as she was trying to mentally get herself ready to step out of the car, like she was getting ready to stand before the firing squad. "What is this place?"

"Crucible," Constance said.

"Okay, but who's house is this?"

"This is your new home," said Mr. Handler, as he stuck a wrought iron key into the front door.

Nick looked to his mom in disbelief as she motioned for him to follow Mr. Handler inside.

CHAPTER 4

Paul Pappas had been away on business for almost two weeks, and Nick couldn't wait to see him. So he spent the first hour of Ms. Leonard's second-grade class counting hash marks in the clock face as the red hand swept past them. Then, mercifully, his dad surprised him and pulled him out early to go to a ballgame—the Mets had a home game.

They sat over the first base dugout with matching hats and giant foam pointy fingers. Paul encouraged Nick to throw his peanut shells on the ground and agreed to buy him a soda if he didn't tell his mom. Nick sang "Take Me Out to the Ball Game" on top of Paul's shoulders with such enthusiasm he made it onto the Jumbotron. A perfect day at the park.

At the house that night, Paul and Constance danced around to Motown classics while the tangy smoke of BBQ brisket wafted in from the grill. They invited over neighbors and cousins to feast with them, just because.

Before long, the house was filled with laughter and boozy conversation. It used to be like that all the time when Paul was around. He hadn't turned into the uptight salesman yet, suspicious of everything and everyone.

After dinner, Paul led the kids in a game of hide-and-seek. Dante was there, and so was his next-door neighbor, Manolo. Nick loved playing hide-and-seek with his dad.

In the first round, Paul was It. Manolo and Dante made it to home base, but Nick was wearing socks and couldn't make it across the wood floor in time, and his dad tackled him and tickled him until he turned red. He was now the seeker.

Nick was banished to the balcony to count, and the cool autumn air nipped at his skin. It didn't take long for him to find Dante, who always hid in the wardrobe, or Manolo, who was lying underneath the dining room table. Paul wasn't so easy to find. He never was.

Nick looked for his dad in the broom closet, behind the paisley curtains, underneath his bed—but he couldn't find him. This only fueled his determination. He went deeper and checked the garage, the laundry bin, the bathtub, working up a sweat in the process. Dante and Manolo soon lost interest and left to play video games. Nick yelled out to the entire house. "Daddy . . . I give up. Where are you? Daddy?" Fun turning to fear.

The front door creaked open, bringing in a gust of chilled air. Constance entered, wiping tears from her eyes. Nick had been so focused on finding his dad that he hadn't noticed his mom left. He looked at her, worried, "Is Daddy out there?"

Concern and confusion knitted her brow. She crouched to Nick's level and put her hands on his little shoulders. "Honey . . . Daddy went to heaven."

Nick's eyes bolted open.

He was wet with sweat, and his skin was hot—either the heat was cranked up to a hundred, or his fever was back. At that moment, he wasn't sure what was worse, his nightmare remix of old memories or waking up feeling like he was running a marathon inside a sauna.

Shafts of morning light spread across a mass-produced pastoral landscape, the only art in his new bedroom. The muted yellows and greens somehow added to his anxiety.

"The agents are here."

Nick turned to find his mom standing in the doorway. She had changed clothes and showered since he had laid down—however long ago that had been. Once again, he had no sense of how long he had been out and didn't remember falling asleep. He propped himself up, noticing his sheets felt like a used washcloth.

"What agents?" he said, his throat so dry that it hurt to talk.

"Get dressed and come downstairs," said Constance.

Thankfully, Nick had taken off his pants and shirt before crawling into bed and had something dry to slip into. As he stepped into his pants, he felt the blunt edge of his smartwatch in his pocket dig into his thigh. In the chaos of the day, he had forgotten he grabbed it. He immediately swiped it open and tried to call Dante, but there was no signal. He dropped it back into his pocket, taking care to turn it off to conserve battery.

Downstairs Nick was greeted by Mr. Handler, "Good Morning, Mr. Pappas. I apologize for the early call, but we must get you processed. Time is simply not on our side."

"Are we going somewhere?" Nick asked "And can I get some water first? I'm beyond thirsty." Without a thought, Nick turned on the faucet and motioned to drink directly from the sink.

"Manners," said Constance, slightly annoyed, as she gestured to the cupboards. "We have glasses."

"I'm afraid we must go into town for this . . ." said Mr. Handler. "I promise it won't be long."

"In that case . . . ."

Nick turned off the water and grabbed a glass, filling it with ice for the road. As he reached his hand into the freezer, Mr. Handler paced the floor behind him. Nick could feel his green eyes drill into the back of his skull.

"And if you brought a computer or any electronic device, be sure to take it with you."

"How's that your business?" said Nick, defiant.

"Nick!" warned Constance.

"What!? It's a legitimate question—"

"He only had his phone, and you took that . . . ." Constance said to Mr. Handler in an apologetic tone. Then, with resignation, "C'mon, Nick, hurry up, let's go."

Nick's mind immediately went to the smartwatch in his pocket. Mr. Handler took his phone, so it stood to reason that if he found the smartwatch, he would probably take that, too, and then Nick would have zero chance of figuring out what was happening.

He would have to hide it, but how? Especially with this bearded old man staring at him?

He recalled a show he'd watched with Dante on a serial killer who tricked the police by putting his phone in his fridge so it didn't give off a signal while he went out and did his crimes. *So, if it worked for that guy . . . .* Nick thought as he dropped his glass of ice.

The glass exploded when it hit the floor, sending shards spiraling across the kitchen.

He used the distraction to transfer his smartwatch from his pocket to the ice maker.

"I'm sorry, Mom. It slipped. I'll clean it."

Mission accomplished.

✕

The car ride to Main Street was short, less than five minutes. They parked outside a single-story office suite lacking any meaningful characteristic or personality. Mr. Handler led Nick and his mother through a glass door that jingled as they entered.

Official-looking men and women wearing varying shades of gray labored furiously behind monitors and Frankensteined electrical components.

“They’ve been at it all night, trying to get ahead of this thing,” said Mr. Handler.

A woman in a dark blazer handed Nick and Constance a printout while lab technicians stuck SQUID sensors, the kind usually reserved for lab rats, to their heads. While it jarred Nick, his mom didn’t even flinch.

“What is happening?” asked Nick.

“Memorize that page,” said Mr. Handler, ignoring his question.

Nick glanced down at the sheet. The header read: *Theo Alexander*. It was formatted like a police file, with stats and bullet points. Nick ripped the sensors off his head, “I don’t want to do this.”

“Nick! Please stop. They’re helping us,” said Constance.

“I don’t want their help!”

"Think of us as a sort of witness protection program," said Mr. Handler, "for Enhanced Humans . . . and their families."

Mr. Handler walked over to a nearby monitor and swiveled it around so Nick could see. Cold sweat seeped through Nick's pores as he took in multiple windows open on display. It was every social media account he had ever opened. Even the burner accounts he kept hidden from his parents. "Do you recognize these, Mr. Pappas?"

Nick nodded, feeling his stomach turn a bit.

"This computer is now the only place they exist," said Mr. Handler. "We've scrubbed them from the internet. The same will soon be true for every picture you ever posted, every mention of your name—anything at all to do with Nick Pappas. As far as the internet is concerned, you never existed."

Another lab tech, this one a large man wearing a static-cling hazard suit, placed Nick's hand inside a silicone mold connected to wires and reattached the sensors to his head.

This time Nick didn't fight it. His mind was too busy processing the total destruction of his digital life. He hadn't thought about it until that moment, but the internet had become like a second brain, holding memories of his life, pictures of his family, and chats with friends. A record of his interests, a map of places visited, and where he spent his free time playing and building virtual worlds—and just like that, it was all gone.

Mr. Handler nodded, and the lab tech in the bunny suit tapped a button on his tablet computer. Nick's fingertips suddenly felt like they were pricked with a thousand tiny needles all at the same time. A moment later, the tech removed the silicone from his hand and gave him back his paper.

"Ow! What the hell just happened?" asked Nick, examining his hand.

"We altered your fingerprints," said Mr. Handler. He used the silver tip of his cane to point to the paper in his and Constance's hands, "Those are your new identities. You are now Theo Alexander, and that is your mother, Alice. You have an hour to memorize the bios printed on the page before they are destroyed. It is of utmost importance that you never tell anyone your true identity or reveal any details of your past. Understood?"

"What if I do?" challenged Nick.

"There will be consequences for not sticking to the script. I'd say ask your father, but . . . ."

CHAPTER 5

"Theo" and "Alice" (the names would take some getting used to) walked through the crown jewel of Crucible: the disturbingly picturesque Town Square Park. Robins chirped between peals of laughter from grade school kids chasing each other around a perfectly manicured playground.

They had spent the morning being scanned by Mr. Handler and his team of gray-suited minions. Everything from brainwaves and eye movement to the gait of their strides had been recorded and scrutinized by sensitive machines—all while being tasked with memorizing the details of their new given identities.

According to their new bios, Constance—now Alice—was a recent divorcee who had been a stay-at-home mom in Poughkeepsie for the last fifteen years and was now in the process of getting certified to teach. The agency even arranged for her to student teach at the local high school to keep up appearances. Nick—now Theo—was a bit of a loner who preferred books and nature to video games and TikTok.

Their likenesses had been inserted into AI-generated pictures and videos meant to simulate memories that never were. Constance and Nick saw themselves as Alice and Theo in their nonexistent house in Poughkeepsie, where, apparently, they'd had a golden retriever named Riot. Nick watched a deepfake of himself at ten playing with Riot. In the video, he accidentally threw Riot's tennis ball into a pond, and the dog dove snout first into the water and came back up with a frog. Theo thought it was hilarious.

Mr. Handler explained that watching the fake videos would stimulate real memories, thanks to mirror neurons and a cocktail of neurotransmitters activated by microbursts of subtle electromagnetic current being pumped into their brain via the SQUID sensors on their heads. The entire experience was surreal and unsettling, leaving Nick—Theo—exhausted. Constance, now Alice, suggested they walk through town to get their bearings and some ice cream. But what should've been a peaceful walk through a serene Norman Rockwell mountain town was only adding to Theo's unease.

Somehow in the light of day, Crucible had an even more artificial feeling to it. Everyone was smiling and waving as they went about their business—it all felt too perfect.

They left the park and crossed Main Street to get to a string of storefronts decorated with antlers and American flags, one of which was a place called American BullShirt, a clothing store specializing in rugged outdoor wear. The window display featured lots of plaid and pants with too many pockets.

Alice grimaced at Theo's shabby clothes, his sweat-stained and slept-in attire had to go. "We'd better get you some clean clothes."

"Not from here."

"C'mon, Pigpen," Alice said, as she pulled Theo inside the store.

Metal hangers screeched as Alice sorted through every last shirt on the rack. "There's gotta be something here you respond to . . . ."

"Nope."

Theo sat on a nearby bench lined with angled shoe mirrors and watched as the sales clerk went to the back for inventory. They had the store to themselves. Theo held his face in his palms, clearly struggling. "Why didn't you tell me who Dad really was?"

Alice glanced toward the back to make sure the sales clerk wasn't listening to their conversation—she was bobbing along to some fast-paced country music blasting through earbuds. "It was for your own protection," said Alice.

"Lotta good that did."

"It kept you safe."

"My entire life just got erased!"

Alice forcefully hooked a shirt back on the rack. "Keep your voice down."

She plopped down beside Theo with a heavy sigh, searching for words. "As bizarre as it is, this is a good thing. Your father fought for this. An insurance policy for when everything gets screwed to hell. He wanted us here."

"You had no right to lie to me. I deserve to know who my dad is. And who I am."

Alice pulled on a frayed piece of fabric on her sweater, guilt hitting her. "You're right."

That wasn't the response Theo expected. He had been gearing up for a fight. But instead, Alice rested her head on her son's shoulder, reminding him that she was just as raw as he was from the hell of losing her husband and being thrust into this bizarre situation.

"I met your dad the first time I ever visited New York," said Alice. "I was working as a reporter back in Vegas, trying everything I could to break out of the local news market . . . but I kept getting assigned these awful human-interest stories. This time it was the Clark County Stallions march to the glee club finals."

"I hate those stories . . . . They're so dumb and boring," Theo said as he settled in.

"Exactly! So, at the time, a radical organization called The Pantheon was making noise in Times Square, and I had this strong feeling the situation was about to boil over. I called my news director and pitched the idea of covering the story. I was on him relentlessly for better assignments—and finally, he agreed—only if I promised to stop harassing him, and I was right. As soon as I checked into my hotel in Times Square, The Pantheon attacked. With more firepower than most countries, a dozen of the nastiest Enhanced Humans you've ever seen did their best to terrorize the city—and would've succeeded, if it weren't for your father."

Theo closed his eyes, imagining Alice's words. He saw his father, Odysseus, speeding through the sky over Manhattan, dodging missiles as they exploded next to him. At the same time, masked men wearing high-tech jetpacks bombarded him with directed energy strikes.

"Through dumb luck, my cameraman and I had front row seats," Alice continued. "The window of our room on the fifty-fourth floor faced the battle. Our live feed was picked up around the world, even broadcast on a

350-foot screen downstairs, where thousands had gathered to watch."

In his mind's eye, he pictured his mother addressing the camera, microphone in hand, as the aerial combat continued behind her. Odysseus launched one of his pursuers into the side of an adjacent skyscraper, and his jetpack exploded upon impact. The blast wave rattled her window and sent a massive chunk of concrete crashing to the street below.

Despite Odysseus's efforts, The Pantheon was gaining ground. Alice was close enough to see the pained expression on his face and knew he was struggling. Eight more men in jetpacks showed up to avenge their fallen comrade. They surrounded Odysseus, blasting him with energy so concentrated it burned the sky.

Explosions set off building alarms, and security went floor by floor advising people to evacuate, but Alice refused, doubling back after getting her camera operator onto the elevator. When she returned to her room, Odysseus had moved out of her view. Based on the position of the jetpack gang, she surmised he was near the hotel's roof.

She aimed her camera at the street below to show the chaos and destruction the battle in the sky was causing. As she adjusted the focal ring, a white van with open hatch doors instead of a roof came into focus, something most people wouldn't notice, even from street level. The only reason Alice noticed it from six hundred feet up was because of the strange-looking cannon protruding from the opening, aimed at the sky.

A voice on Alice's earpiece crackled; it was her news director yelling at her to get out of the room. Alice ignored him, zooming in on the van as much as the camera could. In the driver's seat was a beautiful Latina woman, talking into a headset. Alice scowled with recognition. "Countess Blood."

Countess Blood was a suspected higher-up in The Pantheon organization and a known terrorist whose hatred of Odysseus was well documented in the public forum. Alice was transfixed. She watched the strange weapon as it tracked Odysseus's every movement across the sky. Countess obviously had a clear shot but wasn't firing. *Why?*

"The Pantheon has the building surrounded!" shouted her news director in her ear. "Odysseus isn't fighting. He's hurt. You have to get out of there!"

That's when it dawned on her: The weapon *was* being fired. It was somehow draining Odysseus of his powers. A heavy explosion shook the building, causing it to sway and knocking Alice over. Debris fell from above. She knew she had to act now. *But how?*

Talking into her earbud, she addressed her news director back in Vegas. “Can you get us back on the national feed?”

Within minutes, Alice was live across the world once again, including on the giant screen downstairs playing to the Times Square crowd. She aimed her camera at the van revealing Countess Blood and her weapon. Everyone saw what she was doing, including Odysseus. He immediately realized this was the source of his power drain and, with every last bit of energy, changed his focus from the jetpacks to the van.

Odysseus tore into the van and weapon. Even in his weakened state, the metal shredded at his touch. With his strength returned, he took out the rest of his frustration on the remaining jetpack gang members, disarming every last one. Somehow, in the confusion of battle, Countess Blood managed to escape.

Before Odysseus retreated into the night, he flew up to Alice’s window, held his hand to the glass against hers, and mouthed, *Thank you.*

“It was all over for me then and there,” said Alice. “I was head over heels for your dad.”

Theo looked off, but not from emotion—he was smarter than she gave him credit for and knew she wasn’t telling him the whole story.

"And you know who my news director was? The same man who brought us here."

"The weird guy with the silver cane?"

"He's been very good to our family."

I don't think so, thought Theo, as he rolled his eyes. *Not by the way he talks about Dad.*

Some years ago, his mom told a similar story about her time as a reporter in Vegas. Curious, he tried to look up some of her old stories, but there was no sign of her work. She claimed it was pre-internet. But he didn't buy it then and wasn't buying it now.

"You must understand that everything we did, all the lies, was to protect you," Alice said, tears forming. "Your father was a hero and constantly at risk. That was his choice, as was putting family first. He wanted to be a part of your life but didn't want you to have any part of his. You saw what happened to him, and I promised never to let it happen to you."

Theo let it all sink in. He wanted more details about his dad, but seeing his mom's pain, he let it go, for now. "How long will we have to be here? In Crucible, I mean."

"It all depends . . . ." said Alice.

"Umm . . . I was gonna close the store for lunch. Are you gonna buy anything?"

They looked up to find the sales clerk, one earbud out, listening for a response.

"We'll take a plaid shirt . . . oh, and some underwear," said Alice.

"Mom!"

CHAPTER 6

Theo bolted awake, out of breath. His dog Riot had attacked him near the pond of his old house in Poughkeepsie, and he couldn't get away. *Wait, that's not right*, he thought, *we never lived in Poughkeepsie. Riot isn't real.*

Theo shook his head, trying to make sense of the fake memories taking root in his mind. Shafts of morning light rimmed the soulless painting on his wall again, and one thing became clear to him: He needed to get the hell out of Crucible as soon as possible.

But to have a chance, he would first need to contact someone back home and find out more information. There would be logistics involved; he needed help.

As much as it pained him to admit it, he no longer trusted his mother. She had lied to him his entire life about his dad being Odysseus and most likely her career as a journalist, *so what was preventing her from lying about other things?*

He needed an outside source, someone independent of his mother—and certainly not Mr. Handler. He needed to find a place to learn more about Odysseus, The Pantheon, and Crucible—if it hadn't been scrubbed off the internet. What he needed was Dante. Nobody on the planet knew more about Enhanced Human culture than that kid, and he was the only person left who Theo trusted.

He glared at the dismal pastoral painting. His mind was made up: He had to find a cell signal or internet access—a connection to the world. He buttoned up his hideous plaid BullShirt shirt and headed downstairs to the freezer to retrieve his smartwatch.

He fished around in the icemaker, deep in thought, when . . . .

"What're you up to?" said Alice.

Theo spun around like he'd just been shocked by a cattle prod in the freezer. He hadn't seen his mom sleeping on the couch and didn't have a lie ready in the hopper.

"Nothing . . ." he said as he palmed his smartwatch. " . . . just gonna go out for a run."

"Did you see the bikes?"

He looked at her as if it was the setup for a joke. Alice pointed. "Out on the side porch."

Theo craned his neck to peek through the picture window, where he could make out the edges of four bikes—each one a different size. They were used, obviously meant for a family with young children. More than once, Theo had wondered about the people who had lived in the house before them. More than once over the last few days, he would get glimpses of who they were—the gummed-up pink sparkle toothpaste in his medicine cabinet, the faint smell of cat pee halfway up the stairs, and now the orphaned row of bicycles.

"We need to put your driver's license on hold. We want to keep low and not draw attention to ourselves."

"Draw attention? How does getting something that every kid my age has draw attention?"

"Just let it be. We don't have a car, and I'm not planning to get one any time soon."

Theo felt a new layer of frustration starting to build; it took everything he had to keep it suppressed. Alice saw that he was trying and kept her cool, too.

"For now, take the bike. You should explore the town. It's the only day you'll have. You start school tomorrow."

"School?!" Theo said, indignant. The thought hadn't occurred to him until this moment and his frustration returned twofold. "You're gonna make me go to school? After everything that's happened?"

"Nick! Argh—I mean—Theo! Please. Classes go year-round here; you need to stay up to date with the class, or you'll fall behind."

"Can't I take a week off? My dad just died—"

"I think it's better for your mental health to be around kids your age. Besides, I'll be working out of the house, dealing with estate stuff . . . ."

"Whatever," said Theo, as he pushed open the front door.

"I love you," called Alice. "Check in with me in a few hours."

"Can't. No phones. No cell service, bye."

He slammed the door as he stomped off. Outside, Theo picked the biggest bike and rode it off the porch, hopping down the stairs with the confidence of a BMX pro.

Fueled by a cocktail of rage, confusion, and hormones, he pedaled toward town as hard as he could. If he were going to find a cell signal, that would be his best bet. As soon as he turned onto Main Street, he took out his smartwatch and waited for bars to appear on the screen. They never came.

He spent the next half hour walking his bike up to every storefront on Main Street, looking for a signal. The coffee shop was his first stop, followed by the bakery, the Fluff and Fold—he even went back to the American BullShirt store. No reception anywhere.

With his watch raised high above his head in a trance, Theo accidentally found himself standing outside the office building Mr. Handler had taken him and his mother to the day before. Fear immediately washed through him; his heart was beating like a jackhammer. The last thing he needed was Mr. Handler seeing him outside his window waving a smartwatch in the air—that would almost certainly qualify as "not sticking to the script."

Theo couldn't see inside the office's windows and wasn't sure if anyone had seen him. He decided the best course of action would be to pocket the watch and ride away as fast as possible. But, before he could implement his plan, bells jingled. The office's glass door flung open, and Theo came face-to-face with an elderly man using a mop to steer a wheeled bucket that sloshed around with soapy, gray water.

"Can I help you?" asked the elderly man, as he wiped his mustache with his sleeve.

Theo's eyes drifted past him into the building, his jaw agape with what he saw.

The entire office was empty.

No monitors, no weird electrical equipment, no workers running around in shades of gray. Everything was gone. Theo tripped over his bike, trying to get a better look.

"You okay, son?" said the elderly man, extending his hand to help Theo steady.

"Where did everybody go . . .?"

"Everybody? Not sure what you mean."

"There were people here yesterday!" said Theo, "with equipment and computers—"

"This building's been empty for years."

Theo stared at the bells on the door, certain it was the same building from the day prior.

"I haven't seen you around here before. Who are your parents? Let me call someone—"

Stranger danger set in, and Theo mounted his bike. "Sorry . . . I was thinking of someplace else. Have a nice day."

Theo could feel the elderly man's stare as he pedaled away. The entire episode left him uneasy. Exhausted, he wheeled to Town Square Park and sat against the massive trunk of a centuries-old ponderosa pine. Sitting beneath the old tree, he could see most of the town. Crucible couldn't have been more than a couple of square miles, nestled in dense, old-growth forest, which was held in a steep mountain valley.

He hadn't noticed before, but on the bike, it was evident that Main Street was pitched at an angle, with Town Square at the very top and the coffee shop anchoring the bottom.

It was the only road in or out of town. Not something you see very often.

Theo's thoughts drifted to the empty office building. *Where did Mr. Handler and his crew go overnight? And why would the janitor lie about it?* Nothing made sense anymore, but Theo was determined to figure it out. He watched as the sleepy Sunday morning crowd strolled into town. They could be summed up into two categories: young families with strollers and designer dogs and blue-haired power walkers stopping for cheap coffee.

Finally, he spotted a kid his own age. She was in a gold sweatsuit, riding a bike with thick tires and a matte-black frame. As she got closer, Theo saw she had a phone to her ear, chatting away. It took him a beat, then he realized—that meant *she had a signal!!*

Theo jumped on his bike and chased after her, hopping the curb to cross the street. Oncoming traffic honked as he cut in front of them. The girl looked back and saw Theo pedaling after her and sped up, casting a sly smile his way as she turned off Main Street. She had striking features: high cheekbones, cinnamon skin, and long, wavy hair peeking out from behind her gold hoodie.

"Excuse me," Theo said as he panted. "Please wait! I just wanna ask you a question!"

The girl banked hard, turning off the pavement into the forest. She used a dirt embankment as a ramp to launch herself over a thicket of bushes, where she landed on a dirt trail and kept peddling. Theo couldn't believe what he had just seen. *What the hell?*

Not one to back down from a challenge, Theo followed her movement, banking hard and going full blast into the dirt ramp. Unfortunately, as soon as his front wheel hit the embankment, his confidence level dropped to zero. He knew his jump wasn't going to end the way hers did, as he came down hard on the oblong edge of a massive boulder jutting into the trail, sending him tumbling over his handlebars and into a grove of barbed bracken.

He lay in the brush, feeling his blood rush to fill the fresh scratches on his skin.

Scared more than hurt, Theo hopped back on his bike and peddled up the mountain trail. Although he was down for less than a minute, it was all the time the girl needed to disappear. Theo kept riding the path up for another few minutes—although it felt more like a half hour to him, once his adrenaline levels from his fall started to subside.

Ready to admit defeat and head back home, he glimpsed the edge of a stone wall just past the tree line. It was covered in moss and vines and looked like it had been there since the beginning of time.

He walked his bike along the wall, following it to a large stone structure. It was a magnificent two-story building about the size of two Dollar Generals stacked together. Intricate geometric patterns were carved into a grand entrance archway—the entire building was crowned in ornate stone grotesques depicting dragon-like demons.

For its age, the building was in impeccable condition. A gentle smoke curled up from its chimney. Theo moved closer enough to peek inside one of the windows, where he saw a row of mahogany shelves filled with books; he couldn't believe it. This was a library?

What luck, he thought to himself. Most libraries have computers available to the public. He could use them to go online and contact Dante.

He wheeled toward the archway entrance, where he was surprised to find a rack full of at least half a dozen other bikes, including one with thick tires and a matte-black frame—the girl in the gold sweats was here! Theo dropped his bike and ran inside.

CHAPTER 7

The unmistakable musty scent of old books greeted Theo like a warm hug as he crossed the threshold of the imposing archway. He took in the ancient-looking building as late afternoon light poured in from an ornate stained-glass oculus, bathing the antique oak tables in the open mezzanine in rich amber tones.

Two-story shelves stuffed with aged volumes clung to every wall, and stacks of worn, leatherbound books took up floor space in every nook and cranny—including the mantle of the grand fireplace, whose mouth was taller than Theo, he noted as he passed.

To his surprise, there were actually young people around his age inside—maybe ten of them. Some were lost in the written word, while others were hunting for the next volume. Most sat around the long wooden tables thumbing their devices while posterboards waited to be decorated. *There must be a project due tomorrow*, Theo thought. Having been a member of *The Last-Minute*

Club for most of his academic career, he could smell his own kind.

He surveyed the faces for the girl in gold sweats but came up empty.

But his attention was soon taken away as he noticed that along the far wall stood a row of wooden cubicles with computers nested inside—exactly what he was hoping for. As he made his way toward the back, he felt both the sting of his road rash and the judgmental gaze of library occupants—he might as well have been on stage under the glare of a spotlight. With every step, he became acutely aware he didn't belong there and began to break out in a sweat as he hurried toward the bank of computers.

He had always heard that in small towns, everyone was up in everyone else's business, but to experience it firsthand with a pack of wild teenagers was panic-inducing. He ducked into an aisle to regroup and instead ran into the girl in gold sweats—literally.

She was leaning over a rolling cart organizing books for return with a set of earbuds in, and Theo knocked into her, causing her to fall face-first onto the parquet.

"I'm so sorry. Are you okay?" Theo said, reaching out to help her up. "I didn't see you."

She swatted his hand away, opting to lay on the floor a little longer with her back to him.

"I guess this means we're even?" Theo said, trying to be flirty.

When she didn't respond, he tried to contextualize his comment, "I was the guy following you on your bike earlier . . . . I biffed it on the jump. Remember?"

"What are you talking about?" growled a throaty baritone.

Theo stared at the ground with his eyebrow raised; her voice was much more masculine than he had anticipated. The girl in gold sweats finally pushed herself to a stand, and when she turned to face Theo, he saw that she was actually a he.

The guy was about Theo's age, only slightly taller with a more muscular build. He rocked a fresh fade and had icy blue eyes that looked backlit from inside his skull.

"I don't have a bike, man," said the boy in gold sweats.

"Right," said Theo, taking in the boy's outfit. He was dead sure it was the same exact sweatsuit the girl on the bike had been wearing, but out of self-preservation and utter embarrassment, he decided to move on. "Well . . . see you," said Theo, rushing past him.

"Just watch where you're going next time," growled the boy in gold sweats.

At the computer cubicle, Theo made himself as small as possible while attempting to sign into his old email accounts. But, just as Mr. Handler said, they no longer existed.

Unwilling to accept he had been completely erased from the internet, he tried typing his old name into a search engine. When no results came back, he tried going to his school account—somehow, somewhere, the agents had to have missed something. But not only did his school account no longer exist, but he had also been erased from his class photo hosted on the school's splash page. They'd completely wiped him from memory.

"You must be new here . . . ." Theo looked up from his screen, unsure where the laidback voice was coming from, or if it was even addressing him.

"Is someone talking to me?" asked Theo, calling into the empty space.

"Uh, over here," said the voice from a neighboring cubicle.

Theo turned to find a gold hoodie sitting two chairs over, face hidden by a thick, wooden privacy divide. He'd know that sweatsuit anywhere.

The voice continued, buried in her screen. "Save yourself some time. You won't get on any social media in this town. It's restricted and near impossible to set up an account."

"They're called privacy divides for a reason . . . . You spying on me?" bristled Theo.

"Always assume everyone is in this town."

"I'm Theo," he said, leaning his chair back to try and steal a peek at the girl.

"Jerry," said the voice.

"How did you get a cell signal?"

"What?"

"I saw you talking on your phone earlier—"

"No, you didn't," said Jerry, scooting back to look Theo in the face.

When their eyes met, Theo could feel his cheeks flush and skin prickle with sweat. Jerry was not the girl he was expecting to see. She had full lips, mocha skin, smokey eyes, and a nose ring that sparkled in the light of her cubicle monitor. Her hair was wound in tight braids streaked with blonde and shaved on one side—*and yet*, she wore the same exact sweatsuit as the boy at the book cart and the girl on the bike.

Jerry registered Theo's distress. "You good?"

"Yeah . . ." Theo stammered, "I just thought you were a girl I saw earlier . . . but you're very clearly not—"

"Let me stop you there. First of all, don't lock me into a genre," said Jerry. "My pronouns are they/them, and I know for a fact you didn't see me earlier because I've never seen you."

"I guess I was confused because of your outfit. I didn't mean anything—"

"My outfit?" said Jerry, growing combative. But rather than engage, Theo's mysterious new friend quickly left the cubicle and disappeared down a book aisle.

Theo stood up to follow.

"Yeah . . . . Are gold sweatsuits a thing here? In Crucible?"

A chorus of voices replied, "Not everyone. Just our thing."

Theo whipped his head toward the voices. Stepping out from another row, one section over, he found the boy from the cart, and the girl from the bike, in their matching gold sweatsuits.

"What the hell?!" Theo said, as he shot up to his feet in a state of shock. His eyes darted across the floor, unsure if he was the only one seeing this.

"Everything okay?" asked Jerry, reemerging from the first aisle.

"Where did they come from?"

"Who?

Theo gestured to where the boy and girl were standing but were no longer there. He searched past a librarian cart and the surrounding area. "You didn't see a boy and a girl wearing the same thing as you just now?"

"I didn't see anyone, and keep your voice down," said Jerry. "This is a library."

Theo rubbed his hands across his face, trying to figure out what was happening. There had to be an explanation—it was just three people wearing the exact same gold sweatsuits, messing with him, right? Or maybe Jerry was right, and he was hallucinating people in sweatsuits. Maybe they were library spirits here for his soul.

"You sure you're good, Theo?" said Jerry. "You look a little pale."

"Who are you? How are you doing this . . .?"

Jerry smiled with a devilish gleam in their eyes. "I don't know what you're talking about."

Simmering anger, festering in Theo's core since his father's death, finally bubbled over. He could feel it burning through his veins. His muscles tightened, and tears welled up in his eyes. He could feel his temperature rising as he clenched his fists.

"Really?" said Jerry, "Oh, I see . . . so, now you're a macho man, huh?"

As Jerry disappeared back into the aisles, the boy in sweats crept up behind and whispered in Theo's ear, "Violence is never the answer."

The girl countered in his other ear, "Don't listen to him. Punch them in the nipples."

"Stop!" yelled Theo as he crashed his fists down onto the cubicle. The wooden desk splintered upon impact, and the monitor toppled to the floor, sending a metallic clank echoing through the mezzanine.

"You're gonna have to pay for that." Jerry was back, and the boy and girl in sweats had vanished again, leaving no evidence they were ever there. Embarrassed and scared by his loss of control, Theo ran.

Theo rumbled through the library, madly searching the valleys of books and magazines for the boy and girl in gold. Either they were here, playing some malicious game of hide-and-seek, or Theo was losing his grip on reality. And given the way things had been going, either could be true.

"Stop it! Stop it, all of you!" Theo screamed as he picked up speed.

He rushed the exit like a linebacker, hitting the door with such force the entire entrance archway tremored. Everyone may not have seen Theo enter the library, but they certainly saw him leave. He hadn't even started school yet, and he already had a reputation of being a complete loser.

CHAPTER 8

Theo pushed himself as he focused on the road ahead—there was an intensity burning inside of him as his legs worked like pistons, peddling his bike with every ounce of energy he could muster. Feeling powerless in his life, he was taking out all of his frustration on his own body, pushing himself—and his bike—to the brink of collapse.

It was the only road in or out of town, and yet there were no landmarks, no mile markers, nothing that would give a sense there was any sort of civilization anywhere.

Theo grunted as he pushed even harder, peddling with such force the crankshaft of his bike was spinning free, with no resistance from the gears any longer; he was flying.

He could feel the sweat in his clothes turning cold in the mountain air. He could already hear his mother complaining about how she would have to do laundry on a Sunday night so he'd have clothes in the morning, but consequences be damned.

He looked out onto the horizon, knowing he was running out of time—his mom's idea of going out to explore the town had turned into an all-day affair. If he weren't home soon, she'd send a search party out looking for him, or worse, she'd come looking herself. He pulled out his smartwatch to see if it had any bars, but of course, it didn't, and the battery was running low. He would have to put a pin in trying to find a connection for a while until he found a charger.

But that wasn't why he was on this final mission before going home. He had gotten it into his mind that if he could somehow find the security checkpoint that they'd passed through the night they arrived in town, maybe he could get a read on who those men operating the station were. Maybe there was something there he could use.

But as he kept on peddling and peddling further and further, the last bit of sunlight sunk behind the vast mountain range that held Crucible so tightly in its grasp, and he knew that he wasn't going to find any trace of the checkpoint. Instead, the road seemed to stretch out into infinity and to God-knows-where—if it even had an end to it at all.

Finally, the lactic acid in his muscles got to be too much, and he clutched his brakes, his tires skidding to a stop in the middle of the single-laned road. His lungs burned as he sucked in the cool mountain air. The asphalt glistened with the evening mist of the forest settling in around him. All he could hear was the chorus of insects buzzing.

That same simmering anger from before returned, still festering inside—his temperature rising once more as he clenched his fists. Theo wished he could lash out at someone.

"What in the hell is this place?! I want to go home!" Theo screamed aloud to no one.

He gripped hard onto the handlebars of his bike, feeling the rage coursing through his nervous system. He let out a guttural scream that rippled across the forest, temporarily quieting the buzz of the insects. He stood there in utter silence.

Steam began to rise off his body. Like a match head that had just been extinguished, gray tendrils rose off his skin into the darkening sky. What felt like blood started dripping from his hand, and he glanced down at his bike; it was the rubber from the handlebars melting beneath his fingers. He pulled them off in shock, frantically wiping his hands.

Somehow, for a brief second, his entire body became like an oven.

Fear set in. His emotions suddenly felt like a chain reaction put into motion, like a piano falling down the stairs he couldn't stop. As he felt himself going into a full-on panic attack, *a shimmer of light* streaked past the corner of his eye. It was bright and effervescent, like the bloom of a Fourth of July firework, and lasted less than a blink.

Theo froze, adrenaline heightening his senses. He zeroed in on the canopy where the light had been, with the overwhelming sensation he was being watched. Hunted.

His mind immediately turned to Jerry and the gold sweatsuit gang. Had they followed him out here? Was the entire gang there, or was it just Jerry?

The entire ride up the mountain, Theo had replayed the events in the library on an endless loop, getting himself angrier and angrier with each push of the pedal. The anger was mainly directed inward. Even as it was happening, he knew that Jerry was baiting him. They were obviously playing some sort of "Embarrass the New Guy Prank" on him, trying to get a reaction, and Theo took the bait . . . hook, line, and sinker.

Tomorrow at school was going to be bad—not only would he be the laughingstock of his class, but he half expected to be arrested for destroying federal property at the library. Those computers weren't cheap, and he still hadn't worked out what he would tell his mother.

The shimmer of light whipped past again, a trail of golden sparkles in its wake.

It dawned on Theo that this was the same light he saw in the woods the night they'd driven into town. But what was it? He set his bike down, drawn to the light's presence—like a call to the void. But as he stepped to the edge of the road where the tree line began, all traces of the shimmer dissipated, and Theo was left standing in the dark, staring into a tangled web of shadows that caused him to feel the nerves in his spine sharpen.

Twigs snapped ahead of him. There was something large moving just beyond his field of vision. Theo froze. As his eyes adjusted to the lightless world under the canopy, he could make out an oversized silhouette moving toward him in the distance.

"Hello?" said Theo. "Is someone out there?"

Theo looked back to his bike sitting in the middle of the road, gauging how long it would take him to get to it if he needed to make a hasty exit. *It all depends on if I'm being tracked by an animal*, he reasoned, *or something else.* He scanned the ground for a makeshift weapon, a fallen branch the size of a wand was the only thing nearby. *Maybe it has thorns.*

As he reached down for the branch, the silhouette mirrored his movement.

Reaching down for its own weapon.

It was definitely a human. And by its movements, it had malice toward him. Theo took a slow step back, and the silhouette followed suit.

"What do you want?" yelled Theo.

The figure ignored him as it moved closer. Unconvinced he could fight the silhouette off with a twig, Theo sprinted toward his bike. The silhouette bolted after him.

In the dark, Theo couldn't see where he was placing his feet and got hooked on a tree root, twisting his ankle as he fell hard into the cool soil of the forest floor.

The silhouette stopped. He could feel it watching him from the darkness.

Theo flicked on his smartwatch flashlight to assess his injury and was horrified to find the silhouette do likewise. In the glow of the watch, Theo finally saw who was chasing him: *It was himself.*

An exact replica of Theo, mimicking his every move. Fear flooded his veins, and he screamed. The mimic opened its mouth in a scream, but no sound came out.

Theo willed himself off the ground and back to his bike, leaving his doppelganger behind him in the inky cloak of the forest, imagining it was at his heels with every step.

Examining his hands as he raced down the mountainside, Theo started to question his sanity. Maybe it was possible he had imagined seeing himself in the forest, just like he imagined the girl and boy in gold sweats in the library or daydreaming he was really a kid from Queens named Nick whose dad was away on business.

Theo was no longer sure of who he was or what was real. The only thing he knew for sure was that he had to find a way to leave Crucible, no matter the cost.

Gliding down the lone black road back to town was made easier by the night sky. Away from the omnipresent glow of NYC, Theo could see the white tail of the Milky Way spiraling in on itself, illuminating the path home. It made him think of his family. His grandparents were into stargazing, and his Uncle Ron used to make his telescopes, but Theo had never caught the bug. He knew the basics and could pick out Orion and Venus, but his favorite asterism to look for was the Big and Little Dipper. His dad once told him it was a father and son bear, using their tails to play catch with the North Star. He liked thinking of it that way; it comforted him and made him smile.

However, tonight, he couldn't find any of them. Not a single recognizable constellation in the night sky. He chalked it up to the stress of the evening and kept pedaling home.

Theo glanced at his smartwatch and eased his bike onto the side porch. It was already 9:30 p.m., and the battery was at 8 percent, nearly dead. He peered into the picture window with the hope that he'd be able to sneak into the house and creep up into bed without any fanfare. The living room light was on, but he didn't see his mom.

As he went to power down the watch, he noticed a single bar appear on screen—a sliver of wi-fi, maybe enough to message Dante. He'd spent the whole day searching for a signal, and he could've found it on his front porch the entire time. Irony was a cruel playmate.

"Text Dante," he quietly spoke into the smartwatch.

A red microphone graphic indicated it was listening.

"I'm being held against my will in some town called Crucible. They took my phone and erased me off the internet. Send help."

Theo hit send and watched the swirling circle of death process the message.

"C'mon . . . c'mon," he said, lifting the watch into the air higher in a vain attempt to help it leap into the cloud.

"Hand me the watch, Mr. Pappas," said Mr. Handler coldly.

Theo twisted around to find the immaculately dressed man emerging from Theo's very own front door. His cane knocked the porch slats ahead of every step as he made his way closer. Theo's impulse to run was thwarted by his mom closing in behind him, having exited the back door. "Do as he says, Theo . . . ."

Theo held onto the watch, stalling for a few extra seconds, praying it would be enough time for his message to send. Mr. Handler held out his hand expectantly. The light spilling out of the picture window cast dramatic film noir shadows across his face, exaggerating his hard features and leaving his eyes sullen and pupils black.

Not one to wait, he snatched the watch from Theo's hand, tossed it to the porch, and speared it with his silver cane, causing the face to shatter.

For a brief micro-expression, Theo saw a glimpse of the sadistic rage lurking just beneath Mr. Handler's polished surface, and it frightened him almost as much as what he saw in the forest. It was a controlled madness—pure evil.

"I owe you an apology, Mr. Pappas," Mr. Handler said in a measured tone. He took out his pocket square and folded it over a few times. "I thought I made it clear that you were to surrender your electronics. Obviously, I failed to communicate the importance."

Mr. Handler shoved the pocket square into Theo's hand and, through gritted teeth, said, "Pick it up."

Theo moved quickly to scoop the pieces of the watch into the cloth. His mother approached Mr. Handler's side. "I'm so sorry about this. I promise I didn't know."

Mr. Handler remained silent, letting his black pupil death stare do the talking.

"He's a good kid; he's not going cause any more trouble."

Theo handed the broken smartwatch to Mr. Handler, neatly tied up inside his pocket square. "I'm sorry, I was just trying to talk to my friend. I followed every other rule—"

"Like staying away from the forest?" snapped Mr. Handler.

Theo swallowed hard, the hairs of his neck standing on end. *How did he know?*

"This was your last warning," said Mr. Handler, carefully pocketing the watch. "Do not violate the script again. I will hear about it."

Alice reached for Theo's arm as Mr. Handler buttoned his suit jacket and moved off the wooden porch toward his black Town Car, hidden in the shadows across the street. Theo kicked himself for not seeing it earlier.

The two of them made their way inside and locked the door. Alice sat behind the table in front of stacks of papers and sighed.

"What was he doing here?" asked Theo.

"Checking in. He got reports you were riding around some security checkpoint? We were about to come to get you."

Theo racked his brain. He didn't see any checkpoint, but he must've been close enough for them to see him?

"I said to check in with me after two hours!"

"I'm sorry, mom, I—"

"You were gone all day! Do you know how worried I was?"

Alice tried her best to hold back tears, the stress of the last forty-eight hours searching for a way out. Theo wasn't sure what to do, so he stood there.

"This is all for you, Theo. To protect you. Please stop fighting it."

"I just wanna know the truth."

"What truth!? We are in a witness protection program for families of Enhanced Humans, end of story. If our true identities get out, we're dead. Now go upstairs and take your shower. You have school in the morning."

Theo lingered at the bottom of the stairs, his mind spinning with a thousand questions: What did he see in the forest? Who were the weird sweatpants kids in the library? How come there was no outside internet? Who was the man with the silver-tipped cane?

All of which would have to wait for another day. He'd pushed his mother to her limit today, and frankly, he was exhausted.

CHAPTER 9

Theo shrugged on his backpack and squirmed a bit under his scruffy flannel, feeling hot under his collar.

"Try to be back by dinner this time, please," Alice said, as she hugged her son goodbye from the side porch while juggling a cup of coffee.

"I don't feel so great."

"It's just first day jitters."

"I think I have a fever."

"Not according to the thermometer."

"We don't know when that thing was calibrated—"

"You're going to school, Theo!"

Theo nodded in defeat. As he mounted his bike, he noticed the rubber grips of his handlebars were still grooved in the shape of his hands from the night before. He forced a smile as he glanced back at his mom. "When do you start your student-teacher deal?"

"I'll be in the sixth-period middle school science class all week . . . ."

"Right. See you there, I guess," Theo said, hopping his bike down the wooden steps.

As he jumped over sidewalks and zipped through tree-lined streets on the way to school, he found himself enjoying the ride. If he had ended up in Crucible under different circumstances, he might have savored the small-town lifestyle. Back home, he'd had to catch two buses to get to school.

His feelings on the subject changed as he racked his bike under the flagpole and witnessed kids of all ages entering a pristine, two-story brick cuboid on the edge of Town Square Park. The building itself was gorgeous, but the energy of the students was off.

It was the quietest schoolyard Theo had ever heard in his life. Gone were all the pre-school games of tag and jubilant playground chatter. Instead, most of the kids just looked at their feet as they marched along to their destination—even the kinders. They weren't just weighed down by their overstuffed book bags; there was something heavier inside holding them down.

As he walked the halls, searching for the locker he was assigned, he passed teachers and staff that seemed more like prison guards than educators. Furrowed brows and downturned lips. He couldn't shake the feeling that he would run into Jerry or one of the other gold kids from the library, which filled his stomach with dread.

At one point, he witnessed a crisply dressed third grader drop his bagel schmear and stare at the floor like he just saw his best friend get shredded in a hailstorm of enemy fire. The kid was broken over a bagel, and Theo knew he would suffer the same fate if he didn't find a way out of this place fast—a task made slightly more impossible with the loss of his smartwatch to Mr. Handler the night before.

The lockers were on the fourth floor outside the music room. As a jazz fusion band warmed up with scales and *almost* recognizable pop melodies, Theo raced through his combination for a fifth time, failing to crack the code again.

"Did you start at zero?" a voice said.

Theo turned to find a gawky kid of Indian descent staring at him as he tried his combo again. The kid wore a baggy graphic tee and cargo pants filled with God-knows-what. He couldn't have been a day over fourteen, and his eyes carried so much intensity it made Theo self-conscious.

"Of course, I did," lied Theo.

The kid pushed his way to the lock, squeezing Theo out. "Eh, you gotta finesse it a bit . . . . The locks are old here."

Lightning fast, the kid pulled the lock. "You sure you started at zero?" he said, handing the lock to Theo. "My name is Shivansh Patel. You're Theo."

"That's right."

"We have English together. I'm in with the juniors."

"Great," Theo said, moving books into his locker.

"You just moved here from Poughkeepsie, right?" said Shivansh with a smug look.

"Uh, yeah . . ." said Theo, suspicious, "how'd you know that?"

The bell rang. Theo glanced at a nearby wall clock mounted underneath a security camera. "Nice to meet you, but I gotta go."

Theo rushed off, but Shivansh followed, "How you liking Crucible so far? Boring, huh?"

Theo picked up the pace, speed walking as he looked at his sheet of classes. "Can we do this some other time, maybe? I'm trying to find—"

"—Mrs. Diamond's class. I know."

Theo stopped, annoyance transforming into anger. "What's the deal? Are you trying to mess with me? How do you know all this?"

Shivansh walked past Theo to a metal door, "I told you, we have English together: Mrs. Diamond."

He pushed the door open and bowed, sarcastically inviting Theo inside. "One of my electives is being her TA. I *may* have read your transcripts."

Theo followed after Shivansh, his face red with frustration as he watched Shivansh take his seat at a group table. Shivansh whispered something to the table—they all chuckled and watched Theo as he stood near the back of the class, unsure what to do.

The classroom window overlooked the park, and its beige walls held posters of famous quotes from literary giants in whimsical typography: Wilde and Woolf, Scott and Shakespeare. A plastic sphere housing multiple cameras and sensors was mounted over the smartboard—*probably for remote learning,* Theo thought.

"Everyone quiet down now, please," announced a cheerful, Southern drawl.

The teacher stood up from her desk, commanding immediate attention. "You must be Theo."

"Good morning, ma'am."

"Good morning to you, Theo. Welcome to your new home. I'm Mrs. Diamond. Everybody, please welcome our new friend."

The class shouted obligatory words of welcome, a cacophony of *What ups* and *Hey Theo's* that came off disingenuous. But, despite his classmates' unenthusiastic greeting, Theo instantly felt a little bit calmer. Mrs. Diamond had an easy smile and kind eyes, making him feel safe. He reckoned she was in her late forties based on her crow's feet and skunk stripe streaking through her black ponytail, but her aura was youthful.

"We're happy to have you here," said Mrs. Diamond. "Coach Kurts was supposed to find you earlier to let you know that you'll be spending the day doing some placement tests before you start the current unit."

"I was told my transcripts had been sent over," Theo said pointedly to Shivansh.

"They were . . . . The school just likes to do its own assessment. It's not graded; it's just a tool to help us know where you're at."

"Make sure there's a chaperone," yelled a voice.

"Don't bend over around Kurts," added another.

Theo turned as people chuckled. He felt like an animal at the zoo, on exhibit, standing up there for everyone to gawk at.

Mrs. Diamond glared at the class. "Inappropriate."

To Theo's surprise, the class immediately went silent.

"I can show him to Mr. Kurts's office, Mrs. Diamond," called out Shivansh.

"No, thank you, Mr. Patel. I think Theo can find his way to the gym just fine."

As Theo left, he made a mental note not to get on Mrs. Diamond's wrong side, if all it took for her to gain control of a teenage classroom was a raised eyebrow.

Theo found Coach Kurts's office—it sat behind a plexiglass window with wire mesh woven in diamonds, overlooking the basketball court. The door next to the window was ajar, and, as Theo knocked, it flew open to reveal Coach Kurts standing there decked out in the standard white polo shirt, red Adidas track pants, and matching kicks.

"Theo! You found the place," he said with the smile of a car salesman.

"Thanks?" Theo said as he took in the P.E. teacher. Kurts was a bulky meathead straight out of central casting. His balding crewcut and neatly trimmed mustache suggested he was a no-nonsense tough guy, but the undercoat of white lurking beneath his cheap hair dye also revealed he had soft spots in the armor.

"Mrs. Diamond said I would be doing some sort of test?" Theo said nervously.

"Ah, they're nothing. Mrs. Diamond get you all worked up?"

Coach Kurts took Theo by the shoulder and led him through his office, past the crowded equipment cabinets and baskets of scrimmage jerseys, and into a stuffy inner office. The office resembled an interrogation room without windows or mirrors—but it did have a camera array tacked in an upper corner of the room, the same spherical device he saw in Mrs. Diamond's room.

There was a desk in the middle where Kurts pointed Theo to sit. On the desk sat a booklet, scratch paper, and a pencil.

"Alright, this is pretty standard stuff . . . . Just go ahead and work your way through that little booklet there and you'll be on your way back to gen pop in no time." Kurts laughed. He pointed back to the main office. "I'll be in there. Just holler if you need something."

The door clanged shut with the same metallic heft of a prison gate.

Theo sat there, flipping through the booklet, confused by what he saw on the pages: *1 to 5. 1 you Strongly Agree, 5 you Strongly Disagree . . . I consider myself open-minded.*

There were hundreds of these vague questions. He could feel his temperature rising and felt like he was suffocating in this airless dungeon. It had to be a mistake. He'd gotten the wrong test. Theo rolled up the booklet and got up to discuss the misunderstanding with Coach Kurts, but the door was locked.

He jiggled the handle, stopping to fan himself with his shirt.

"Can I help you?" crackled Kurts's voice from a loudspeaker somewhere inside the room. It sounded to Theo like it came from the sphere.

"Umm . . . I think I got the wrong test," Theo said, treading lightly toward the strange device. He could hear it whir as it slowly turned, tracking his movement.

"It's the right test."

Theo stood directly underneath the device, close enough to see a reflection in its multiple irises and sensors. It resembled the eye of some alien bug designed by Apple.

"I thought I was taking a placement test? This feels like some sort of psych evaluation?"

"They're just questions, buddy," said Kurts over the loudspeaker. "Don't worry about it. Holler when you're done." The speaker crackled, and the room went silent.

Theo sat there for what felt like hours, going through the pages, heating up like the proverbial frog in a slow-boiling pot of water.

The booklet was more like a novel; somehow, they had fit nearly six hundred questions in those slim pages, ranging from *Do you enjoy country music?* to *Do you think that gross misdemeanors should result in corporal punishment?*

The test was weird enough, but the thing that was really getting to Theo was the bizarre camera array watching over him. He felt he was being studied the entire time, not just by Coach Kurts. He stared at the sphere, almost getting lost in its electric eyes. *Who is watching? And more importantly, why?*

CHAPTER 10

Theo rubbed his palms across his temples, pushing the sweat into his hair. It had been sweltering in the bizarre test room, and he wasn't finding it much better in the hall.

Coach Kurts led him upstairs, past clusters of kindergarten still-lifes and student poems tacked to construction paper. The aesthetic had a sort of madhouse feel to it.

Their walk ended at a row of trophy cases on the first floor and the sound of chatter.

"Chow's in there," said the coach, chucking a thumb toward a paint-chipped double door. "Now, my back teeth are floating . . . I gotta use the can."

Coach's eyes went to Theo's collar as he walked away; it was wet with perspiration. "You need to wash up or something, kid?"

"I'm fine. I just need some water," Theo said, self-conscious as he touched his neck.

Coach raised an eyebrow. "Come back down to my office after lunch, we'll finish up."

More tests!? He understood taking a foreign language placement test or a math assessment but failed to see how asking if he liked curly fries or crinkle-cut was relevant. He was being evaluated for something beyond academics, but couldn't wrap his head around what for or why. But not much here made sense.

As he looked into the cafeteria, the air hit Theo like a steam bath made of burnt canola oil. Inside, nearly two dozen hormonal teenagers, many of whom Theo recognized from the library the day before, fed in a marina fish-like frenzy—gossiping and giggling between bites of prepackaged and overcooked institutional slop. It was the most animated he had seen anybody in the town to date. He made a beeline toward the food counter, trying his best to remain under the radar.

Another spherical camera array perched in the corner of the room tracked his movement as he grabbed a plastic tray from the stack—the camera slid along the metal tube counter. Theo could see the iris diaphragms on some of the lenses focused on him.

It made the base of his nerves tingle. *What the hell is going on here?*

Like every kid Theo's age, he was vaguely aware that he was under constant surveillance. He knew that every cell phone, car, doorbell, elevator, and intersection had a camera and that he left a digital trail everywhere he went. Still, it never felt personal—more like some amorphous algorithm running in the background, trying to optimize ways of selling him useless junk he didn't need or couldn't afford.

But this felt much different than that. The sphere felt personal. It was like the cameras were someone's eyeballs, stalking him from some dark hiding place. It triggered the same sense of dread he felt seeing himself in the forest the night before.

He scoured the counter for water or something cold to drink but couldn't find anything.

"'Sup, Theo tomatillo!"

Theo startled and turned to find Shivansh next to him, reaching for one of the sweaty food plates on display under the heat lamps. "Y'know? Tomatillo, cause you look hot." Shivansh cringed to himself, realizing his dad joke read more like a pick-up line. A long beat passed before he offered Theo a cold bottle of water. "Here, you look thirsty."

Theo grabbed the water, beyond grateful, "Oh, thank God! How did you know?" As he chugged, Shivansh filled his tray with some sort of dry meat sandwich sitting under the hot lamps.

"Sloppy Janes," Shivansh said, examining the odd-looking sandwich suspiciously. "Gotta love plant meat."

"That's what that is?!" Theo said, his eyes moving to the pizza.

"The sandwiches are better than they look . . . but stay away from the pizza."

Theo heeded Shivansh's advice as the sphere watched the two boys walk away from the lunch line together. They were cut off by a kid as tall as an NBA center throwing his trash away, nearly upsetting their trays full of Sloppy Jane.

"My bad, Shiv," said the kid.

"It's alright. You just remembered your math test revisions are due. You're distracted."

The kid frowned and took a step toward Shiv, "Stay out of my head, Shiv."

Shiv swallowed hard. "Won't happen again."

The kid grabbed his bag and awkwardly hustled out of the cafeteria.

"What just happened?" asked Theo, confused.

"That's DeShawn Haight," explained Shivansh. "He'll be in the upper school next year."

"That kid isn't in high school yet?"

"He's in the middle of a growth spurt."

"What did he mean to stay out of his head?"

"I'm not sure," shrugged Shivansh, " . . . people are weird here."

Theo sensed Shivansh holding back. "Why's everyone in this town so damn secretive?" he asked, defeated. "Nobody can ever give me a straight answer to anything."

"We should sit," said Shivansh, his eyes darting to a sleepy security guard patrolling the lunchroom perimeter.

Few species are more territorial about their feeding ground than the adolescent human, and most of the standard brown bench lunch tables appeared occupied.

"Where do you normally sit? It's packed."

Shivansh nodded to a frosted window adorned with painted security bars. "Windowsill."

"What about over there?" Theo gestured to a far table hosting only a boy with a girl in his lap, neck nuzzling. They seemed older than the rest of the kids.

Shivansh shook his head, "Sorry, that's Anita and Fernando's table."

"They brought it from home?"

"They prefer to be alone."

"I'm sitting," Theo said, marching off toward Anita and Fernando's table.

Theo was over it. All of it. The tests. The lies. Sticking to the script. His mom, Crucible, The Pantheon. If the kids in the lunchroom had a problem with him sitting down, so be it.

He dropped his tray with a loud smack that sent Sloppy Jane flying to the far corners of the table as he plopped down on the bench. Anita and Fernando untangled themselves enough to glare at Theo, as he blotted the sweat off his brow with a brown paper napkin.

"Go back to making out. I'm not here," Theo said, tossing the soaked napkin onto the table next to his tray. He dug into his Sloppy Jane, surprised it was good.

But as he chomped on his food, he couldn't help but stare at the annoyed couple. Up close, Fernando and Anita were stunning. He'd never seen people this beautiful out in the wild before. They looked like they belonged on display in the Louvre.

"Hey. Can I ask you guys a favor?" said Theo, taking another big bite out of his Sloppy Jane. "If I needed to make a phone call, could I maybe use one of your phones?"

Fernando and Anita looked at each other with disgust. *Is he serious?*, they seemed to be thinking. Their eyes tracked the security guard, who was now looking in their direction.

"I'm asking for a friend," said Theo, suddenly aware of the sphere watching him. His burst of bravado had exhausted itself, and he was now afraid he said too much, and Mr. Handler would be waiting on his doorstep when he got home.

"Hey, guys . . . this is Theo," said Shivansh with a nervous titter, slinking up behind Theo. "He's new here, obviously. He likes to joke around. Funny dude, huh?"

"I'm Anita," the girl said, unphased, extending a hand. It was covered in a lacy black glove Madonna might've worn in the '80s. As Theo shook her hand, he realized she was completely covered, wearing jeans, a long-sleeve blouse, and lace gloves—which made him feel even hotter than he already was.

"Are you okay? You don't look too good. . . ." she said as she pulled her hand away.

"I'm fine. Just warm. It's warm in this school, right?"

Fernando looked to Anita, motioning with his eyes for her to look at the security guard, who had finally stopped staring their way.

Shivansh was in on their silent conversation and seemed relieved. Theo was both impressed and horrified at their silent prison shorthand. He also felt left out.

"You were in the library yesterday," said Fernando, like an accusation.

"I don't think so," said Theo, feeling heat ripple through his body. *Was that yesterday?*

"I thought I saw you talking to Jerry," said Fernando. "You know Jerry?"

"It's a small town," Anita said, "everybody knows everybody. You know?"

"How do *you* know Jerry?" Fernando asked pointedly.

"I don't know . . . ."

"You don't know if you know Jerry?"

"It's sweltering in here," Theo said, fanning himself with his shirt.

"Why don't we just ask Jerry?" Anita said, nodding past Theo.

Theo turned to see Jerry in the lunch line, clad in their patented gold sweatsuit.

"I gotta go." Theo shot up to leave the table in a bolt of panic. The pressure of a new school, new friends, living under a microscope—Theo felt the walls closing in and desperately wanted some air.

"Don't leave yet; we have a new mystery to solve," said Fernando.

"Yeah. Who's that woman with them?" Anita asked.

"I think it's a new teacher," said Shivansh.

Theo spun around again to look—Jerry and his mother Alice walking toward them, less than a table's length away!

"There he is," said Alice with a wave and a smile. "Theo, I want to introduce you to Jerry. They work at the library and play basketball—your two favorite things.

I invited them over to hang. You all are welcome to come, too."

"This is your son?" Jerry said, barely containing a snicker.

All Theo could do was stare at the horror unfolding in front of him.

"Theo was having a hard time remembering if he was in the library yesterday . . . or if he even knew you," Fernando said mockingly.

"You don't recall breaking a computer and running out of the library yelling?" Jerry said.

"What?" said Alice. "Is that true, Theo? Did you break a computer?"

Theo fumbled for a response but couldn't find any words. His breathing grew labored.

"Theo, I'm waiting," demanded Alice.

"You know, you cracked the glass in the archway, slamming that door when you stormed out. That can't be replaced," Jerry said with a smirk as Alice looked at Theo with shame.

Theo could feel the eyes of other students in the lunchroom on him. His heart raced as he poured sweat. *It is so hot.* Shivansh was the only one who seemed to notice his distress. "Hey guys," he warned, "something's happening with Theo."

Theo's head was spinning, his field of vision narrowing.

Out of the corner of his eye, just beyond Jerry and his mother, he thought he saw both the girl and boy from the library in gold sweats creeping along the walls, taunting him.

That was the last thing he remembered before he blacked out.

CHAPTER 11

Theo jolted awake, bathed in sweat, blinded by a harsh white light beaming into his pupils.

Cold, calloused hands were holding him down while the metal beak of a surgical speculum pried his eyelids apart.

"Hi Theo, my name is Dr. Limley," said a sterile voice. "Your mother called me to help you. Just stay calm; you're safe and sound at home."

The light revealed a handsome older man, maybe in his late sixties but shockingly fit for his age. Theo sat there, dumbly taking him in—he wore a blue surgical mask that complimented his eyes and a knee-length lab coat over a seasoned twill suit.

Theo searched the wall for the soulless pastoral painting he hated so much, just to confirm he was back home—or rather, back in the tract-house prison they were calling home.

Alice took his arm as Dr. Limley released his eyelids.

"Baby, it's me. You're okay. You just had a fainting spell."

Theo turned toward his mother, sitting opposite the doctor on the other side of his bed, and blinked moisture back into his eyes. She was cradling his teddy bear in her lap, the lone physical artifact from his life as Nick Pappas.

Reality came rushing back in, and—all at once—he was assaulted by the memories of what had happened in the lunchroom. It released a torrent of neurotransmitters that jumpstarted his nervous system and launched Theo up to a sitting position.

"I didn't break that computer on purpose," he blurted out.

"Don't worry about that now. Just rest," said Alice.

"What's happening to me?"

Alice looked to Dr. Limley, who carefully packed his scuffed leather Gladstone bag.

"Doctor, he's going to be okay, right?"

"Oh, yes, Mrs. Alexander. Young Theo has been under a lot of stress and not getting enough rest or electrolytes. As a result, he got a little overheated and had a spell. Give him some food and water; let him rest. He'll be fine tomorrow."

Alice tucked the teddy bear in bed next to Theo and approached Dr. Limley. "He was in pretty rough shape at the school," she said in a hushed tone. "Are you sure he's okay?"

"Bring him by for some blood work if it would help ease your mind, but he's healthy enough to get back to school tomorrow. And it's good for him to keep up a routine."

Theo couldn't believe what he was hearing. "How do you know I'm okay?"

"Your vitals are all normal," said Dr. Limley. "Your temperature, pulse, blood pressure—"

"Is it going to happen again? How long was I out? What if I hit my head?"

"Shivansh caught you as you fell," said Alice. "You were out for less than a minute."

"You've just been sleeping," added Dr. Limley, "and I encourage you to do more of it."

"Stop gaslighting me!" yelled Theo.

"Theo!" said Alice. "Don't be rude to the doctor."

He couldn't help it. What the doctor and his mother told him simply didn't ring true. The last thing he remembered, he was in the lunchroom eating Sloppy Jane, and a blink later, he was in his bed with Dr. Limley in his eyeball—and based on the angle of the sun seeping through his window, his best guess was that several hours had passed in between. He had no memory of waking up or getting home or of any dreams occurring during the time he was unconscious.

"He's not making any sense," Theo protested. "Back home, if someone passes out cold and loses hours of their life, they aren't dismissed! Maybe you're the one who needs to be checked out."

"Maybe you're right there, Champ," said the doctor with a condescending smirk. "Look . . . I know you're scared. And that's normal. I'd be worried if you weren't, but you have to trust me. I'm good at my job, and I promise you you'll be okay if you get some rest and hydrate."

The doctor winked at Theo as he removed his mask and put on a porkpie hat. "I'll check in with you tomorrow, Champ."

"I'll walk you out," said Alice, following the doctor out of the room. As she left, she gave Theo "the look." That nuanced glare only a mother can provide that says, *I know you're sick, but you messed up, and there will be consequences.*

Theo tried to sink back into his pillow, but he could hear murmurs from downstairs, and it was apparent his mother and Dr. Limley were talking about him.

He tossed his sweat-covered sheets aside and went to his bedroom door to eavesdrop, but all he could make out were keywords with upsetting medical terms with "-osis" suffixes.

He looked at his hands; whatever happened on the bike to cause him to melt the rubber a couple of nights ago couldn't be normal. Add to that the sweats and fainting spell—he didn't need a doctor to tell him there was definitely something wrong with him.

When he heard the front door creak open, he went to his window to continue his spy campaign.

He had a clear view of the water tower and terracotta roof tiles on a row of lookalike houses across the street.

He caught a glimpse of his reflection and was taken aback by what he saw. He couldn't tell if it was the lack of sleep, stress, or everything combined, but he was starting to look like a man—and not just any man. At that moment, he looked exactly like his father. Maybe it was wishful thinking or just a cruel trick of the light.

He knew his father would've had some bogus home remedy (that somehow always worked) to cure him. No amount of fake memories or gaslighting by a townful of weirdos would ever take away the fact that he was still Nick Pappas, son of Paul Pappas. God, he missed him. Tears formed as he grabbed his teddy bear off his bed, remembering his dad.

His reverie was cut short as he spotted his mother walking Dr. Limley to the sidewalk in front of the house. Theo hugged the wall to ensure he wouldn't be seen if they looked up at his window. They stayed at the edge of the driveway talking until a fast-moving SUV turned the corner and raced toward the house. The blacked-out, armored vehicle stopped in front of them hard enough to make the tires squeak.

Mr. Handler stepped out of the back, using his silver-tipped cane to steady himself. He straightened his pinstriped jacket as he approached Alice, his eyes darting up to the second-story window. Theo took a step back, unsure if Mr. Handler saw him or not.

As the immaculate man spoke to Alice and the doctor, Theo watched both of their body languages shrivel, like Mr. Handler was sucking the energy out of them with his words.

They all turned to the SUV as the back window rolled down, revealing Jerry inside. Somehow the gold sweatsuit-wearing teen was involved in this drama.

Jerry was talking, but Theo couldn't hear what they were saying. Whatever it was, it enraged Mr. Handler. He pointed at them with his silver-tipped cane, yelling as he marched toward the vehicle. Dr. Limley followed him like a wounded puppy. Theo changed position to get a better look inside the SUV as Mr. Handler opened the door, not trusting that he saw Jerry in the backseat—but he compromised himself in the process.

For a fraction of a second, he and Jerry locked eyes. The expression they exchanged wasn't adversarial or threatening. It was vulnerable and pleading. Jerry looked frightened.

Unsure what to do, Theo dropped to the floor.

He waited until he heard the SUV's engine rev up and disappear into the neighborhood.

When he was sure the coast was clear, Theo raised himself back up to the window, where he saw Alice crumpled on the pavement, sobbing.

It became clear to Theo that Jerry would be a key piece to figuring out Crucible, and he made it his new mission to find out everything he could about them.

CHAPTER 12

Theo was late for Mrs. Diamond's first-period English. His mother had ambushed him an hour before his alarm went off to inform him that he had to report to school early to finish his "placement tests" with Coach Kurts. He didn't have the strength to protest.

Back within the Coach's tiny room again, Theo found that the tests consisted of more of the same psycho-babble as the day before—only this time it was short answers: *Is it ever okay to break the law? How do you define a hero?* But the questions didn't bother him as much today. Partly because he decided to entertain him-self with the answers: *"How do I define a hero? Anyone who could tolerate being married to your mom."*

Mostly, he was just happy to be out of the general population, tucked away in the interrogation room, away from the prying eyes of his fellow students who witnessed his collapse in the lunchroom. Nevertheless, he had a sneaking suspicion people would be in his business even more than before, demanding to know details of his medical condition.

His suspicion was confirmed when he crept into English for the last few minutes of class. He could feel everyone's eyes on him, followed by the hiss of their whispers. He imagined all the scandalous rumors they'd have heard about him: *He has hyperactive sweat glands that cause him to smell like feet. He blacks out whenever he gets aroused.*

Theo had been assigned a seat at Shivansh's table, which he figured Shivansh had something to do with by the way he was flagging Theo over with a toothy grin. *Possibly the only perk of signing up to be a teacher's assistant as your elective,* Theo mused.

"Happy to see you feeling better, friend," said Shivansh, as Theo unzipped his bag. *Here we go,* thought Theo, *I'm gonna have to talk about blacking out for the rest of the week.*

"You probably don't want to talk about blacking out, so we won't," said Shivansh.

Theo softened at his perceptiveness. Somehow the kid always seemed to know what Theo needed and was touched that Shiv called Theo "friend" (even though Theo felt they were still at acquaintance level at best, it was still nice to hear). He was the only kind face Theo had encountered in Crucible and would need his help getting intel on Jerry.

"Thanks for catching me," said Theo.

"I got your back!" said Shivansh. "Cuz . . . you fell on your back?"

Theo thought a beat and laughed to himself. Then, before Theo could take out his notebook, the bell rang, and everyone popped up from their seats, rushing to get out of the class.

"Theo, stay a minute," called Mrs. Diamond from her desk, not looking up from her book.

"I'll see you at lunch," said Shivansh, as he packed up his laptop and left.

"Wait, I want to talk to you about—"

"Jerry? Yeah, I know."

Pushing aside the need to unpack how Shivansh knew that, Theo lowered his voice. "I was hoping we could talk in private before lunch."

"Sure . . . ." said Shivansh, as he abruptly turned and marched out of class without setting a time or place to meet up. Theo shook his head, *this guy is my only hope?*

Theo approached Mrs. Diamond's desk as the rest of the class filed out. He watched her run gel-tipped fingernails along the last lines of a chapter. Finally, she closed the book, savoring the last words. "I just love Pushkin."

"I don't know him," shrugged Theo.

"You will. We do a whole semester on 19th-century Russian literature."

“Neat,” said Theo, a little more glibly than he intended.

“I heard about yesterday.”

Mrs. Diamond took off her glasses, forcing eye contact. She peered into Theo’s eyes as if she was probing his brain. “I just wanted to check in with you. See how you’re feeling.”

“I’m fine.” But, seeing she didn’t buy it, he continued, “I mean, as far as I know, I am.” Theo anxiously looked toward the wall clock, desperate to break the teacher’s constant gaze.

Mrs. Diamond furrowed her brow. “How are you adjusting to Crucible?”

“Honestly . . . It’s too early to tell.”

“It’ll take time. When I first came here, someone told me that whenever you move cities, it takes about six months before you feel like it’s your home—I found that to be true.”

Theo wasn’t sure what to say. There was no way he was going to be here for that long.

Mrs. Diamond pulled a flyer printed on glossy cardstock from her desk and offered it to Theo. At first glance, it looked like a knock-off Caesar’s Palace ad—regal stone statues in full armor looming over flowing fountains, but the caption read: *Crucible High Invites You to an Evening You Won’t Forget.*

"The back-to-school gala is in two weeks," explained Mrs. Diamond.

"I thought this place was year-round?"

"We still have school years. We're about a month into the new one, and I wanted to invite you and your mom to the gala personally. It's Grecian-themed. Think: toga."

"Thanks," said Theo, folding the flyer in half, already self-conscious about the toga.

"The good news is . . . you already have a mask."

"What do you mean?"

"You know . . . your family?"

What mask? Theo thought, his mind straining to find meaning behind her cryptic question. *Does she have me confused with someone else? What does she mean by "your family"? Does she know who my family is? Is it a test to get me to reveal who I am?*

Theo suddenly became aware of the sphere perched above them—the silent witness, always there, always watching.

Sensing his discomfort, Mrs. Diamond smiled. "Hope you can make it."

The late bell rang, and Theo left the classroom.

"Crap," he said as it dawned on him in the hall that he didn't know where to go next. He dropped his bag to the ground to search for his schedule.

"What do you want to know about Jerry?"

Theo spun around to find Shivansh standing behind him. "You scared me," he said, raising his hand to his heart to steady it. "Aren't you gonna be late for class?"

"No, but you are. It's my free period."

"I don't even know what I have next," Theo said, rummaging through his bag before remembering his schedule was crumpled in his pocket. "I think it's—"

"P.E.," said Shivansh.

"Right," said Theo, as he read it off his slip, confirming Shivansh was correct.

"How'd you know that?"

"I saw your schedule yesterday. Remember?"

"And you committed it to memory?"

Shivansh shrugged.

"You always seem to know what I'm about to say before I do," Theo said, putting on his bag.

"I guess I just pay attention."

Theo waved off his observation as he moved past the lockers toward the stairs. He could hear the lower school rehearsing in the music room. It was "The Swallow of Rhodes," a Greek folk song he heard as a child. *An odd choice for the Gala*, he thought, *but I guess a chorus of kinders shouting could make anything sound cute.*

Shivansh walked by his side much quieter than before as if he was deep in thought.

"So, how long have you known Jerry?" asked Theo.

"Long enough."

"You good friends with them?"

"Good enough," Shivansh said, getting weary of the conversation's direction.

"What's the deal with the gold sweats?"

"I don't know if this is a good idea," said Shivansh, stopping.

"What?! Don't you think it's weird that Jerry runs around in the same clothes as those other two kids? Are they part of a gang or something?"

"In Crucible, it's better to stay out of people's business. Less you know, the better."

"That doesn't seem to apply to me," said Theo. "The whole school's in my business."

"It's not my secret to tell," said Shivansh with intensity. Theo recognized the pain and confusion he carried in his face, and it mirrored his own. "Hey, I didn't mean anything—"

"Jerry is a good person. They're not who you think—"

The hydraulic whir of metal cut him off. Theo and Shivansh turned as an elevator door slid open and a security guard armed with a taser stepped off. Theo recognized him from the lunchroom the day before.

"Morning, Phil," said Shivansh.

Phil pointed to earbuds in his ear and mouthed "*on the phone.*"

“I didn’t know there was an elevator,” Theo said as he ran over to board it.

“We’re not supposed to use it.” Shivansh grabbed at Theo to pull him out.

“It’ll be faster,” Theo said, slapping him away.

As the door slid closed, Theo reached out to select the basement floor but found no buttons. Where a control panel should be was just oiled metal buffed to a mirror shine.

“How do you get downstairs, that’s usually where all the secrets are stored?”

“You don’t,” said Shivansh, as he looked around nervously.

“Surely this thing goes to the basement.”

“Basement access denied,” announced a computerized voice. “Exit now.”

“What!?” shouted Theo. “It’s voice-activated?”

“We need to go. Now!” Shivansh warned, pulling Theo toward the door as it flung back open. Theo dragged his feet, yelling to the elevator, “Take me to floor one.”

“Access denied,” repeated the elevator. Only this time, the warning came with an alarm.

Hidden lights pulsated, turning the cube blood red. A klaxon blared. Shivansh used all his strength to pull Theo out of the lift as the door slammed shut.

"Are you trying to get us pruned!?" Shivansh yelled in a panic.

"Pruned?"

"You can't keep going like this, Theo."

"What did I do?! I tried to take an elevator."

"You're rocking the boat! And Crucible is a boat that does not like to be rocked!"

Footsteps approached, loud and fast.

"They're coming. Get to class! Meet me after school at the library."

Theo bolted to the staircase while Shivansh turned to face the approaching shadow. As he rounded the corner to go downstairs, he caught Phil the security guard running up on Shivansh and feared the worst.

CHAPTER 13

Returning to the scene of the previous day's crime wasn't the afternoon Theo had planned, but when he didn't see Shivansh or Jerry at lunch, his curiosity made it impossible for him not to go back to the library. The last time he saw Jerry, they were in the back of an armored SUV being verbally assaulted by Mr. Handler—and he hadn't seen Shivansh since they got busted for playing on the forbidden elevator he still felt guilt over.

Theo sighed as he coasted up to the stone entrance. Only one other bike was chained to the rack. It had a black-matte frame and fat tires—he instantly recognized it as the bike the girl in the gold sweatsuit rode. He had the overwhelming feeling that he should turn around and run away, but his determination beat his flight-or-fight response.

Yes, it was uncomfortable being back at the library and facing Jerry and their weird sweatsuit friends, but if he was going to get out of this town, he would have to face his fears. Theo let his bike fall to the ground and marched up to the entrance archway with purpose, stopping to examine the antique window above the gothic entryway.

As Jerry had told his mom, there was a hairline fracture in the curved stained glass, slicing through the intricate geometric flowers. *All that damage came from me*, he thought. He put that all aside as he took a deep breath and pushed open the heavy wooden door, half-expecting an ambush by Jerry and the sweatsuit gang.

To his surprise, the library was eerily empty. Nobody was sitting at the harvest tables lining the mezzanine or moving through the book stacks. All he could hear was the crackle of wood burning in the grand fireplace.

"Hello?" said Theo, moving deeper into the aisles.

His voice echoed off the oculus.

"Shiv? Jerry?"

Perfect, he thought. *Shivansh set me up. He lured me back to the lion's den to be eaten. Either that or Phil, the security guard, got him. Then again, maybe he's just late.*

Theo moved to the computer cubicles to inventory the damage from his outburst. The terminal was closed off with yellow caution tape, and a handwritten note in Sharpie read: *Temporarily Out of Service.* The computer had been removed from the station.

Theo ran his hand across the vintage desk, fashioned from thick hickory. He had left a crater the size of his fist where it made an impact that splintered the depth of the wood in multiple directions—he had nearly destroyed the thing! Theo felt a flush of pride at his feat; he had no idea he possessed that kind of strength. He had never been particularly sporty, only playing the occasional pickup game with Dante and usually coming in somewhere toward the middle of the pack in most P.E. competitions.

Theo examined his hand, and there were no bruises or cuts. There wasn't even a callous.

His mind wandered. A slow-burning thought rose from the depths of his consciousness that he couldn't ignore: If his dad was an Enhanced Human, what did that make him?

Theo's brain exploded in revelation. Why hadn't he seen the connection before? The fevers. The testing. The constant monitoring. Was he an Enhanced Human? Do those traits even get passed on from parents? Why was he really in Crucible?

With that, he darted to a working terminal and double-clicked to open the library catalog. His fingers rapidly typing: *O-D-Y-S-S-E-U-S*. The internet may be throttled in Crucible, but maybe he could find out information the old-fashioned way: books.

No titles came back with his father's name. He tried searching author, subject, and keyword next and got a smattering of hits. The books he pulled were mostly about Homer's epic poems. He would have to get more creative with his search.

Next, he tried *Enhanced Human, Odysseus of Queens, The Pantheon, Crucible, Are Enhanced Powers Genetic?* The titles of a few academic journals returned, but when he flipped through the pages, they were filled with black marks where information had been redacted. Some books had entire pages missing. This only strengthened his resolve.

He tried a dozen other keywords that led to dead ends. And then Theo caught a glimpse of the tape covering the damaged cubicle. The words: *New York City Crime* popped into his head. The search directed him to newspaper archives stored on microfiche, which Theo didn't know existed until he retrieved sheets of film from oversized filing cabinets near the check-out desk. Unsure what to do with it, he held a sheet to the overhead lights, squinting to read the micro-photos imposed on the film.

A patronizing giggle broke the silence. Theo was startled and turned to find the girl in the gold sweatsuit behind him, placing a stack of books on the check-out counter.

"That's not how you do that."

Theo lowered the film, slightly embarrassed. He kept his eyes trained on the girl, waiting for her to disappear again.

"Is Jerry here?" asked Theo, bracing himself for Jerry and the boy in gold sweats to pop up behind him. They seemed to travel in a pack.

"Just me," said the girl.

Theo got lost rediscovering her striking features. Up close, her green eyes were hypnotic. Her skin was smooth and golden brown and she smelled like lavender and vanilla. She put an impatient hand on her waist. "You need help with the microfiche?"

"You work here, too?" said Theo, lowering his guard slightly.

The girl took the film sheet out of his hand and led him to a giant boxy screen that looked like it had teleported out of the 1960s. She slipped the microfiche onto a plate under the screen and hit a button that activated a bright light that passed through the film and projected it onto the screen. Finally, the micro-images became big enough to read.

Theo delighted as headlines came into focus: *CRIME WAVE CONTINUES, ENHANCED HUMANS OUT OF CONTROL; HEARING SET FOR CRIME BOSS.*

"You use the wheels to navigate and focus," she said, nodding to the two silver knobs in her hands. Turning one knob left or right allowed her to go up and down the film. Turning the other allowed her to focus. "Have fun," she said flatly as she went to leave.

"Wait," said Theo as she stood from her chair. "Uh . . . I like your bike."

Even before the sentence hit her ears, Theo knew it was the wrong thing to say, but it was the only thing his flustered mind could conjure to keep her there a bit longer.

"Me too," she said, as Theo went red. Then she turned to go. "Is that all, then?"

"No," said Theo, nervous. "I'm trying to find out more about Enhanced Humans."

The girl just scoffed. "Good luck—"

"So, you've tried before?"

From her nonchalant shrug, Theo pushed further, asking, "You have a censored internet and a library filled with books that have been redacted, and you're okay with that?"

"It's not that I'm okay, it's just—"

"Look!" said Theo, sitting in front of the microfiche reader. He turned the silver knob to scroll through the *Times* articles. "There's stuff in these old newspapers that wasn't censored. If we look hard enough, I'm sure we can find useful information."

The girl's eyes scanned the headlines, and Theo watched as something shifted inside her.

"There's another reader," said the girl, as she padded to the oversized filing cabinet.

Her words brought a smile to his face. "I'm Theo, by the way."

"Jenna."

She returned with a stack of microfiche, and the two of them spent the next twenty minutes looking through old *Times* articles. Most of them dated back to the '80s and '90s. They looked through the newspaper-crafted narrative, finding one article that reported that in New York City, a group of militant Enhanced Humans had emerged, seemingly from nowhere, and threatened the social order of the country. In response, the US government revealed their own sanctioned Enhanced Humans to help restore order—but there was still nothing about Theo's father.

About to call it a day, Theo put in one last sheet of film and hit the motherload. Mr. Handler said he'd scrubbed Theo's family's existence, but it looked like he'd missed a spot.

"Wait! That's him! There he is!"

Jenna jumped up to get a look at his screen. Under a headline from 1987 that read *The New and Improved EH, Now with Greater Powers* was an unlabeled picture of Odysseus hovering near the Wall Street Stock Market. He was absorbing energy from the eyes of two masked men in Armani suits.

Jenna's face dropped in disappointment. "Oh. You mean Odysseus."

"Exactly! He should be in all these articles! That's who I've been trying to find."

"From what I hear, I think he's a jerk," said Jenna, suddenly angry. "He's done more harm for Enhanced Humans than anybody in history—"

"What do you mean? What do you know about EH?" Theo said, trying to control his excitement.

Jenna paused to formulate a response before answering with a terse, "Never mind."

She got up from her chair. "We done here? I need to get back to work."

"Where's Jerry?" asked Theo. "Weren't they supposed to be here?"

"I dunno," said the girl, organizing her microfiche pile.

"Surprised to see you alone tonight. Where's that other guy you all hang out with?

"Who? James? We're twins, and he's never far away."

"Good to know. How long have you both lived in Crucible?"

"Too long . . ."

The way she phrased her answer and the sagging tone of voice resonated with Theo. At that moment, he thought that maybe he wasn't alone in his misery in Crucible.

Maybe there were others like him, who had been placed in witness protection, but how could he ask directly? What if he was wrong? What if they were all being watched?

He settled on a vague yet loaded response: "So you want out, too?"

As she was about to answer, the massive wooden door creaked open. Jenna's twin brother, James, stalked in, antagonized.

"You here to break more stuff?" said James, spotting Theo from the threshold. "And who said you were allowed back in?"

Theo looked to Jenna for help, but she grew cold and looked away. He was on his own. He looked back toward James, but he was gone. Theo scanned the entrance but saw no sign of him—or Jenna for that matter, who had also disappeared from his view.

"They asked you a question."

And there was Jerry, completing the trifecta, suddenly on him. Theo vaulted up from his seat, disoriented. How did they sneak up behind him so fast?

"Jerry. I was hoping to find you. I'm not here to cause any trouble." Theo struggled to keep his composure and attempt a rational conversation, all the while trying to anticipate where the twins would pop up next.

"It's too late for that," said Jerry. "We know what happened at the school."

His head was on a swivel, but as Theo blinked, Jerry was gone. Then he was surrounded by the twins again. Their chests were puffed with rage, and their pupils were gray and milky. Each one inches away from him.

"Leave us *alone*!" they echoed in unison, their voices combining in a demonic tone.

For the second time in three days, Theo ran from the library, this time fearing for his life.

CHAPTER 14

Theo pumped his legs as fast as the crankshaft would turn; its metal teeth bit into the bike chain like a buzz saw, causing it to rattle. He glanced back at the library as he fled, fully expecting to be attacked at any moment.

His mind went to Shivansh. Had he set him up? Or had Jerry and their sweatsuit mafia got to him before Theo arrived? He shook the thought; right now, he needed to survive.

As he banked into the woods, the tires kicked up dirt as he pedaled up a steep mound toward a trailhead leading back to town.

His body felt like a furnace, and his fever had returned with a vengeance, punishing his body to make up for the lost time. He dragged his flannel sleeve across the sweat on his brow.

To his surprise, the trail was different than the one he had ridden days earlier. It resembled a tributary, with multiple forks—paths splitting off in endless directions. As Theo sped across the unsteady terrain, it became clear he had taken a wrong turn.

He had reasoned that as long as he kept heading downhill, he would reach the town, but as the trees got thicker and the canopy darker, he realized his logic was flawed.

What he thought was a downward path was full of hills and switchbacks that left Theo disoriented. When he turned around to retrace his steps, he got even more confused about where he was, until the canopy became so thick it eclipsed the sun, and he could no longer see the ground ahead of him. Panic began to set in all around him.

Theo squeezed his handbrakes, skidding to a stop.

Looking up through the trees, it was hard to see much of anything. He dropped his bike and unfastened the top buttons of his shirt to try and get a reprieve from the heat.

As his eyes adjusted to the darkness, the trees seemed to radiate a faint blue aura. It was quiet enough to hear the biomass breathing. He took comfort in the pungent smell of damp soil, a scent usually reserved for fresh rain.

But all of that went out of his mind with the crunch of a branch overhead. He had heard that sound before. It was similar to those nature documentaries he watched as a kid. You know, the ones where a predator was lingering in the canopy, waiting to pounce on its prey below.

Theo froze, eyes glued to the black void above him. The branches continued to move, creaking slightly under the weight of a hidden beast lurking above his head. It moved slowly through the canopy, trying for stealth, but Theo was already alertly attuned to its presence.

He went through a mental Google search of potential predators: Panther? Python? Gorilla? Each animal seemed more impossible to get away from than the last. He tried to remember what to do: *Do you run away? Do you make yourself big? Do you avoid eye contact?*

He couldn't think. It was too damn hot!

Feeling trapped, a pent-up rage surged through his system. He was tired of running. Tired of being bullied and lied to. Tired of being held hostage by this god-awful town. His blood became pressurized, coursing through constricted veins. It was time to make a stand.

The invisible hunter moved closer, snapping branches as it leaped from one tree to the next, but the predator had become the prey.

Theo exploded, balling up his hands and shouting at the unseen terror with his entire being. As he screamed, a ball of fire erupted from his clenched fists, lighting up the black umbrella of the canopy. As the flames subsided, he stared at his smoldering hands in disbelief. Studying them as if they were appendages grafted on from another body. The persistent heat and fever plaguing his body were gone. It was the best Theo had felt in days, and then he laid eyes on the beast.

He only got a glance; it somehow seemed to flicker in and out of existence.

He took the thing in. It was a human. Maybe.

It had more muscle mass and longer arms, but its face was definitely human, expressing fear. It was frightened of Theo.

Seeing the terror he inspired in the creature transformed his anger into regret.

"It's okay," said Theo, "I won't hurt you."

The flames from his fist died out, plunging the woods back into darkness, and Theo lost track of any sight of the man-beast, but he could hear it take off through the trees.

He mounted his bike and chased after him.

"Wait!" called Theo, dodging branches and vaulting over rocks and roots, the sound of the would-be attacker swinging in the trees guiding him through the darkness.

As the cool forest air whipped his face, he thought back to the computer cubicle he destroyed with the strike of his hand. That same energy, born out of anger, caused him to ignite with flame. There was little doubt in his mind now that he had inherited (at least some of) his father's Enhanced abilities. It made him feel both powerful and scared.

Light began to filter through the trees, brilliant streaks of moonbeams that Theo mistook for sunshine. He had been trapped in the forest depths longer than he'd wanted, and his eyes had grown accustomed to the dark.

He heard the roar of an engine and squinted as headlights from a passing vehicle sliced through the tree line as it zoomed past. The beast had led him back to a road!

Theo instantly recognized it as the only road in or out of town. About thirty feet out from the street, the beast stopped abruptly. He could briefly make out its hulking form, then lost it.

Theo skidded to a halt, trying to see where it was perched. He owed it a thank you for leading him to safety and an apology for scaring it half to death. But as he stood there with his head in the trees, a trail of golden sparkles streaked past him.

His eyes were drawn to another shimmer approaching from the opposite direction. A third light appeared from yet another direction.

They coalesced near the location the invisible beast had stopped.

Theo watched from his bike as their eerie shimmers swirled around the base of a pine tree, glimmering like a miniature galaxy. They emitted a faint hum that reminded Theo of being underwater, which lulled him into a hypnotic stare.

Cuttlefish do this to their prey before striking, he thought. *They mesmerize them with a light show. Then, they attack.* It made Theo wonder if his replica was nearby.

As he plotted his escape, he looked to his hands, trying to will the heat to rise back up from within him. Maybe he could fight his way out? Part of him wanted to feel the primal anger course through his body again.

But all of his machismo suddenly left with the sickening snap of a twig behind him.

Theo watched as a silhouette, backlit by moonlight, took shape, mimicking his movement. *He* was back . . . .

Theo pedaled toward the road with every ounce of energy he could pour into his legs.

He could feel his lungs burning, unable to suck in the air fast enough to breathe fully. He rubbed his wrist over his forehead, trying to keep the sting of sweat out of his eyes.

Up ahead, the lights of Town Square were glowing in the night. He'd never thought he'd be so happy to see that mundane, pre-planned shopping village in his life.

Dragging himself toward his tract house, Theo dreamed of running a hot bath, changing his clothes, and trying his best to forget the past twenty-four hours, but as he got closer to his house, he could see his mother out on the front porch—she was pacing back and forth on the phone with frantic breath.

"Mom, what's going on? Are you okay?" Theo said with concern as he dropped his bike in the front yard.

"Someone broke into the house."

"Who would steal from us? We hardly have anything," Theo said, his confused eyes darting toward the house.

"I don't know! Maybe someone found us. Knows who we really are," Alice continued.

"But, whoever it was . . . they were searching for something specific."

"What do we do?"

"Get your stuff. We're leaving. We need to get as far away from here as possible."

Those words were like magic to his ears.

Theo sprinted toward his room, not wanting to give her time to change her mind. As he moved through the house, the feeling of glee that he might finally be leaving Crucible gave way to a sense of violation as he took in the extent of the damage.

His steps slowed as he padded through the living room; closets had their contents tossed, end tables had been flipped, and lamps were cracked in two. From the kitchen's center island, he could see the refrigerator doors were wide open, food and containers everywhere. When they first arrived the house was move-in ready, all the furniture was in place and the shelves fully stocked. So, Theo was sure whoever searched their house weren't the same folks that prepared it.

It could be enemies of my father, but what in the hell were they looking for?

On the stairwell, the drywall had been gashed open and defaced with red spray paint.

In his room, school books and papers were strewn around, his bed was turned over, and his mattress cut open. But all he cared about was his teddy bear. Somehow, it was unscathed and kicked upside down into the corner of the room.

He took the teddy bear from the floor and held it tight, breathing it in as he left.

Back downstairs, Theo found his mom with her coat and purse, ready to go.

Alice called for a car service; they were both more than ready to get out of this town. But no cab ever arrived. Instead, a familiar, blacked-out SUV eased up to the house.

"What the hell?!" said Theo, ready to take on the marines at this point.

"Wait here," Alice said, as she stepped away from the house.

"Are you crazy? What if it's the people who did this?!"

But she was already gone.

Theo stood on the front porch, watching as several official-looking men in suits stepped out of the SUV and met Alice as she approached. They took her toward the back of the passenger side of their vehicle as another SUV arrived, and Mr. Handler stepped out into the cool night air.

Theo watched as Mr. Handler and the men spoke with Alice in hushed tones as she argued wildly, motioning back to Theo, and then to the house. Theo already knew what his mother was going to say as she walked back.

"Theo, I overreacted.... I've been assured our secret's still safe. We need to stay."

Theo couldn't bring himself to look at her, feeling the stress of the day set in and wanting to cry. All he could muster was a meager, "Why?"

The question lingered in the air until Theo finally brought himself to look at his mother, the tears streaming down his cheeks—every day in this town felt like agony, and he couldn't hold it inside any longer.

Alice wiped away his tears and smoothed over his cheeks, wanting to cry herself. "This is still for the best. Remember that."

Theo watched as his mother, defeated and confused, strained to open the front door and enter the house.

Hesitating for a moment, she stood in the doorway and gave a nod for him to follow.

Theo looked down at the teddy bear in his hands, sickened at the thought of continuing in Crucible and tired of clinging to his old life. It was time to put away childish things. He threw the stuffed animal into the trash and then made his way inside.

CHAPTER 15

Theo arrived at school early by choice for the first time he could remember.

Unable to sleep, he was up before the sun, replaying the events since his father's death, taking inventory of what he knew thus far.

To start, his father was not Paul Pappas, but Odysseus—possibly the world's most famous Enhanced Human—who was killed in a Midtown explosion. His mother somehow knew Mr. Handler and allowed him to erase their identities and be taken to Crucible, where they were forbidden to leave under the guise of being "protected." Not to mention, Theo seemed to have inherited at least some of his father's Enhanced abilities. Oh yeah, and he wasn't allowed to talk about any of it.

With his bike secured to the rack, he hopped onto the concrete base of the flagpole and scoured the crowd as he tore through a pack of Pop-Tarts. He was determined to corner Shivansh the second he set foot on campus and shake him down for answers.

Shivansh had ghosted him after school, leading to Theo being ambushed by Jerry and the twins at the library and being stuck in the forest with all sorts of bizarre unpleasantness. He was convinced Shiv knew much more than he let on about the weird happenings in Crucible—and at this point, he was the only person who might be willing to talk to Theo. If he was even still alive.

The bell rang, and Shivansh wasn't there. So their awkward conversation would have to wait. Theo crumpled up the thin cellophane package and braced himself for class.

DOSTOEVSKY was written in neat bubble letters across the length of the whiteboard, announcing the start of Mrs. Diamond's famed Russian literature unit. As the class sauntered in, Theo felt like he could actually hear the sound of eyes rolling.

Shivansh slipped into class halfway through Mrs. Diamond's lecture on the sociopolitical tableau that gave rise to much rich Russian literature in the late 1800s. That ever-present spark in his eyes was dimmed. Instead, he looked different, tired, and disheveled.

"What happened to you yesterday?" whispered Theo, as Shiv took out his laptop.

Shivansh stared blankly at Theo like he had no clue what he was talking about.

"You were supposed to meet me at the library," said Theo expectantly.

Shivansh knitted his eyebrows. After deliberation, he finally said, "We need to talk."

"Let's talk, then," Theo fired back.

"Not here," Shivansh said, typing into his laptop. He turned the screen subtly so only Theo could see. It read: *Next period, meet me in the 2nd story boy's bathroom @ 9.*

Shivansh deleted it off his screen right as Mrs. Diamond appeared behind them. "Is there something you would like to add about the Russian flu outbreak of 1889, gentleman?" she said with an air of accusation in her voice.

"No, ma'am. Sorry," said Shivansh.

Mrs. D leaned over Theo's shoulder and whispered, "I heard about the break-in. I'm here if you need to talk." Theo squirmed, feeling her breath on his ear.

Without skipping a beat, she turned back to address the entire class about the first pandemic of the modern age.

Theo's chest tightened. *Did she know about the break-in because it's a small town and people talk? Or is there some other, darker explanation?* Whatever the case, the entire exchange left Theo with an uneasy feeling he couldn't shake.

⌘

Dodgeball was the game *du jour* in second period P.E. The glossy maple floor of the gymnasium was partitioned down the middle with mini orange traffic cones.

Like most Crucible classes, it was filled with multiple grade levels, and several middle school kids were pleading with Coach Kurts that they were at a disadvantage playing against the upperclassmen. To which the Coach answered with mock tears.

Theo kept his eye on the clock, waiting for the little hand to park on nine so he could ask for a hall pass to meet Shivansh, but at five 'til, the gym doors creaked open, and Dr. Limley awkwardly shuffled in with his porkpie hat and scuffed Gladstone bag.

Theo's stomach twisted. He immediately knew the doctor was there for him.

Dr. Limley shook hands with Coach Kurts, and a few pleasantries later, Theo was being waved over to them. Theo's heart began to race, imagining the possible reasons Limley found it necessary to pull him out of class to talk. *Had his blood work come back bad?*

He watched the clock as he walked over; whatever this was, he had to find a way to postpone it to get over to Shivansh.

"C'mon, Alexander! Put some heat on it," Kurts yelled, encouraging him to move quicker.

Dr. Limley greeted him with the smallest of closed-mouth smiles. "Good morning, Theo."

"Is everything alright?"

The doctor hesitated. "Everything's fine . . . . We just need to do some follow-up."

"What kind of follow-up . . .?" Theo said, nerves tingling. *What is wrong with me?*

By now, every kid in the gym was looking in their direction, and their judgmental stares made Theo grow hot. He could feel his sweat pores starting to open.

"Why don't you come with me into Coach Kurts's office?" said Dr. Limley, gesturing toward the diamond mesh window. "We can discuss things in private."

Theo eyed the clock; it was two minutes after nine. "Can I use the restroom first?"

"Good idea," said Dr. Limley. "I'll come with you. We can get a urine sample."

⁂

Walking through the halls with Limley was one of the most socially awkward situations Theo had ever been party to. It was silent, save for the searing squeak of a Sharpie being pressed against the label of a plastic pee cup. Dr. Limley held the cup away from his face into the light and squinted. "I think I spelled that right."

He handed the cup to Theo and stuck the Sharpie tip into the cap, fixed between his teeth like a cigar. "There you are, Champ." Theo grimaced at the unsanitary act.

"Thanks?" said Theo, his mind racing to find a way to ditch the doctor. No immediate solutions presented themselves. He needed more time. "So, should I be worried?"

"No. We just need a larger sample to run some additional tests. It's standard."

They stopped at the first-story restroom. Shivansh was on level two. This was a problem.

"I'll wait out here," said Dr. Limley.

Theo nodded and put his hand on the door, but instead of opening it, he turned and bolted down the hall toward the stairway.

"Hey! Come back here," demanded Dr. Limley.

But Theo had already committed, and there was no turning back. He ran up the stairs two at a time and flew into the second-story boy's bathroom at full throttle.

He leaned against the door to keep it shut. He felt his skin tickle with sweat as his chest heaved in and out like a bagpipe while he caught his breath.

"Is that you?" called a timid voice from the far stall.

"If 'you' is Theo . . . then, yes," said Theo, between ragged breaths.

A metal lock rattled, and dry hinges groaned as the stall door opened to reveal Shivansh, sitting on the closed toilet seat.

"Remind me . . . why are we meeting in the bathroom?" asked Theo. "That's how rumors get started."

"It's the only place without a camera . . . . At least, I think it is," he said, looking around.

Theo haphazardly scanned the windowless walls and air vent as if he'd be able to spot a recording device the size of a pin tip embedded inside. He shrugged.

"So, what happened yesterday?"

"That's what I wanted to ask you," said Shivansh.

"Don't mess with me."

"I'm not—"

"You said you would meet me at the library after school."

"The library? Why?"

"C'mon, dude. Stop gaslighting me."

Shivansh buried his face into the palm of his hands. "I don't remember . . . seriously."

"Sure," said Theo, starting to lose his chill. "You know what I think? I think you set me up to get jumped by Jerry and the twins—"

"What're you talking about?!"

"Maybe you're the one who robbed my house since you knew I wasn't gonna be there."

"Your house was robbed?" said Shivansh, rising from the toilet seat. He made his way over to the sink to splash water on his face, mumbling to himself the entire way.

Outside, in the hall, Theo could hear his name being shouted by Dr. Limley. He knew he didn't have much time.

"Okay, fine . . . I'm going back to class," said Theo.

"When did all this happen?" said Shivansh, now staring at himself in the mirror.

The tremor in his voice made Theo think that maybe he was telling the truth. Perhaps he didn't remember what they talked about yesterday; then again, it seemed too fantastic to believe—this kid literally remembered everything, committing Theo's class schedule and locker combo to memory with a glance. Theo proceeded cautiously.

"Right after we got busted on the elevator."

"When was that?"

"After English!"

Shivansh furrowed his brow and glanced at Theo's hand. "What's with the pee cup?"

Theo forgot he was holding it and hid it behind him. "Nothing. Don't worry about it."

"I remember leaving Mrs. Diamond's class yesterday," Shivansh continued, "but I don't know what happened after that . . . . Next thing I knew, I woke up in bed, late for school."

His expression was pained. He was obviously struggling.

"You really don't remember?"

Shivansh stared at Theo. "Can you do me a favor?"

"Depends . . . ."

"Think about the last time you saw me yesterday."

The request hit Theo like a bad smell. It was a strange thing to ask someone.

"Hold it in your mind," Shivansh said, getting closer to him. His intense eyes stared holes into the back of Theo's head.

"*Theo*!" called Dr. Limley from somewhere on the other side of the door. The doctor was getting closer.

Out of time and with nothing to lose, Theo granted Shivansh's request. He closed his eyes and called to mind the previous afternoon's events. He saw himself back on the elevator, alarm blaring, as Shivansh pulled him off. His mind's eye watched Phil, the security guard, run down Shivansh as Theo fled the scene. All the guilt and confusion surrounding the moment returned to his body as if it was happening again. He opened his eyes to find Shivansh staring at him as if he could see the memory, too.

The bathroom door smacked into Theo's spine.

"Open up the door," said Dr. Limley from the other side.

"Uh, who is that?" whispered Shivansh.

"It's my doctor."

Shivansh twisted his head in confusion.

"It's a long story . . . ." said Theo, turning to face the door in an effort to keep it shut—cursing the gods that no school bathroom ever has a lock. "You better hide."

Despite his best efforts, Theo wasn't strong enough to keep the surprisingly fit doctor out of the bathroom. Theo's shoes slid across the tile as Dr. Limley muscled his way in.

Conceding defeat, Theo stepped aside and let the doctor all the way inside.

"It was all my fault," said Theo. "Punish me. He had nothing to do with it."

The doctor looked at Theo like he was insane. "Who are you talking about?"

Theo glanced behind him to the row of open stalls. Shivansh was gone.

He had somehow escaped the bathroom without using the door. Theo was baffled.

Dr. Limley was not amused. He looked to the pee cup in Theo's hand.

"Alright, fill it up."

CHAPTER 16

The faint trickle of water turned into a roar as they reached a clearing in the woods. Shivansh motioned to a weather-beaten rope bridge straddling a narrow ravine.

"It's just on the other side," Shivansh said, turning his attention to the rickety bridge.

Theo inched to the edge to get a look at the river below. A gentle mist floated up the canyon wall, caressing his face.

"That must be a hundred-foot drop," Theo said as he peered at the rushing water.

"Closer to two hundred, actually," said Shivansh, taking an exploratory step onto the slippery wood planks of the bridge.

Theo thought back to the Walkway Over the Hudson. He and his mom used to go to the river walk with their dog Riot and bike over the Poughkeepsie Bridge. A bronze informational plaque at the center of the bridge declared the structure topped out at two hundred and twelve feet—about the same height of the precipice he presently found himself on.

He remembered that his mom used to buy him ice cream if he made it across the bridge and back without complaining. The memory warmed him into a smile and calmed his nerves enough to follow Shivansh.

"This doesn't feel safe," Theo exclaimed. His first steps were unsure and caused the rickety bridge to wobble.

"Just keep moving," advised Shivansh.

Theo did as he was told, putting one foot in front of the other to calm the rope walkway.

The air below his feet drifted up like an air conditioner on full blast, refreshing his overheated body. He and Shivansh had peddled uphill for the better part of an hour and left their bikes behind for another half-hour hike into the woods.

Shivansh had been waiting for Theo at the bike rack after school and told him to come with him *"to learn the truth"*—although what that meant remained a mystery. Much like the way he disappeared from the bathroom stall.

Every attempt Theo made to unpack the statement was met with silence or the same canned response: "You never know who's listening." It all felt very cloak-and-dagger.

Theo delighted as sunbeams lit up tiny water droplets hanging in the air, and a psychedelic rainbow bloomed in the sky next to him. The sheer beauty of the refraction took his mind off the precarious situation he found himself in.

Then reality came crashing in on him. All at once, Theo remembered he had never lived in Poughkeepsie. It was a false memory. The day's events came rushing back into his head.

After the bathroom incident, Dr. Limley took him into the little room behind Coach Kurt's office, where Mr. Handler was waiting for him.

Theo panicked and tried to run out, but Limley had locked the door.

"Please don't be alarmed, Mr. Alexander," said the well-dressed man.

"What do you want from me?"

"To see how you are," said Mr. Handler, as he unlocked a thick black Pelican case. "Doctor Limley tells me you've been a little under the weather lately. And yet you had energy enough to make the poor doctor chase you up a flight of stairs."

"I'm feeling better?" Theo stated, trying to play along. Mr. Handler wasn't buying it, and Theo watched carefully as he removed a VR headset attached to a spiderweb of SQUID sensors from a foam cocoon.

"I know these past few days haven't been easy," said Mr. Handler. "That wasn't our intention. Crucible is meant to be a safe haven for you and your mother. A place where you can learn and grow." He jammed the headset into Theo's hands. "Put this on."

Theo knew this wasn't the time or place to resist, so he slipped the strange device over his forehead and stared at a reflection of his eyeball on the black screen before him.

"It occurred to me," continued Mr. Handler, "that you're not sticking to the script because you don't know your lines. But we can fix that for you."

Theo felt Dr. Limley's cold, calloused hands on the back of his head, fastening the sensor netting into place. Next, the doctor placed thick joystick bracelets onto his wrists.

"I know my lines—I swear!" said Theo, squirming around in his chair. "Please, I've done everything you told me. I haven't told anyone anything—"

"Silence, Mr. Alexander! You will sit here until I am sure you're not off-book."

A switch was thrown, and the headset lit up, throwing Theo into a virtual memory of himself in Poughkeepsie as an eleven-year-old boy. In an instant, he watched himself flex in a mirror hanging from his closet door, pretending to be a wrestler.

It was almost like his bedroom in Queens, except his fake dog Riot was licking himself on his bed behind him, and he could see the Hudson River out his window. His real window faced the brick ledge of Dante's bedroom, *or did it?* He was having trouble recalling the details now.

Theo could hear the electric hum of the SQUID sensors broadcasting electromagnetic waves into his brain, helping to graft this new virtual memory over his real memory.

When he went to take the headset off, he felt Dr. Limley pull his hands back down.

"Not yet, Theo," warned the doctor.

Mr. Handler's voice crackled into his ears over the headset earphones, "Let's review the rules: Do we ever talk to anybody about who we really are?"

"No," whimpered Theo.

"That includes our family, doesn't it?"

"Yes."

"Even at the library."

"Yes," said Theo, feeling sick to his stomach.

Somehow Mr. Handler knew Theo had searched for his dad in the library. Either he was watching Theo's every move, or he had spies everywhere. Either way, the invasion of privacy made Theo's skin crawl.

Theo was forced to stay in the eerie virtual vice for what felt like hours, watching deepfakes created by some algorithm armed with a lifetime of social media posts, while Mr. Handler's voice kept repeating the rules of Crucible. "Don't go near the guard shack. Don't discuss Enhanced powers with anybody. Someone is always watching."

The weight of the day crushed Theo, and he fell into the rope siding of the bridge. The rickety structure couldn't take his weight and twisted on top of itself, launching Theo upside down. He tried grabbing the rope but couldn't grasp it fast enough.

He felt gravity push him toward the river below as Shivansh latched on to his arm. Shivansh used all his strength to pull Theo to the safety of the wet cliffside.

As both boys lay on the ground gasping for breath, Shivansh said, "That's the first time that's ever happened . . . you okay?"

"No," said Theo. "Where are you taking me?"

Shivansh gestured to a volumious winter bush at the base of a steep mountain wall some twenty yards away.

"The bush?" asked Theo, incredulous.

Shiv nodded.

Theo pushed himself to a stand, looking at Shivansh with a reluctant shrug.

"Well . . ." Theo said, brushing the damp wilderness off of his clothes, "if you were gonna kill me, you would've let me fall into the river, I guess."

He held out his hand to help Shivansh up.

"You can't tell anyone I took you here," said Shivansh.

"Don't worry. I couldn't even if I wanted to; I have no idea where we are."

Shivansh treaded carefully toward the bush, his eyes scanning the area for trouble.

"You can lighten up a bit, we're the only ones around. Besides, what is this place?"

"You never know who's listening—" said Shiv, making sure nobody was around.

"We're out in the middle of nowhere!" Theo said, doubting that even Mr. Handler could have cameras out here tracking them. Nevertheless, his eyes scanned the bushes, just in case.

Theo raised his arms into a "Y" and shouted toward the sky, "Is anybody out there!?"

His voice echoed off the mountain wall. He turned to Shivansh, smiling, "See?"

Shivansh just glared at Theo, unamused. "You, of all people, should understand the severity of getting caught out here."

"We're not allowed up in the mountains either?"

Shivansh pulled back several branches of the bush, revealing a small opening in the mountain wall about the size of a car door. Theo could feel cold air coming out of the impossibly dark entrance. It was followed by the smell of the stale earth on the inside.

"You first," said Shivansh.

"I'm not going in there," said Theo, folding his arms in protest.

"Fine," said Shivansh, as he crouched down and crawled into the opening, annoyed.

The bush branch he was holding snapped back into place, dusting Theo with a cloud of pollen and whipping his forehead. He sneezed five times in a row, his sinuses in agony.

Leaves rustled in the treetops above his head. It sounded identical to what he heard the other night, right before he came in contact with the strange beast-man. Theo froze, pouring every ounce of concentration he had into trying not to let out another sneeze.

"You coming?" asked Shivansh from inside the cave.

"Yup," said Theo, as he let out a huge sneeze.

Theo jumped through the bushes into the cave opening, his eyes fixed on the treetops behind him as he went. Just like Han Solo, he had a bad feeling about this. Mr. Handler's voice echoed in his mind: *"Someone is always watching."*

Belly-crawling through the black tunnel made Theo feel like he was part of the SEAL teams, although feeling his pants get wet with mud and thinking of the insect life hidden in the darkness pulled him out of the fantasy just as quickly as he'd thought of it.

These were his only pants, and his mom was a stickler for stains.

They rounded a bend, and Theo saw the glow of fire dancing against the craggy cave wall ahead. Shivansh whispered to Theo, "Stay here."

Shivansh slithered toward the glow and disappeared into a rabbit hole, leaving Theo alone with his thoughts, which were preoccupied with whatever lurked in the canopy outside the cave. He wondered if it followed them inside or if it would be waiting for them when they got out. Maybe it was a spy sent by Mr. Handler to follow him.

From inside the neighboring chamber, Theo heard muffled voices arguing—*were people inside this place? Has Shivansh set me up? Again?*

He became seized by a claustrophobic feeling of being trapped. Theo's anxiety spiked, and his heart started pumping fast. Too fast, in fact. He could feel the heat return to his skin. He had to go. He had to move. But he didn't know where.

Outside he heard twigs snap. His mind had been made up for him. There was no going back. He soldiered through the rest of the tunnel into the rabbit hole, which spilled him onto the floor of a spacious antechamber.

"Well, it's too late now. He's here," said a voice nearby.

Theo looked up, squinting into the quivering light of an altar burning with a dozen separate flames. As his eyes adjusted to the candle glare, Jerry came into focus.

They were standing over Theo, arms akimbo, shaking their head in a mixture of pity and disgrace. "I'll never forgive you for this crap, Shiv."

"What were you thinking?" said Anita, stepping into the light.

"Great. You've compromised everything! Now we need a new place," said Fernando, walking by her side.

"No, we don't. He's one of us," said Shiv.

"I'm not dealing with this. I'm outta here," said Jerry, moving toward the darkness Anita had emerged from.

"Guys, stop! You know why we're here, and you know I'm right," Shiv continued to argue his case.

From Theo's vantage point on the floor, it seemed like Jerry went into another room within the antechamber. *And maybe a better exit?* he thought, as he stood up with an assist from Shivansh.

"It's okay. I can leave," said Theo, brushing the excess mud off his knees. "I don't want any part of this. And honestly, I don't even want to know what this is."

"You're not going anywhere," said Fernando with firm eyes and folded arms. "How do we know you won't run out and narc on us?"

“I’m telling you, we can trust him,” insisted Shivansh. “I saw him with Dr. Limley today. He was on the headset.”

Fernando nodded gravely. Apparently, that meant something; time with the headset was a shared experience. Different memories, different lies, same pain.

“I’ll get him some water.” A gesture from Fernando showing he understood.

Theo took in the antechamber as Fernando dipped into the shadows. It was tall enough for him to stand in but not much taller. Beyond the candles was a mess of sitting cushions, blankets, and bedrolls. Next to that was a pile of vintage books stacked along the wall, with volumes ranging on topics from General Patton to crime theory. There was also a silver boombox from the ’90s and a smorgasbord of fast-food empties.

Anita reached her gloved hand out to Theo’s forehead. “You cut yourself.”

Theo touched his head and examined his fingers for blood, startled by her beauty.

“Huh, I didn’t even feel it,” he said, getting caught by her crystal-blue eyes. “It must’ve been the bush on the way in here.”

She grabbed a napkin from a fast-food bag and gently wiped the blood away, maintaining eye contact the entire time. “Didn’t notice it before. You’re cute,” said Anita, as she finished her operation.

Theo didn't know how to respond to the compliment. Was she flirting with him? Wasn't she with Fernando? Was this a trap? Overwhelmed, he pretended like he didn't hear it.

"So what is this, *Huckleberry Finn*?" said Theo. "You all meet in caves and chew tobacco?"

"It's the only place we aren't monitored," shrugged Anita.

"Their signals can't penetrate the rock," said Fernando, handing Theo a bottle of water. "It's like a Faraday cage."

"You're being watched, too!?" said Theo, choking on a mouthful of water. He had suspected there were others like him, but to get confirmation was as if he had just been informed Santa Claus was real. His mind lit up with a thousand questions: *Who is watching us? Why are we all here?* But all he could manage to say was a weak, "I thought I was the only one."

"We all did," said Shivansh, emptying curious green sand from his pocket into a circle outlined on the floor with stones. Silver specks glimmered in the candlelight.

"We were brought here against our will and told we were being put into witness protection," said Anita, as she pulled up her lace gloves and wrapped her arms around Fernando, further confusing Theo over why she called him cute.

"How long have you all been here?" said Theo.

"Most of us have been here about a year," said Shivansh.

"I've been here since I was eight," said Fernando, breaking away from Anita's embrace to pick up a baseball bat wrapped in barb wire from the corner. Theo instinctively backed up a couple of steps, as Fernando stalked the floor with the bat.

"At first, I loved it," Fernando continued. "My parents used to 'work' all the time back home. They were always out of the house, and when they were around, they would fight. But here, things were good, man. We spent time together, watched movies, and had family game nights. Me and my old man played catch in the park—American dream stuff. That all changed a few years ago when Limley showed up with that bastard with the cane. People got weird. Teachers started getting into everybody's business."

Fernando swung the bat into the air. Theo watched his movements carefully.

"We've been working on a way out," Shivansh added.

"You say another word, and I'll kill you, Shiv," said Fernando.

"He should know our plan."

"Stop spilling all of our secrets," bristled Anita.

"Wait," said Theo, confused. "So none of you can leave either?"

"You having a hard time following along with the conversation, sweetie?" mocked Anita, "Have you not noticed that Crucible is a prison for people with Enhanced powers?"

"Everybody stop talking," demanded Fernando.

He moved closer to Theo, getting in his face, "See, our families all knew each other on the outside. We know who we are, and we can trust each other. But you . . . ." Fernando pointed his barbed bat at Theo. "We don't know your family or anything about you."

"Doesn't my word mean anything?" said Shivansh.

"Not since you got pruned," said Anita.

"And his memories helped bring me back!"

"Shiv says you set things right," called a voice from the dark.

Theo saw Jenna and James emerging from the shadows in their gold sweatsuits.

"He's one of us," said Jenna. "I saw his power in the library . . . and his anger." Her familiar lavender and vanilla scent hit Theo's nose, triggering sense memories that both comforted and terrified him.

"Our bro doesn't wanna be here anymore than we do," said James.

"Anyone else in here?" asked Theo, keeping a nervous eye on the twins.

"Nope, we're the only ones that matter," said Fernando.

"Why are they keeping us? Who's responsible!?" said Theo.

"We don't know," said Anita.

"It might go all the way to the president, or higher than that," said Shiv.

"It's pretty simple. They wanna study our enhancements—" said Jenna.

"And control them," finished James.

"What is your power?" said Fernando, looking Theo over.

"I-I don't know," said Theo.

"Don't be afraid . . . show me yours, and I'll show you mine," challenged Anita.

Theo felt himself get warm, fearing what would happen if he couldn't show them. He closed his eyes and balled up his fists, trying to conjure the anger and summon the heat like before. But the only thing that happened was a tiny, disproportionately loud fart escaping his backside under the intense strain. It echoed through the antechamber.

The group hid their faces in laughter.

"What the hell are you doing?" said Shivansh, like a disappointed father.

Theo lowered his eyes in shame.

"Stinking us out ain't a power. I'm afraid I'm going to need more proof than that," said Fernando.

"I can do it," stammered Theo. "I just don't know how."

"Time you learned by example," said Fernando. He yelled, "Anita Dynamite."

Anita jumped to alert like a trained soldier, taking off her gloves.

Fernando swung the bat into her as fast as he could.

In one move, Anita caught the barbed wire bat, absorbed the kinetic energy of the swing into her body, and used it to twist around and punch the cave wall. An invisible energy wave burst out of her hand, warping the air around her and devastating the rock wall. It exploded into a million pieces as if it were hit with a stick of dynamite as it detonated.

Dust and rock fragments blanketed the antechamber.

"What the hell?" said Theo, covering his mouth, coughing as the soot hit his lungs.

"Gemini Gold!" yelled Fernando. "Unite."

"No," said Jenna.

"We're not your dog—" said James.

"—or your pony," finished Jenna.

"Why don't you show him your enhancements, Captain Nothing?" snickered James.

"We talked about this. Good leadership is a superpower, and I don't need anything else," stammered Fernando. "You know what? Screw you. It's time for the initiation. Grim Karma, show us the future."

Shiv's crystal blue eyes lit up with focus as he approached Theo, "Thought you'd never ask."

"Now, let's see exactly what's on your mind," warned Fernando.

CHAPTER 17

"The mantra is Shri . . . Aing . . . Namah . . ." said a soft voice through the darkness.

"She . . . ain't . . . nice . . . ." replied Theo, in a mocking tone.

A sharp, disapproving flick to his temple caused Theo's eyes to shoot open. "Ow."

"Knock it off. This is serious business," said Fernando.

He made a point to glare at Theo before retaking Anita and Jerry's hand in the séance circle and closing his eyes. The twins had opted out of the ceremony, allowing for Jerry's return. Before departing, Jenna exclaimed Jerry was the better choice to "try and figure Theo out."

Theo's eyes racked to Shivansh kneeling over his head, making him uncomfortable with the intensity of his stare. The way the candlelight hit his eyes made them glow white.

Somehow, Theo had allowed himself to be the centerpiece of this ridiculous spectacle, lying shirtless on a bed of green sparkle sand inside a circle made out of uncut obsidian, which jabbed the fleshy parts of his extremities.

"I stuck my neck out for you. Take this seriously," whispered Shivansh.

"C'mon, get on with it, Shiv," groaned Jerry.

Shivansh grabbed a candle from the altar and dripped hot wax onto Theo's forehead. Theo grimaced as the burning sensation spread with the wax along his skin.

"Repeat the mantra in your head silently," instructed Shiv. He pulled more of the mysterious green sand out of his pocket and mixed it with the wax on Theo's head.

"Anytime you notice another thought or sensation, go back to the mantra."

"Got it," said Theo, trying not to laugh at the absurdity of the moment.

Shivansh recited ancient text from a partially decomposed leather book, *probably Sumerian*, Theo thought, although he had no idea.

Theo relaxed and settled in, closing his eyes and repeating the mantra in his head while Shivansh delivered a chilling (and at times hammy) incantation.

Shri . . . Aing . . . Namah . . . Shri . . . Aing . . . Namah . . .

Theo wondered how long this pageantry would go on. His back was already starting to ache, and he was confident the obsidian rocks were going to leave bruises, but what choice did he have? He couldn't just get up and leave. He tried that already.

He heard the others chanting along with Shivansh as he returned to the mantra.

Shri . . . Aing . . . Namah . . . Shri . . . Aing . . . Namah . . .

The mantra boomed in Theo's ears as if some other voice was speaking it from inside his head. It was Shivansh, entering his mind for a second time.

Shri . . . Aing . . . Namah . . . Shri . . . Aing . . . Namah . . .

The voice was divorced from Shivansh's being—with a commanding presence all its own. Neither threatening nor pleasant. It just was.

"Everything you want is here," said the voice, "All you have to do is look."

Theo's eyes sprang open. As he sat up, he found only the warm glow of candlelight flickering in the antechamber.

Everybody was gone.

I must've dozed off, he thought, scanning the cave.

"Shivansh . . .? Anita . . .? Anybody?"

Theo's voice bounced off the stalactites and echoed back to him. "Figures."

He pushed himself up to a stand to look for his shirt, trying to figure out how he would navigate his way back home. As he fumbled along the cave floor, an uneasiness settled over him, squeezing his lungs like he was underwater.

Not only were the other kids gone from the antechamber, but so was everything else.

The blankets, the books, the empty food bags had all vanished. A gust of wind whistled through the chamber, blowing out the candles, leaving Theo alone in the dark.

“Hello?”

Sure they were playing some sort of joke on him, Theo eased further into the darkness, keeping his hand on the cave wall to help guide him. He thought if he could make it to the adjacent chamber, he would discover the entire crew hiding. They would all have a quick laugh, and he could put this stupidity behind them.

But the neighboring chamber never came.

The cave kept going, and Theo kept walking, without knowing how long or how far he had gone. Judging by the temperature, he was heading deep into the earth. At times it felt like he was hiking through a steam shower and he struggled to breathe.

The jagged rock surface under his palm transitioned into a smooth metal that was hot to the touch, and he heard a metallic crunch under his feet.

“Shivansh? Anita? Where are you all?!” Theo felt his stomach churn.

A pinprick of light blinked in the distance, cutting through the dark like a lightning strike.

Ahead he could see a figure, but his vision was hazy as a thick mist surrounded him, making it impossible to focus on what lay ahead entirely.

"Jerry? Is that you?"

The figure turned back to look at him, then sprinted toward the light.

"Wait!"

Theo bolted after it, watching the small dot turn into a blazing sun as they got closer. It was emanating from what looked to be the end of the tunnel. The metal tunnel was cubic and mirrored and reminded Theo of a supersized air-conditioning duct.

High-pitched rhythmic beeping spilled into the chamber from the other side of the light, ricocheting off the metallic walls and attacking Theo's ears in a brutal digital assault, as if thirty alarm clocks were going off around him all at once.

"Please wait!" cried Theo as the figure reached the end of the tunnel. But it was too late. The figure kept running until it was enveloped by the light and disappeared.

Theo slowed as he reached the blinding light, his lungs choking on steam. As he caught his breath, his pupils narrowed to the size of periods, and a room came into view.

He saw a pristine medical facility brimming with strange machines, rows of tanks filled with bubbling liquid where comatose patients floated inside, their breathing assisted via a snorkel device. Official-looking people in lab coats kept a careful eye on them, administering treatments and taking notes. Theo now recognized the beeping he heard as the rhythmic metronome of cardiograph machines.

From a loft above the floor, a well-dressed man with a cane surveyed the activity below.

Theo froze, sensing that if any of these people spotted him, especially Mr. Handler, he would be in real trouble.

As he turned to go, there was a flurry of activity on the floor as one of the cardiograph machines flatlined into one long beep. Lab coats rushed to the errant tank and initiated a sequence that drained the liquid faster than an airplane toilet. Mr. Handler peered down from his loft, leaning on the railing, deeply invested in the crisis below.

Once empty, the tank lid was opened, and he could see the unconscious patient encased in a viscous gel. And while the gel distorted some of his features, Theo recognized the man in the container, and his blood ran cold. The body lying in the tank was his father, Paul Pappas. Odysseus.

Theo shook with anger. His skin flushed. He could feel the fire in his veins, begging to come out, to the point his pores throbbed with pain.

A hand grabbed his shoulder with force.

Theo turned; it was the figure he had followed into the facility. The harsh light of the medical center revealed it wore a gold mask with ghastly features.

Theo tried to pull himself free but couldn't.

Desperate, he grasped at the figure, pulling off the mask to find it was . . . *himself!?*

Theo screamed, exploding into a hurricane of flames.

"Theo!" said Shivansh, "Wake up."

Theo bolted awake, gasping for air, drenched in sweat.

Shiv and Jerry tried their best to restrain his slippery arms as he thrashed around.

"It's okay. We got you," said Shiv.

"Damn, he's hot," said Jerry. "He's burning my hands."

Theo took in his surroundings. He was back inside the antechamber, lying on top of a circle of green sand—the mess of blankets, books, and fast-food empties back in place.

Fernando and Anita stood over him with concerned, somewhat horrified expressions.

"Welcome back?" said Shivansh with a cautious tone.

"He doesn't look so good," said Anita.

"If he dies, you're all helping me bury the body," Fernando stated, a little too honestly.

Theo tried to sit up, feeling disoriented.

"Easy . . . . I got you," said Jerry helping him. "You good?"

Theo took a deep breath, trying to get his bearings. He could see steam rising from his arms. The pain he felt in the dream was still present—fire lurking beneath his skin.

"You . . . keep . . . asking me . . . that."

Jerry poured water on their hands to stop them from burning.

"There was a facility," said Theo, still catching his breath. "I saw my father . . . he's alive . . . he's here . . . in Crucible. We have to tell people."

Shivansh and Jerry exchanged a look of concern about that statement.

"I think you might wanna keep that one to yourself, pal," said Jerry.

Theo rubbed his temples in confusion.

"Why? It was in the vision quest. Isn't that why you sent me? To find the truth?"

"Vision quest?" snorted Fernando, "You fell asleep, bro. You had a bad dream, and now you look like hell."

Theo glared at Fernando, waiting for the punchline.

"He's right," said Shivansh. "There was no vision. This was just supposed to be a gag."

"A gag?"

Shiv held up the "sacred book" he was reading from. He pulled off the leather cover to show it was just a General Patton biography.

Fernando started to laugh, and it spread to the others. Theo looked around at their cackling faces, hurt by their deception and enraged by their dismissal of his vision. What he saw during the ceremony felt more real to him than reality—even if it was fake to them.

He felt his jaw tighten and his eyes swell with tears. Pressure built inside him as a primal rage coursed through his veins, looking for an escape. He wanted them to suffer as he did. He wanted them to know his pain. He balled up his fists, staring at Fernando, who started this mockery and laughed louder than the rest.

Fernando noticed the shift in Theo and raised his barbed bat. "What's up, buttercup?"

The others took note of Theo's wild-eyed look, and their laughter turned to concern.

"Hey . . . we didn't mean anything by it," said Anita.

"We were just messing with you," added Jerry. "Like a hazing, y'know? We all went through it."

"I didn't want to do it," pleaded Shivansh. "They put me up to it. I hate jokes. I'm sorry."

"Why don't you just calm down, buddy?" said Fernando.

That was the lynchpin. You never tell an angry person to calm down.

Theo exploded into flames as he leaped toward Fernando with the ferocity of a tiger.

Anita intercepted him, absorbing the energy of his attack and using the power boost to launch Theo into the cave wall behind them. He hit so hard that his shoulder blades left divots in the rock.

He landed face-first on the blankets below, which immediately caught fire.

Jerry was gone, but the twins were back and quickly went to work putting out the scattered fires.

Theo recovered quickly, barely registering the impact. He leaped to his feet, eyes dancing with a spark of madness. Pure energy shot from his fists, melting the rock below his feet. He felt stronger and more alive than he ever had in his life.

Shivansh, Fernando, Anita, and the twins glanced at each other with frightened eyes, considering what to do.

Seeing their fearful looks overwhelmed Theo with sadness. *What had happened to him?*

He couldn't stand to see anybody get hurt. Dante used to make fun of him because no matter what movie they watched, Theo would end up crying at some point during the emotional arc. When he was younger, his mom tried to refund their annual zoo pass because Theo got upset seeing the animals in cages. He couldn't even watch reality shows because he felt too bad for the people who got cut or didn't get the date. And now he was in a blind rage, ready to kill his classmates.

The flames dissipated, and Theo fell to the ground.

"Grab him. We have to find some way to cool him off," yelled Fernando.

As they moved toward him, Theo pushed past them, knocking them over like bowling pins on his way to the rabbit hole he entered through, still feeling an incredible strength.

While the twins and Shivansh patted out the flaming bedrolls, Anita stepped in front of Fernando, eyeing the spiked bat.

"Give me a hit. I'll go after him," she said with a steely determination in her eyes.

CHAPTER 18

A smoky, red-blood moon greeted Theo outside the cave, casting a spectral light over the mountainside. Once again, he'd lost track of time, and was startled to see the night sky. He scanned the treetops, searching for the beast and listening for the slightest movement.

A sound echoed behind him in the tunnel, loud and fast. The mind-bending "fake" séance had ended in catastrophe. Whatever hope he had of making friends with the other prisoners had been obliterated by his temper. *Why couldn't he control his anger?*

Theo felt the sweat roll down his brow. The heat wouldn't go away. His body felt like a furnace; he was terrified. *What if he had another outburst? What if he hurt someone?*

He tried to pull himself back into the present moment. The others would be out here any second. He reasoned that they would expect Theo to run back toward the bridge, but he'd never get to his bike with them on his tail. He'd have to go deeper into the forest.

He sprinted uphill into a maze of gnarled shadows and leaped up the steep mountainside as if it were a flat road. Maybe it was the adrenaline, but aside from his body heat, he felt amazing. It wasn't just his increased aerobic capacity. All of his senses felt sharpened. He could see deep into the black canopy, as if it were daylight, and differentiate the smells of plants he passed. He could hear the blood moving in his veins and tiny animals scurrying under the foliage.

Instinctively, he knew Anita was on his heels, using the kinetic energy of swinging branches to vault herself forward in physics-defying sprints.

The sudden burst of sensory information triggered his brain to overload. All at once, he tremored with anxiety and struggled to focus on relevant information. The musky scent of wood moss weighed heavily in his mind as he identified a landing spot for his next step forward. It was too much information for him to process.

He hit a small pit and rolled his ankle, sending him flying into a wall of bracken. The fern blockade softened his fall, but not enough to stop him from slamming his head into solid granite rock, which made a sound like a wet washcloth hitting cement.

As heightened as his senses had just been, they were now dulled just as dramatically in the opposite direction. Feeling discombobulated and dazed, he closed his eyes.

When he opened them, he was looking up at the Milky Way. He had an unobstructed view of the stars. Once again, he had difficulty identifying constellations, but at least he was out of the forest. How long had he been out?

"Theo!" yelled Anita from somewhere far away.

Theo put his elbows down to sit up, but they went through the ground! He looked beneath him and saw he wasn't on the ground but laying on top of the canopy in a nest of thatched branches a hundred feet in the air.

"Theo! Where are you?!" said Fernando.

With this new context, Theo could pinpoint Fernando and Anita's voices as coming from the floor below. *So how did he get up there?*

His weight shifted, and the limbs making up his nest started to bow and crack. He clung to the most prominent branch he could reach, feeling its twigs stab his shirtless body.

"Did you hear that?" said Jenna.

"He's up there," finished James.

"Let him go," demanded Anita.

'Let him go?' thought Theo. *What were they talking about? Weren't they chasing HIM?*

A concussive blast ripped through the air, and the tree convulsed, violently swinging back and forth like a pendulum. Theo held on for dear life.

"Drop down, Theo. We'll catch you," said Fernando.

"No!" yelled Theo.

"Do it again," said Fernando.

Through a gap in the branches, Theo could see the twins charging toward Anita; she took their kinetic energy and channeled it into the base of the tree trunk.

The bark exploded like it had been sent through a wood chipper, and the tree swayed.

Anita hit the tree a third time, this time delivering a knockout punch. Again, the tree creaked and moaned as it teetered over.

"Jump Theo!" said Anita.

Theo let go of his branch, but his pants got hooked on another limb, and he fell with the tree in a symphony of shaking leaves and snapping wood. He prepared himself to get skewered under the massive weight of the ancient timber.

Right before impact, hands latched onto his feet and swung him back up to the canopy.

Hanging upside down from his new perch, Theo watched the fallen tree crash to the ground with such force that it uprooted three of its neighbors. A wall of dust and foliage exploded through the forest, reaching as high as the canopy.

Theo twisted and squirmed to try and see who was holding his legs, but he already knew who it was. Blood pooling in his head from hanging upside down started to make him dizzy, not to mention the throbbing he felt from his head wound as it intensified.

"Let me go!" demanded Theo.

The beast-man hoisted Theo up even further until they were face to face. Up close, in the light of the stars, Theo was shocked to find that the beast-man wasn't a beast at all . . . or a man . . . .

He was a boy.

More precisely, a teenage boy with a lean and very muscular build and the thin, scraggly beard of an adolescent. Theo guessed he was about fifteen or sixteen.

"Call your friends off," said the boy.

"They're not my friends," said Theo.

Another concussive blast split the air, and the tree shuddered with Anita's deadly punch.

"They're coming," said the boy. "Call them off—"

The boy froze midsentence, raising his head to the sky. He sniffed the air like a dog, and his face blanched. He was clearly spooked by whatever scent he had just picked up.

"It's too late," said the boy.

He dropped Theo and leaped out of the trees, sending Theo freefalling through the canopy like a dead-drop ride at Coney Island.

The boy went into a synchronized dive, catching a branch, and scooped Theo up to slow his fall before letting go again. He repeated the action a second time, right as Theo was about to hit the ground, and laid him down gently behind Anita and Fernando, who were still staring up at the canopy, searching for him. Then, without taking a beat, the boy-beast disappeared back into the trees.

Jenna and James witnessed the entire controlled fall and ran to give Theo aid.

"Damn, you alright, bro?" said James, taking Theo's hand.

"What'd he do to you up there?" asked Jenna, grabbing Theo's other hand.

The two worked as one to pull Theo to a stand and stabilize him. Theo needed the help. His brain felt like a pinball being smacked around the machine. A field of floating dots clouded his vision as his vestibular system worked to find balance.

"Looks like Nature Boy's back in town," said James.

"Never saw him that up-close," finished Jenna.

Anita rushed over to see how she could help. Fernando stayed behind at the base of the tree, his attention firmly fixed on something deep in the woods.

"Man, you're burning up again," said Jenna, placing the back of her hand against his forehead. James squinted at Theo's head, studying it carefully.

"Yo, is that . . . steam coming off your head?"

"Are you gonna blow up again?" said Jenna, taking a step back.

Feeling a rush of anxiety, Theo couldn't catch his breath. His throat tightened. His skin was flush. Sweat beads prickled his pores. He was nearing a full-on panic attack.

"Bigger problem! The Mirrors are here—! Everybody! Back to the cave!" yelled Fernando.

Jenna and James took off in a sprint. Fernando was right behind them. A strange flicker in the darkness caught Theo's eyes. A streak of iridescent sparkles.

The shimmer bloomed all around them and disappeared just as quickly.

The creatures were back.

"C'mon," said Anita, "we have to get out of here!"

All Theo could do was stare at her. He was frozen. Sweat bled through his clothes, and steam rose from his skin. His hair was completely soaked.

The shimmers got bigger and brighter fast, blinking in and out of the darkness like a swarm of angry fireflies. They were working their way toward them.

"Go without me," said Theo in between ragged breaths, not comprehending why she was helping him after his behavior in the cave.

"No," said Anita, taking off her gloves. Leaves touching Theo's skin began to smoke and blacken. He could smell the glue in his shoes melting in toxic waves of plastic fumes.

"I don't know what's happening to me," Theo's voice quivered. His eyes met Anita's. "I don't know how to control it."

"It's okay," assured Anita. "I can take it."

She smiled at him, and for an instant, everything else in the world melted away, and it was just them. Anita reached out her hand to smooth back his hair, but Theo flinched, "I don't wanna hurt you."

"You can't," said Anita. "Just let it out."

Anita wrapped her arms around him as she tackled him to the ground, covering his body with hers, just as Theo burst into flames—sending a ball of fire screaming into the night.

Anita absorbed the brunt of the explosion, sending her tumbling into the bushes. The outburst provided him with instant relief as if he'd just had a demon exorcised.

"Are you okay?" said Theo, fearing the worst.

Anita shook and nodded as she saw a light dance toward them through the forest. In a hushed tone she warned Theo: "Stay down."

The strange flickers of light reappeared within arm's length of them. The two watched as they swirled and surrounded them, hypnotized by their prismatic luster.

The strange light beings slowly started to take shape: three distinct figures, each one taking on the form of a young man and woman. Theo instantly recognized them as himself and Anita, and they were mimicking their every movement.

"Stay back," said Anita, as she moved toward the strange creatures.

They surrounded Anita, forming a triangle around her, and all at once, Theo saw thousands of copies of Anita, stretching into infinity. The beings weren't morphing into her and Theo. They were made of mirrors! The entire time Theo thought he saw his replica, he had really been staring at his own reflection in their looking glass bodies.

Anita took off her sweater, revealing a tight crop top with a lot of exposed skin. *She's trying to increase her ability to absorb energy*, Theo thought. *Damn, she looks good.*

"Come and get me, assholes," she said, squaring off in a fighting stance.

The creatures motioned for her. As they attacked, mirrored appendages—similar to leathery mirrored bat wings—unfolded behind them, making them three times as big and intimidating.

A brilliant light shone from their abdomens, like miniature galaxies swirling inside glass cages. Anita attacked the Mirror closest to her with a vicious stepping overhand. What should've devastated its flesh was instead swallowed up by it. She cried out in pain as her hand was sucked into the mirror's body, torn apart atom by atom as if the galaxy inside its belly was a black hole.

She used the energy from her molecular unraveling to kick the other mirror creature closest to her. The impact caused a dazzling energy wave to scream through the trees, obliterating everything in its path, but it wasn't enough. Her leg and foot were now fully absorbed into the Mirror, and the rest of her body was soon to follow.

Anita let out a blood-curdling scream—"*Run*!"—as it closed its bat-like wings around her.

The third mirror creature turned toward Theo. He was next.

Theo looked for an escape, but it was too late. The mirrored demon stood over him and Theo saw his terrified reflection in its strange body.

As it stooped over to swallow him, Theo was enveloped by a cloud of green dust.

The last thing Theo saw was a luminous, all-consuming white light, and then, nothing.

CHAPTER 19

An ethereal white glow gave way to a cloud of flickering green dust. As it settled, Theo quickly realized he was now on the floor of his bedroom, and someone was on top of him.

He felt a surge of panic jet through his veins before he recognized it was Shivansh. Theo tensed to scream, but Shivansh threw a hand over Theo's mouth.

"Wait here and be quiet!" said Shivansh in a frantic tone.

He reached into his pocket for another fistful of the peculiar green sand. It shimmered in the light as he tossed it in the air and yelled something mystical in Sanskrit.

Shivansh then dove headfirst into the electric dust cloud and vanished.

A second later, a new dust cloud exploded near the ceiling, and Shivansh tumbled out of it, holding Jerry in his arms. They came down hard on Theo's mattress.

Jerry landed, with Shiv, crashing down on top of them, elbows first. Jerry groaned in pain.

"Are you okay?" asked Shivansh.

"I'm fine. Go-go-go!!"

Theo lay there on the floor of his room in awe of this sorcery as Shivansh repeated the sand ritual and returned with Fernando. This time the dust cloud portal burst open inside the drywall, blanketing the room in a fine, baby powder-like particle cloud.

With no wall left to support it, the bland pastoral painting, Theo's lone room decoration, came crashing down, and the glass frame shattered into pieces on the floor beside him.

"I was starting to like that thing . . . ." mumbled Theo.

"Sorry," said Shivansh, pushing aside the frame. "Still working on the landings."

"Where's Anita?" asked Fernando, spitting drywall powder out of his mouth.

Shivansh's silence said it all. And it clearly wasn't good news.

"What happened to her?" said Jerry, still recovering from the elbow landing.

"The Mirrors got her," said Theo, too weak to sit up.

Fernando fell to the floor and buried his head in his hands.

"That can't be true! How the hell did you let that happen?"

Shivansh put a comforting hand on Fernando's shoulder, who sat hugging his knees.

"We shouldn't talk about it here," warned Jerry.

Shivansh repeated his mantra: "You never know who's listening." He took in the wreckage of the room, a weight settling over him. His face and posture sagged, and he somehow looked older than his age. He pulled a beaded pouch out of his tattered Union Bay cargo pants. It had once been filled with green sand, but now it was empty. He dumped the last of the pearly grains onto the floor. "What have I done? It's all gone."

"This shouldn't have happened." Shiv hid his eyes as tears formed. "Since the pruning, I haven't been able to see clearly." Pausing to compose himself, Shivansh turned to the others, "I need more sand, but to get some . . . . I just can't go through that again."

Theo wanted to know what "that" meant, but his mouth wouldn't work. All the energy in his body had been spent, and he was in a state of virtual paralysis. Despite his best efforts, he could no longer hold his eyelids open, and his entire world faded to black.

When his eyes shot open again, he was in his bed, wearing only his underwear.

Every muscle in his body ached, and he had the worst migraine of his life—the kind of headache that blurs the vision and brings a fresh wave of pain with every pump of the heart.

The only thought on his mind was getting water. He was dehydrated on a clinical level.

Theo eased himself up to a seated position, causing his now-busted mattress to squeal. Yet, to his astonishment, his room was somehow clean. There were no signs of the pulverized drywall or green sand. Even his awful pastoral painting was off the floor, hanging over his bed on a different wall—minus its cheap, Walmart glass frame.

He heard rustling in his closet and reflexively pulled his covers over his bare flesh. It was Jenna! And for some reason, she was rummaging through his dresser drawers . . . .

Never far away from her, Theo looked for James. He caught a sliver of him snooping through his medicine cabinet in the bathroom across the hall.

As Jenna got to his drawer of boxer briefs, Theo cleared his throat, "Can I help you?!"

Jenna and James both stopped in their respective tracks.

"He's up," they said in unison.

Theo smacked his mouth, trying to moisten it.

Jenna nodded and approached the bed with a cold bottle of Gatorade, as James entered the room from the hall, taking care to close the door as gently as possible.

Theo chugged the entire bottle in one go and was still left feeling thirsty. "Got any more?" he said, letting the bottle fall to the floor.

"Hey, we just cleaned up, man," said James, motioning to the spent bottle.

Jenna picked it up and put it in one of half a dozen overstuffed trash bags lined up along the baseboard, evidence of the chaos that had transpired.

"Thank you," said Theo, feeling slightly embarrassed. "You didn't have to do that."

"It wasn't for you, bro—" said James.

"You get caught, we all go down," finished Jenna.

"Where'd the others go?"

"Home," said the twins in unison.

Jenna fished another bottle of Gatorade out of her tote bag and handed it to Theo. He tore open the lid and swallowed as much as possible in one swig.

"What were you doing going through my stuff?" said Theo, between gulps.

The twins glanced at each other with guilty eyes. Theo clocked the exchange. It made him suspect they were caught in the act. "Which one of you took my pants . . . if you don't mind me asking."

"Umm . . ." started James.

"It was Jerry's idea," finished Jenna.

"Ain't nobody got time for this," said James, running toward Jenna.

She caught her brother in her arms—and in an instant, the two dissolved into each other and transformed into Jerry! Or, as Fernando called them, Gemini Gold.

The entire metamorphosis took less than a heartbeat. Theo sat there on his bed, watching this in a state of disbelief. His jaw literally dropped.

Finally, the mystery of the gold suit mafia was solved, and it pissed Theo off.

"That's just great," said Theo, feeling the Gatorade slosh in his stomach. "This is your Enhancement? Pretending to be three separate people?"

"Please don't," said Jerry.

"Don't what?!"

"Pretend like you know what you're talking about."

Theo kicked his blanket off and swung his feet to the floor, forgetting he had no clothes on. He then immediately fumbled to get back under the covers.

"I just saw you smush together . . . or whatever the hell just happened."

"Maybe we should discuss this when you're in a calmer state—"

"Oh, screw you! You're in the wrong here."

"I was just trying to help—"

"By stealing my clothes and ferreting through my stuff while I sleep?"

"That wasn't me. That was James and Jenna."

Theo stared at Jerry, beyond annoyed. "Are we running through a 'Who's on First' routine here? Don't you mean that was you? Aren't you all one and the same?"

"No. They're them, and I'm me."

Theo squinted as he tried to wrap his mind around that statement. Jerry handed him the clothes he wore earlier; they had been washed and neatly folded.

"They were covered in mud . . . and blood," Jerry said. "I thought you could use a refresh. You don't have too many other options here. You dress like a cartoon character."

Theo softened. He was touched that they had cleaned his clothes.

"How's your head?" Jerry asked.

Theo rubbed his forehead where he had hit the rock, and it too had been cleaned and bandaged while he was out. It was still tender to the touch. "Good . . . I think."

With that, a cascade of memories was triggered.

Theo remembered back to the forest; images of Anita being pulled apart by the mirror demons haunted his mind's eye, and her scream echoed in his ears.

"What happened to Anita? What were those things out in the forest?"

Jerry pressed a finger softly against Theo's lips. "Shhh . . . later."

They looked down toward their other hand, where a boxy, cell phone-like device blinked in their palm. Theo recognized it as a bug detector. *That's what the twins were doing in my stuff,* Theo thought. *They were scanning for surveillance equipment.*

"Did you find anything?"

"It looks like someone removed most of it," said Jerry, glancing to the walls, "but you can't be too careful." They flashed a Mona Lisa smile and took Theo's hand into theirs. "I'm glad you're okay."

Holding Jerry's hand made Theo buzz with excitement. He squeezed a little tighter. "Why are you helping me? You were all hate back in the library," said Theo.

Jerry remained silent, formulating a response.

"I misjudged you," they finally said. "People like us . . . we need to stick together."

Jerry leaned in and kissed Theo on the corner of his lips, on the skin between his chin and cheek. It was unexpected and sensual, and Theo wanted more. As he went in . . .

"Theo, is that you?" asked Alice, knocking from the other side of the door.

“Don’t answer it,” whispered Jerry into Theo’s ear. Their breath made his skin tingle.

But Alice didn’t need him to answer. The door was unlocked. As she entered the room, Theo jumped out of bed. “Mom! Get out!”

Alice’s eyes darted past her son to the bed, “I didn’t know you had company.”

Theo turned to see Jenna and James sitting on the bed. Jerry was gone.

“Hello, ma’am,” they said in unison.

Alice took in the scene with a suspicious glare, “It’s getting late. Why don’t you wrap up whatever this is that you’re doing,” she said, stepping out of the room.

Theo looked to Jenna, then James, pulling up his sheets around him as they smiled.

A split second later, Alice reappeared in the doorway with a furrowed brow, “Theo, why are you in your underwear?”

“We were just leaving,” said Jenna, standing, caressing Theo’s cheek as she left.

“Later, bro,” said James, mimicking his sister’s actions; he gently touched Theo’s other cheek and followed after her.

Theo watched the twins walk out. He was more confused than ever as his mom took in the freshly pulverized drywall. Even though the dust had been vacuumed, it would be hard not to notice a missing wall and the half-dozen trash bags lined against the baseboard.

"Oh, I can't wait to hear this explanation . . . ." she said, as she placed her hands firmly on her hips.

CHAPTER 20

A beam of light streaked across the outer edge of Theo's eye toward his pupil, causing him to squint.

"Keep it open," said Alice. She held his chin firm to keep his head from squirming and shined a flashlight into his other eye.

"How is a light supposed to tell you if I have a concussion?" said Theo.

"If your pupil doesn't constrict, or if it gives a slow response . . . that could signify intracranial pressure or some other brain stem injury." She clicked the flashlight off and set it on the wobbly kitchen table, exchanging it for a cheap ceramic coffee cup.

"Did it constrict?" Theo asked nervously.

Alice ignored the question. She sat back and glared at her son with suspicion. His forehead had a gash and was swollen to the size of a baseball, his arms and neck were covered in tiny scratches, and his pants looked like they had been set on fire. She sipped her lukewarm green tea, making a slight slurping noise.

"So . . . you say all this happened playing tag in the woods?"

Theo reached for a glass of ice water sitting beside him. He rattled the cubes around to get them to fall into his mouth. "Yup."

"And the missing wall . . . the bags of trash . . . your burnt pants . . ."

"Roughhousing," said Theo, crushing the ice between his teeth.

"Roughhousing," repeated Alice.

She took another long sip of tea, keeping her eyes firmly fixed on Theo. An uncomfortable beat passed, and Theo felt the need to fill the silence: "Yeah . . . we were sort of doing a WWE reenactment. I was The Rock. Got carried away."

"And all this happened with the twins?"

"Just the wrestling part."

Alice raised her eyebrow. "I see."

It suddenly dawned on him where his mother was steering the conversation. "Whoa—hey! No-no-no. Not that kind of wrestling. It was all PG."

"You were in your underwear."

Theo sprung out of his seat. “Can I go now? Are we done?”

“Sit down,” demanded Alice.

Theo sighed and slumped back into the uncomfortable wicker chair, resting his head on the lacquered beechwood tabletop.

Theo studied his mother’s heavy expression while she searched for words, wondering how many details of his evening he should share if she kept pressing him.

“You know, I’m trying to make it work here. Chipping in at the school, keeping the house in order, and now I have to worry about whatever it is you’re mixed up in.”

“I’m not mixed up in anything,” Theo said, sounding more defensive than he intended.

“Then why aren’t you telling me the truth? I thought we could talk about anything.”

“What?!” Theo cried. “You’re one to talk! You’ve been lying to me my whole life.”

“It was for your own protection—”

“Stop saying that! I don’t believe you! You’re a hypocrite!”

“Theo, what has gotten into you?”

“This town! I hate living in this town!”

“Lower your voice.”

"I just want answers! Why is that so difficult to understand?"

Alice sat back in her chair, knowing she needed to tread carefully. Theo was shaking with adrenaline, trying to tamp down his anger, afraid he wouldn't be able to control it.

He looked toward his empty water glass as if he'd somehow find answers inside.

Finally, in the calmest voice he could muster, he said, "How about this? You tell me the real reason you brought us to Crucible and who that dude with the cane is, and I'll tell you about what I was really doing out in the forest."

Alice nodded. They looked at each other for a beat, sitting in silence under the yellow light cast by the cheap acrylic chandelier.

"I can't," said Alice, defeated.

"What's wrong? Worried 'they' might hear us . . .?" Theo pushed his chair back and moved into the kitchen, riffling through the drawers and tossing out silverware.

"What are you doing? Stop—" she said, as forks and spoons rattled across the floor.

"Huh, is there a mic in here?"

Theo opened the cabinets, looked under the sink, and turned over the trash can, recklessly searching for a listening device.

"Or maybe here? You think maybe your friend with a cane left a device to watch us? Maybe you're in on it with him!"

"Theo, stop. You don't know what you're talking about," said Alice, exasperated.

Alice went to Theo with a calming touch to the shoulder as he paced in the middle of the kitchen, the frustration getting to be way too much for him.

"I just want out of this place . . . . It's not a town. It's a prison."

Alice thought for a long moment, realizing he knew more than she thought he did. She rubbed her hand on his back in the way only a mother can. "We can't leave . . . not yet."

Theo pushed passed her and snatched a bottle of aspirin from the counter. He could feel himself heating up and grabbed his glass and went to the sink to fill it under the tap.

"I'm sorry I have to be so mysterious," she said, putting the silverware back in the drawers.

Theo felt himself getting angrier as the tepid water filled the glass.

"But your dad wanted it this way. He trusted the program, and we have to see it through."

Theo had stopped listening, focusing on the sound of running water as his rage continued to build within.

Suddenly, the glass he held cracked and shattered into pieces, slicing the fleshy part between his thumb and finger. The water ran over his hand, steam rising as it touched his skin. He looked down as water mixed with blood, circling the drain.

"You cut yourself. Come here and let me take care of it," said Alice. Walking over, she took his hand into hers and patted it dry with paper towels to examine the damage. "It's not that bad. Looks like you'll live," she stated, trying a feeble attempt at mom humor to diffuse her own concerns.

"You get your anger from me, kiddo. Your dad was always so calm. So measured, it used to piss me off sometimes, actually." She watched in awe as his body heat cauterized the wound. She nodded to herself as if this action justified everything they'd been through.

A peculiar knowingness crept its way into her expression. "I think I understand what you're going through." She made it a point to make eye contact with Theo before adding, "That's why we're here." She cut the water off to fish out the glass shards.

Theo suddenly felt exposed and caught, never having shown his mother that he was anything other than the little boy she'd known his entire life. Now, she suddenly saw him as something more, something closer to the man she always hoped he'd grow to be.

Broken from his trance of anger, he caught his reflection in the kitchen window, the night making it appear more like a black mirror. The fury and hatred in his eyes looking back at him shook him to his core. But there was something else there, too, something he had never noticed before: He looked exactly like his father did in the microfiche picture he found in the library.

It triggered a memory from the dream he'd had while under the phony séance in the cave; it felt so real. He could almost feel his dad's presence in the town.

"Have you ever thought . . . maybe he's still alive somewhere?" said Theo, emotional.

Alice shook her head. "I wish he were. Believe me. But he's not."

"I wish he was here. I wish he were alive and with us so I wouldn't have to go through this alone."

"You're not on your own . . . . I'm here. I can help," Alice softly pleaded.

"Can you start by getting us the hell out of here?"

Alice carefully pulled him into her arms and embraced him. Theo tensed, afraid he would still be hot to the touch, but his mom either didn't notice or didn't care.

"All I can say is . . . just hold tight for now. I'm trying to figure a way out of this."

Theo returned the embrace, wanting to believe his mother's words—but a lifetime of secrets and her seeming allegiance to the program that kept them trapped here made it almost impossible ever to trust her again.

Deep down, Theo knew that the only person he could truly trust in Crucible was himself.

CHAPTER 21

Main Street glowed in the morning light. Dew drops glistened across perfectly staged storefronts, and backlit American flags flapped in the gentle mountain breeze. Theo could smell the coffee and freshly baked bread as he biked past Café Crucible. For a brief moment, he was seduced by the idea that this tiny town was a slice of paradise.

Fernando disabused him of that notion, sticking his barbed bat into Theo's spokes as he cut through Town Square Park. He had been hiding behind the park's star attraction, the centuries-old ponderosa pine, knowing Theo rode past every day on his way to school.

The front tire immediately seized up, catapulting Theo into a tangle of roots and wet grass. His one clean outfit was soiled again with more mud and blood.

"You couldn't take a joke. Now we're all paying for it!" shouted Fernando.

Theo rubbed the pain out of his elbow, his head spinning as he tried to catch up with what Fernando was talking about. He had obviously been waiting in the park for some time, hyping himself up into some sort of caffeine and testosterone-fueled frenzy.

"No good morning?" said Theo. He pushed himself to a stand and hobbled over to his bike to assess the damage. The barbed wire punctured his tire, but the spokes had snapped his bat in two. Theo considered it a draw.

Fernando puffed himself up even more, enraged he wasn't being taken seriously.

"Did you hear me?!" said Fernando, stalking toward Theo.

"I heard you, I heard you . . . ."

Unflapped, Theo lifted his bike onto its back wheel and moved off toward campus.

A curious thing had happened to Theo overnight: He'd actually had a good night's sleep. After his heart-to-heart with his mother, he fell into the kind of peaceful slumber that babies are accused of having. There was no waking up or night terrors. Instead, it was blissful and restorative, and Theo woke up feeling great. No fever. No soreness.

Moreover, all the little scratches from his forest adventure had healed, and the gash on his forehead had disappeared. There was no trace of where he'd sliced his hand on glass—he didn't even feel angry. He characterized his mood as chipper, a word no saccharine-averse teenager would ever use to describe themselves. But here he was, enjoying a beautiful morning in the park, and Fernando wasn't going to ruin it. He began to whistle as he wheeled his bike along its back tire.

But Fernando wouldn't be ignored. He stepped in front of Theo, forcing him to stop.

"You're the reason Anita got erased," said Fernando, jabbing a finger into Theo's chest.

Memories from the previous day pulsed back into Theo's brain; violent images of flames and mirrored demons rattled his core. His brief respite from the hell of Crucible was over. It wasn't that he'd forgotten what had happened, just that his focus had shifted.

Somehow, the quiet charm of the morning had diverted his attention and lulled him into a momentary feeling of comfort. Maybe it was all the brain programming Mr. Handler had forced Theo to endure and the hours of reliving fake joyful memories in Poughkeepsie via virtual reality. Or maybe siloing off the trauma was a coping mechanism—the only way his subconscious brain could come up with to survive.

Either way, his contentment was replaced by dread and guilt. His shoulders tensed.

"What do you mean, erased?" said Theo, fearing the worst.

"The Mirrors," said Fernando in a hushed but angry voice, scanning the park to ensure no one was in earshot. "That's what they do. Anybody tries to leave this place, the Mirrors get hold of them and wipe their memories clean—"

Theo perked up. "You mean she's alive?"

"I wouldn't say that. She's a freaking zombie," bristled Fernando.

"Where is she?"

"If she got on the bus this morning, she's probably at school."

Theo dropped his bike and started running. Fernando called after him, "She won't recognize you, man."

⁂

Theo found Anita sitting alone in the cafeteria in front of a plate of cold pancakes. She was at the same table Shivansh had identified as belonging to her and Fernando.

She stared out the barred window, watching two squirrels chase each other around a tree trunk. A wistful aura clung to the air around her, making the scene resemble Nicholas Sparks at his melancholic best.

Theo approached with caution. "Hey, Anita . . ."

Anita smiled at Theo as he took a seat across from her. He examined her carefully, studying her smooth, creamy skin and golden-brown hair pulled back into a messy ponytail. There was no sign she had been spaghettified by demonic mirrored creatures less than twelve hours before—pulled apart one painful atom at a time.

"I think they're flirting," she said, nodding to the squirrels.

Theo glanced at the rodents. He didn't have the heart to tell her it was two males fighting over territory. One would probably kill the other before the day was through.

"I'm Anita," she said, extending a gloved hand. "What's your name?"

Theo's heart sank; what Fernando said was true. She really didn't remember who he was. He wondered how much of her memory had been erased by the mirror creatures.

"Hey . . . I'm Theo," he finally replied.

"Nice to meet you, Theo. I just moved here from Detroit with my dad."

Theo felt an overwhelming sadness move through him. This wasn't right, and it shouldn't be allowed to happen. He scanned the faces of the cafeteria, wondering how many of these other innocent kids, some as young as six, had met a similar fate.

Another terrifying thought entered his brain: What if his own memories had been erased? He would have no way of knowing. Theo felt his body deflate as if some hidden force was squeezing the air out of every cell. He slumped.

A heavy hand clasped his shoulder. "Gotta second, pal?"

Theo turned to see Fernando standing behind him. Anita lit up the room with her megawatt smile, a faint glimmer of recognition in her bright blue eyes. "Hi! I'm Anita."

"Fernando."

"Hey, you remind me of someone . . . ." Anita squinted, trying to recall some distant memory. "Have you ever been to Detroit?

"No, sorry . . . ." said Fernando gently.

"Oh, okay." Her attention drifted back to the squirrels as the thought she was reaching for disappeared into the impenetrable recesses of her subconscious.

Theo and Fernando's eyes met, both displaying mutual heartache.

The omnipresent surveillance spheres tracked Theo and Fernando as they walked outside the music room toward the lockers. From this angle, Theo noticed each row of lockers was painted a different color of the rainbow. He had assumed all of the lockers would just be green like his. Meanwhile, inside one of the practice rooms, some aspiring rocker gave the drum kit hell and provided the perfect sound cover for their conversation.

"How long's this been going on?" said Theo, picking his words carefully. The last thing he needed was to be recorded breaking one of Mr. Handler's rules.

"Since always."

"Will her memories come back?"

"Some might. But I wouldn't count on it. Being erased is way worse than any pruning."

"Pruning?" Theo repeated, remembering he had heard that expression before.

"It's the headset with the SQUIDs. It screws with your mind," Fernando said. "Replaces old memories with new, or just takes them all away."

Like they did to Shivansh and me, Theo thought to himself. "Have you ever been pruned?" said Theo, louder than he'd intended.

"Most of us have."

Fernando glanced to the sphere, uneasy. Theo nodded in acknowledgment and adjusted his volume to a stage whisper. "Have you told your parents?"

Fernando laughed. "They're either in on it or pruned themselves." He guided Theo down the first row of lockers, painted red. The elevator shaft was visible at the end of the aisle.

"No. I haven't told my parents," said Fernando. "We're on our own."

Theo felt a surge of fear seeing the elevator again. The way light bounced off the red lockers made the metallic doors of the elevator resemble a shimmering portal to hell. It also reminded him of Shivansh. He never got a chance to thank him for saving his life and found himself missing Shivansh's commentary on the day's events—what he had expected to happen by bringing Theo to the cave.

"Have you heard from Shiv?"

"Nah," said Fernando. "Using magic puts him in a bad place." He stopped in front of a locker with a fist-shaped dent in it. "Give him time. He'll come around."

"What about Jerry . . . or the twins? Theo felt a wave of genuine concern. "And are *you* doing okay?"

"Don't act like we're cool," said Fernando, twisting the wheel of his combo lock.

His abrupt shift in tone caught Theo off guard. He stuttered to get back on defense: "Y-you're the one that asked me to come out here and talk."

"I just didn't want you hanging around Anita," said Fernando, underscoring his sentiment with a well-timed fist into his locker to coax the door open.

"I don't really think that's up to you—"

"I don't care," exclaimed Fernando. "Just leave her alone!"

Theo watched Fernando wrestle his overstuffed backpack out of his locker and slam it shut again. The action made him seem like a petulant little kid.

"What happened to Anita wasn't my fault," said Theo.

"We were fine until you showed up. We were happy."

Theo could see the affection in Fernando's eyes and understood his anger. The truth is, Theo had felt a connection with Anita and didn't care that she might've been otherwise romantically entangled. He was blinded by her beauty and intoxicated by her Enhanced abilities, and—by the way—she had come on to him. But Fernando didn't need to know that.

Theo softened. "Look, man . . . I didn't mean to step on your relationship—"

"Just stay the hell away from us!" Fernando snapped. He shouldered his bag and stomped off down the hall, leaving Theo to marinate in his thoughts.

He stood there for a second, trying to determine what drum pattern the aspiring rocker in the practice hall was attempting. *Was it "Umbrella" or "Walk This Way"?*

"Good morning, Mr. Alexander," said a sharp English accent.

Theo spun around to find Mr. Handler standing behind him in a bespoke pinstriped suit. His silver-rimmed glasses matched his cane top, which, up close, Theo saw was a disturbing vulture with a dead snake in its beak.

"I heard you were starting fires in the forest last night," Mr. Handler said, with a bemused grin on his well-manicured face. He brushed a finger across his cane and clucked his tongue with a patronizing tut-tut, telegraphing his disapproval. "Now, you know better than that, Mr. Alexander."

Theo scanned the area, looking for help from other kids or a possible escape route, but couldn't find any. Fernando was right again; they really were on their own.

Mr. Handler buttoned the top and middle buttons of his suit jacket, making sure the third button remained open as style demanded. "I've gone out of my way to ensure you and your mother were looked after. You were made to feel at home here. Yet, I have not seen an ounce of reciprocation. Where is the gratitude? What would your father think? Rest his soul."

Theo swallowed uncomfortably, "I'm sorry . . .thank you?"

"Ah . . . you see, that wasn't so hard now, was it?" Mr. Handler pinched Theo's cheek. "Now be a good lad and run off to class . . . ." The bearded man smiled wide as he turned and poked the elevator button with his cane.

"Oh, and Theo, stick to the script. Bad things happen to people who don't."

The doors slid open with a digital beep—the same one Theo had heard in his fever dream. As Mr. Handler stepped onto the elevator, Theo noticed something very out of place amidst the erudite man's bespoke wool suit—a slim, blue nylon cord protruding from his hip pocket.

Mr. Handler addressed the onboard computer and stepped on, "Take me to the basement."

The metallic interior of the elevator was exactly like the metal ductwork Theo had been chasing himself through the night before. At that moment, Theo knew without a doubt that what he saw in the séance was real. His father was alive in Crucible.

CHAPTER 22

The sweet stench of Sloppy Janes permeated the teacher's lounge, and Theo loved it. He was on his third round of the meatless wonder with eyes on a fourth.

An insatiable hunger had snuck up on him in P.E. that prevented him from focusing on anything but food the entire morning. He tore through all the Pop-Tarts in the second-story vending machine and "borrowed" Coach Kurts's protein shake in the communal teacher's fridge, killing the powder-heavy beverage in one long slurp. But the hunger remained.

"Did you get taller?" Alice asked, stirring a packet of Splenda into a fresh cup of weak coffee. Her cafeteria spoon made the Styrofoam squeak.

Theo shrugged. "Are you gonna eat that Sloppy Jane?"

Alice sighed and slid her plate over to his side of the table. "Are you sure you don't want to sit in the cafeteria? You won't make new friends in here with me."

"I'm sure," said Theo through a mouthful of meat-less filling.

His encounter with Mr. Handler had shaken him, a feeling amplified by the fact that Shivansh was absent from Mrs. Diamond's English class, and he hadn't seen Jerry or the twins all day. The only people he knew in the lunchroom were Anita and Fernando, and who needed that drama? He felt safer here with his mother.

At the far table, the kindergarten teacher was ranting to her colleagues about how drunk the head of school had been at last year's gala and how embarrassing it was when he got handsy with one of the room moms. A dia-tribe took an interesting turn when Alice leaned to Theo and whispered: "The head of school is her husband."

Moved to tears, the kindergarten teacher excused herself from the table and worked her way over to the elevator near the copy machine. The doors slid open.

"Take me to three, please," she said, dabbing her eye with a tissue.

"Access denied," replied the computer.

One of her colleagues yelled after her, holding up a blue-roped security lanyard in his sausage hands. "Hey, Nancy? You forgot your badge."

Theo watched with rapt interest as she grabbed her blue nylon lanyard.

He had attempted to track the elevator shaft all the way to the basement, the floor Mr. Handler had requested earlier that morning, by walking down the neighboring staircase. On the top floor were lockers and music. The third floor was lower and middle school classrooms. The second floor held the lunchroom and teacher's lounge, and the gym was on the ground floor. It begged the question: Where was the basement?

The stairwell provided few answers. It ended inside the gymnasium, and there were no other doors or any indication that there was a basement level underneath. When he learned that it opened into the teacher's lounge, he got an idea: *You need a security badge to operate it.*

He noticed a blue cord sticking out of Mr. Handler's pocket, the same lanyard all the teachers wore to protect their security badges. If he could somehow get his hands on one of those badges, he might be able to get down into the basement, if the basement even existed. Still, he couldn't shake the thought that the answers he sought were down there.

His theory was all but confirmed when he witnessed the kindergarten teacher enter the lift with her badge in hand. "Take me to three, please."

The elevator replied, "Access granted, Nancy. Have a nice day."

Theo smiled at his cleverness. Now, all he needed was a key card and to come back when the school was empty.

Getting through the last two periods of school on a stomach full of Sloppy Jane was a grit test, but somehow Theo made it without letting air out of his back tire, as it were.

The previous day's events played on a loop inside his head: The nightmare he had during the séance. How his body exploded with pure energy. Witnessing Anita torn apart by mirrored demons and being teleported away by Shiv.

But most of all, he thought about Jerry. Theo was touched by how they stayed behind with James and Jenna to take care of him, and the memory of their kiss excited him.

Jerry still remained a mystery, and Theo craved to know more. If nothing else, he needed to talk to them away from the prying eyes of spheres and spies at school. He needed their help tracking down Shivansh and repairing things with Fernando. At the end of the day, everyone in the cave had been through an ordeal together, and this rag-tag group of Enhanced prisoners was the only chance he had of getting out of Crucible.

Without his bike, the library seemed much further than he remembered. Theo was relieved to see Jenna's matte-black bike with the fat tires parked in the bike rack . . . or maybe it was Jerry's. He still wasn't sure how it worked with them sharing a body.

The library had a smattering of young people inside starting on their homework—the after-school rush. On a cursory sweep of the mezzanine, Theo didn't spot Jerry or the twins, but walking among the aisles, he picked up traces of lavender and vanilla and knew they were nearby. He finally found Jenna in the 500s—natural sciences on the Dewey decimal system—where she was organizing volumes on the solar system and periodic elements on a book cart.

"Tag," said Theo, tapping her shoulder. "You're it . . . ."

Jenna stared at him blankly. Theo's face blanched with embarrassment.

"You know . . . like hide-and-seek?"

Jenna furrowed her brow and moved her head in an angry, rhythmic nod.

"So, what, you're pissed at me, too?" said Theo.

"She's wearing earbuds, bro," said James, sneaking up behind him. He lifted his sister's hair to expose her plugged ears. "Can't reach her when she's lost in the groove. It's her happy place." Jenna rolled her shoulders in time, adding to her stank-face nod.

"Oh, well . . . that's a relief," said Theo.

"But to answer your question, yes, we are pissed at you."

"Why?" said Theo, exasperated.

"Because that's what happens when you make a mess of things."

"I-I'm sorry," stammered Theo. "I don't know what happened. I just found out I have Enhancements. I don't know how to control them—"

James waved his arms and whisper-yelled, "When are you going to learn to keep your mouth shut? You trying to get us like Shiv and Anita? Damn! Just, take a step back, loser."

Theo regarded James's words, letting the hurt of his accusations wash over him. "You think I meant to get them erased?"

"I dunno. Did you?" James said, as he crossed his arms.

"What?! No!"

"Methinks the lady doth protest too much," said Jenna, nodding to the beat in her ears.

James's left arm and leg suddenly jerked to the side violently, sending books flying off the shelf. Jenna involuntarily mirrored his movement, her right arm and leg forcibly flailing around as if they were possessed.

"What's happening?" said Theo, backing up. Both of their faces twitched in pain before freezing in expressions of terror. They ran face-first into each other, melting into Jerry.

This is going to take some getting used to, Theo thought, slightly creeped out by the whole process.

"You have some nerve showing up here," said Jerry.

They squatted down to pick up the fallen books, resuming Jenna and James's work. Brushing off the bizarreness of the situation, Theo stooped down to help them.

"I wanted to see you again."

"You've seen me," they said, dismissive.

"I'm a little confused," said Theo. "Last night, I thought—"

"Last night was a mistake," said Jerry. They slammed a book on Venus down on the shelf. The sound ricocheted off the oculus for all to hear.

Theo knitted his brow, unable to comprehend why Jerry acted this way. "I thought you said . . . we had to stick together?"

Jerry just shrugged. Apparently, the sentiment had changed overnight.

They picked up an aged volume off the ground with a torn spine, a casualty of their metamorphosis. They brushed past Theo to get to the check-out counter.

Theo lingered in the aisle, trying to process his emotions, doing his best to stifle the impulse to cry as his chin trembled with hurt. He watched Jerry pull a set of keys jangling on a large ring from the front desk and move toward a steel door behind the counter. Theo shook his head. None of this made sense.

He charged the check-out counter with a head full of steam.

"Did I do something to upset you?"

"No, I just don't think I trust you," said Jerry, not bothering to turn around to look at him. They unlocked the steel door with a series of metal clunks. It opened into a workroom with several book desensitization machines, office supplies, and a computer terminal.

"What did I do?" demanded Theo, entering the room with them.

"You can't be in here," Jerry said. "Staff only."

"I'm not leaving until you tell me why you're acting like this to me."

"Fine."

Jerry placed the broken book on the worktable and scribbled something on a Post-it note. Theo crossed his arms, waiting impatiently for them to talk. Instead, they took their time, throwing away an abandoned water bottle and straightening chairs.

They leaned over the computer to power it down, closing out a YouTube video on the Jersey Transit System of all things.

"Oh, c'mon," said Theo, "talk to me. Tell me what I did."

Jerry pushed past him, cut the lights, and held the door open expectantly. Theo got the hint and shuffled passed Jerry; they stared straight ahead like he wasn't there.

"You talk about trust," said Theo. "At least I never lied to you."

"I never lied to you either," snapped Jerry.

"You told me the internet was censored here. That there wasn't access to social media."

"There's not."

Theo motioned to the workroom, "Then how are you streaming YouTube videos?" Theo felt himself heat up as he challenged them. The anger was returning. "You know what? Forget it. You don't wanna talk to me. You wanna play games? Have fun. I'm done." Theo turned on his heel and marched toward the exit, proud he stuck up for himself.

Jerry called after him: "You have no idea how close you're being watched right now."

"And you have no idea how little I care," said Theo.

"You need to chill."

Jerry put the keys back on the front desk and slammed the drawer shut.

"I need to get out of here, and I will," said Theo. "With or without you and your friends—"

"See? That's what I'm talking about! Everything is about you. *You* need to get out of here. *You* need to use the internet. *You* need to speak your mind and blow our cover—YOU! YOU! YOU! There are a whole lotta other people here in just as much pain, trying to figure out how to get out! Whose chances are being blown by your self-obsession."

"Oh yeah, like who?! You!?" Theo fired back.

"Like Anita. Like Shivansh. That's why I don't trust you," said Jerry, shaking.

"What happened to Shivansh?"

Jerry looked at the ground. "Nothing good." Their voice hardened. "Using his power comes at a cost."

Theo rubbed his face in frustration. "If I find a way out, I promise you I will come back with help and free everybody."

"You have no idea who you're dealing with."

"Are you talking about the old guy with the cane?"

"You mean Judge?"

"That's his name!? Jesus, I've been calling him Mr. Handler."

"Wilding Judge," said Jerry, shaking their head. "He's director of operations—"

More like judge, jury, and executioner. But Theo kept that thought to himself.

"He doesn't stand a chance if we work together against him."

"I'm not worried about him. He's second shelf. There's someone else, Someone above."

"Who?"

The massive door at the entrance creaked open. Theo watched as a trio of middle school girls talking a mile a minute burst in, bringing a gust of wind with them.

When Theo looked back at Jerry, they were gone.

"Jerry . . .? Jerry?"

He didn't think he'd ever get used to how they and the twins seemed to vanish in and out of rooms. He glanced around, making sure nobody was watching him, then leaned over the counter, grabbed the keys to the workroom out of the drawer, and left.

CHAPTER 23

Theo spun the large ring of keys around his finger, considering the many different sizes and shapes as they jangled. A tinge of guilt crept in for stealing them from under Jerry's nose, but he'd had enough of this cryptic place and its baffling citizenry. The time for action had come.

"Mom, you here?" shouted Theo as he stepped through the front door. The house was dark and silent.

"In the kitchen," her voice called out in a flat tone.

Theo found her sitting at the cheap dining room table. She had a faraway look in her eye and barely acknowledged her son as he stood there.

"Is everything okay?" Theo said.

"Oh, I'm fine, just tired. School stuff, you know . . . ." she said quietly.

"Why are you sitting in the dark?"

"I think I'm going to get to bed early. There's sandwich stuff in the fridge, so help yourself." As she excused herself from the table, Theo could tell something had happened. He worried that all of his extracurricular activities had put his mother in danger. *What if she's been pruned? What if Mr. Handler . . . Judge . . . took his anger out on her instead of me?*

"Oh, we have the Back-to-School Gala Friday . . . you should think about what you want to wear," she said, as she trailed off up the stairs to her bedroom.

"Okay? Good night . . . ." Theo replied, unsure what to make of her behavior.

He glanced out the picture window to the side porch. The remaining bikes were meant for women or children, but they would have to do since his ride still had a flat tire. He'd wait until he was sure his mom was sleeping before he enacted his plan.

⁂

Theo stopped as he entered his bedroom. Gone were the bags of trash that Jenna, James, and Jerry had cleaned up for him. The absent wall was now replaced with fresh drywall and paint. His bed had been repaired, and the glass to his terrible pastoral painting replaced. There was even a new addition: a full-length dressing mirror mounted on the sheetrock.

He checked his dresser drawers, which were now filled with a bank of neatly folded blank tee-shirts and blue pants cut from a stretchy canvas material. His closet was stocked with rubber-sole, high-top sneakers.

"Mom, did you do all of this?"

His query was met with silence. An uneasiness settled over him.

Theo shrugged and gave in to it; whether it was his mom, the program, or Wilding, he desperately needed the clothes. His one American BullShirt shirt and charred cargo pants had been put through the wringer. As he slipped off his shirt, he caught sight of himself in the mirror; gone were the spindly arms and bird chest of a boy, replaced by the sculpted pectorals and protruding biceps of a man.

The sudden transformation startled him but didn't stop him from flexing, conjuring up fake memories of when he pretended to be a pro wrestler in Poughkeepsie.

He pulled on the new clothes, enjoying the fresh feeling of soft fabric on his skin.

That's when he heard the whir.

A faint electric hum. He knew the sound well but couldn't place it. He moved closer to the patch of wall that had been replaced and listened. Nothing.

He stared at himself in the mirror, concentrating on the sounds in the room. It was so quiet he could make out his stomach gurgling and the filament vibrating in the lightbulb overhead, but the hum had stopped.

Shaking it off, he moved to his closet to get some shoes.

The sound returned.

It reminded him of the subtle grind computers used to make processing data, spindles and actuators spinning at speed to read data.

It sounded like it was coming from . . . his new mirror???

Theo approached the wall mirror and tried to take it down, but it wouldn't budge. He cupped his hands around the sides of his eyes to look into the glass without the glare of his bedroom light and was unsettled to find it was actually a one-way mirror.

There was something on the other side, although he couldn't tell what.

Taking care to shut his door, Theo wrapped two of his new shirts around his fist like a boxing glove and punched the mirror.

The first strike bounced off the glass, the second cracked it, the third sent shards to the floor, and Theo came face to face with a surveillance sphere.

The same Draconian orb that followed him around school and town had been placed in his bedroom, its fly-eyed sensors and lenses monitoring every metric Theo had to offer.

It sent Theo into a rage. He spit on the sphere and flipped it off.

"I know who you are, Wilding Judge! And I'm not afraid."

Theo covered the sphere with a blanket and bolted out of his room with the library keys in his pocket.

※

Theo eased his new bike, designed for a little girl, to coast as he approached the library. Its old-world design looked creepier than ever, cast in deep shadows by the full moonlight.

The ride there had been fraught, with Theo fighting off goosebumps with each push of the peddle, especially as he rode through the path in the woods in the dark. He kept expecting Mr. Handler to pull up in his armored chariot and send him back to reprogramming. Or, even worse, have the mirror creatures materialize out of the ether and swallow him whole. And being tickled by the frilly handlebar tassels the whole way didn't help his unrest either.

But to his surprise, he arrived without incident.

He tried a few keys before finding the right one. He rolled his eyes as the massive wooden door creaked open like it wanted to give away his cover.

His senses were on high alert as he stalked down the dark entryway and passed the front desk, where he could still smell the lavender and vanilla of Jenna's presence. Even in the dark, he could still read the tiny subtitles on the spines of books he passed.

He laid eyes on the workroom door and again produced the key ring. He made entry without incident and quietly stepped inside.

He kept the lights off and squeaked a worn-out office chair over to the computer desk.

As the outdated desktop monitor fired up, he could feel the charge of excitement and fear. He knew if he were caught here, it would most likely be the end of him.

The computer flickered to life, the harsh blue light of the screen searing his eyes.

To his surprise, he was on the home screen with only a click. He couldn't believe it wasn't security protected. He'd been guessing at passwords the whole way here and was slightly disappointed he didn't get to try any.

Theo set his fingers on the keyboard. He had planned to try to reach the one person he always counted on through thick and thin, his best friend, Dante.

And he finally figured out how.

Theo had been erased from the internet, and all of the usual social media sites were restricted in Crucible. But, for some reason, YouTube was working.

When he saw it on the screen earlier in the day, his mind immediately recalled Dante's food review channel.

The kid thought he was going to be the next Food Network sensation and started a review series to find the best sandwich in Queens two summers ago, nearly giving himself heart disease in the process. His rating system was simple. If he liked your sandwich, you got four crowns. If he hated it, you got no crowns.

Dante was always on that stupid channel, arguing with people in the comment section.

"It's all about engagement," he'd tell Theo. "That's how the algorithm sends you to the top."

And he was right. He'd managed to get close to 5,000 followers, and his channel came up in most search engine sandwich searches made in the greater New York City area.

Theo clicked around and made his way to the most recent upload on the page. A video posted a day ago entitled: "Hoagie, Grinder, or Sub?"

Theo played the video, tears quickly forming in his eyes as he watched his friend laughing and talking with a mouthful of a meatball sandwich. He felt silly but couldn't stop the emotion.

"We're gonna break format a little today," started Dante. Pausing to wash down his bite with a Coke. "A lotta people ask me what the difference between a hoagie, a grinder, and a sub is, and I have a lot to say about it . . . ."

"Such an idiot . . . ." Theo laughed to himself.

His attention shifted to the comments section, where people actively argued back and forth with snarky barbs.

> SandwichSnob85: "Nobody asked this fat ass to explain sandwich types."
>
> StrawberryPiazza: "Save yourself time: Subs = soft bread. Hoagies = hard bread. Grinders are like pastrami."
>
> SandwichSnob85: "Pastrami?! Grinders are just subs served hot, idiot."
>
> StrawberryPiazza: "Your mom is hot."

Theo noticed that Dante had replied to someone only minutes ago!

> DantetheGreat: "Guys, let's keep the discord friendly . . . ."

Theo felt a surge of excitement as he hovered over the keyboard.

He hopped onto the comments as a guest, using a nickname only Dante called him from their stint in Little League: "Snot Rocket."

Dante had been calling Theo that since he sneezed while at bat, got snot all over his hands, and blew their shot at state championships with a strikeout.

SnotRocket: “Dante, it’s me, Theo . . . .”

DantetheGreat: “Who?”

It took Theo a disturbingly long second to remember that it wasn’t his real name.

SnotRocket: “It’s Nick. Best friend for years! I need your help, man!”

StrawberryPiazza: “Your mom needs help.”

Theo sat there a minute, his anxiety racing in the quiet hum of the workroom, watching the comments as people continued arguing on the hoagie vs. grinder thread.

And then, Dante replied. Theo took a deep breath as he read.

DantetheGreat: “Nick . . . what do you want?”

Theo’s heart sank . . . . *Maybe he’s joking?* Or maybe Dante thought it was a hoax?

He typed back.

SnotRocket: “It’s really me—Nick Pappas. I’m being held in some town called Crucible, and I need you to help me get out of here.”

Theo waited as the thought bubbles pulsed in the reply section.

DantetheGreat: "Listen, SnotRocket, I don't know a Nick Pappas."

Theo stared at the screen for a moment in utter disbelief. The harsh blue light cast a pale glow over his face as a tear streamed down his cheek. He'd risked everything to break into this place only to find himself berated by his one connection outside Crucible.

SnotRocket: "Please, Dante . . . you're like a brother to me. I love you, man. Please! Call the police. Let them know what happened. Send help."

DantetheGreat: "NO ONE WANTS YOU HERE! UNSUBSCRIBE!"

Theo felt like the wind had been knocked out of him. The sadness washed over him. His best friend since he was in preschool had just disowned him.

SandwichSnob85: "Are we still talking about sandwiches here?"

Theo closed the tab and wiped his history before shutting down the computer and leaving the workroom. At that moment, he knew he could never go home again.

Just like Fernando had warned, he was truly on his own.

CHAPTER 24

Theo flipped off the camera as saliva slid down the lens, warping the image.

"I know who you are, Wilding Judge! And I'm not afraid."

The video froze. Theo looked like a hulking madman in the oddly stopped frame, about to cover the sphere with his blanket.

A thick, scarred voice bellowed from the darkness: "Screen off."

Theo disappeared. The floor-to-ceiling image was replaced by a thoughtful impressionistic painting on a rich mahogany wall so natural you'd never know it was computer-generated.

Wilding stood from a leather chair and buttoned his jacket. The office was decorated with sleek, modern furniture and smooth marble floors. Nearly every surface turned into a touch screen on command. His posture changed as he approached a massive stone desk where a slender silhouette sat with his back to him.

The silhouette gazed out of a glass wall overlooking a command center. Faint clicks and coughs from an army of agents crunching data could be heard below.

They were situated in front of an enormous, curved, two-story screen divided into tiny squares that cycled through every hidden camera in Crucible. Visible vector boxes analyzed everything from facial recognition and body temperature to walking gait and oxygen levels of unsuspecting residents.

"So . . . you saw the evidence," said Judge, reaching for his cane.

"We always knew he would be a challenge to contain," said the silhouette.

"Not like this. He's resistant to our programming. He seems impervious to whatever we throw at him."

"That's why I intervened," said the silhouette.

His hand caught the light from the curved screen below as he lit a tobacco pipe, highlighting lumpy, varicose skin with a purplish hue. It shimmered like it was covered in mucous and reminded Judge of a tongue.

"With respect," said Judge, choosing his words carefully, "I don't think our impersonating his best friend on YouTube will deter him for that long."

"You don't see what I see, Wilding."

"I've been tracking him since he was a babe," argued Judge. "He's everything like his father. He won't stop until he makes contact with the outside."

"Don't underestimate the power of social pressure. We have him where we want him. He's broken. He craves connection and will fall in line to get it."

Puffs of smoke wafted into the air above the man as he remained facing away from Wilding, not deeming him important enough to look at during their conversation.

"I recommend we turn him off," said Judge calmly.

"Let me understand this. You can't figure out how to do your job, so you recommend we kill the boy?"

"He's too powerful."

"Too powerful?" laughed the silhouette. "That's precisely why we need to manage this. To maintain the balance!"

Judge shifted, uncomfortable. The dynamic between the two men poked holes in the well-heeled veneer of his outward appearance.

"What about the mother?" said Judge. "I'm no longer convinced she's friendly to the cause."

"We visited her earlier this evening; adjustments have been made. I don't anticipate her being a problem moving forward, and she knows what's at stake."

The silhouette pulled his sleeve back over his purple flesh as he exhaled another lungful of smoke.

Wilding watched it curl around the air in tiny clouds as it dissipated.

"Everything will proceed as planned," said the silhouette.

"Yes, sir."

"And if I have to intervene again . . . you'll be the one that gets turned off."

"Understood," said Judge.

The silhouette put his hands on the desk to help himself to a stand. There was something very unusual about his dimensions, his body was too skinny for his tall frame, and his skull was grotesquely elongated—twice the size it should be.

Nonetheless, he was impossibly intimidating, clinging to the shadows like Nosferatu.

"I think it is time that he found the mask."

CHAPTER 25

"Do we have to do this?" said Theo.

He tugged on his bedsheet toga, cinching the loose strap back into place over his shoulder. His mother had insisted they walk to the gala—parading down Main Street for the entire town to see—and Theo was over it.

Alice playfully squeezed his biceps. "Look at you. Someone's been working out."

"Mom . . . please don't do that," said Theo. He was already self-conscious enough and didn't need his mom drawing further attention to his body.

"Am I embarrassing you?" giggled Alice.

Theo ignored her, but as they walked further, he cringed at the sidewalk near the gym. It was crowded with people in Grecian costumes: white robes and sandals with calf straps.

He suddenly felt underdressed. "These people went all out."

"Just smile and ask lots of questions . . . and you'll be the belle of the ball," assured Alice.

The Crucible High Back-to-School Gala was *the* social event of the year. In high society terms, this was Alice and Theo's coming-out party. She spent a good deal of the walk over underscoring how this would be an excellent time to make a new first impression on the town, and if they had any hope of fitting in with those that mattered, they had to nail it.

And Theo was more than game.

After Dante severed his lifeline to the outside world, Theo decided to embrace Crucible. Fighting the town had led to the worst week of his life and destroyed all his new friendships.

He still hadn't seen Shiv since the cave incident, and he'd barely talked to Anita, whose mind was still recovering from being erased by the mirrors. Fernando was still pissed off at him, and Jerry and the twins literally disappeared every time he tried talking to them.

Theo's primary goal of the night was to make things right, and he was glad to be on the same page with his mother for once. They'd hardly spoken the past few nights since he walked in on her sitting in the dark. So, to see her laugh both delighted and confused him.

They were handed plastic laurel crowns at the check-in table and sent through a tunnel of white paper streamers dangling from the gym doorway. Dance music blared from a tinny PA system on the other side—*Probably Earth, Wind, and Fire*, Theo thought.

"Theo!" slurred Coach Kurts as they entered the gym, slapping him on the back.

Both Coach Kurts and Security Guard Phil were dressed as Greek hoplite soldiers, standing sentry at the door in plastic bronze helmets, breastplates, and skimpy skirts.

"Welcome to 'An Evening to Remember,'" said Phil in an unironically flat voice.

Kurts slurped from a red plastic cup glistening with condensation as he looked Alice up and down with elevator eyes. "Whoa! This your mom?"

"Alice," she said, turning on her charm. "You must be Coach Kurts. Theo told me so much about you."

"Uh-oh, I hope he left the naughty parts out," said Kurts, holding Alice's hand longer than anybody wanted to see.

"I'm gonna look for my friends," said Theo, extracting himself from the awkward scene.

Theo only cared about finding one person: Jerry. It had been two days since he stole their keys and broke into the library, and he was trying to figure out the best way to give them back. He had smuggled the sizeable key ring into the gala, carrying them in his basketball shorts under his toga, where they kept digging into his thigh. His plan was to both confess his crimes and his affection for them. He also had wild fantasies of finishing what they started in his room underneath the stars in Town Square Park.

About three hundred families attended the school, and it seemed to Theo like most of them were inside the gym. Moving through the crowd, he was surprised by all the different accents and languages he heard. He hadn't noticed how multicultural the school was before—diversity was not the first thing that leaped to mind when walking down Main Street Crucible—but there were actually families from around the world in this tiny town. But as they laughed, talked, and danced, they all seemed to belong together.

It filled Theo with nostalgia for his old life. He longed for the sense of community he felt back home. In Queens, he knew every kid on the block, his mom was active on the school fundraising committee, and his dad used to coach Little League. The weekends were a wall of parties and playdates . . . at least before his dad got too busy.

The last couple of years had been hard. His dad spent a lot of time "on the road," and when he was home, he was preoccupied or in a bad mood. He and Theo's mom would bicker all the time, and Theo never knew what might set his father off so he stayed out of his way.

But given what he's learned since losing him, it all made sense, looking back on it.

Theo walked the baseline of the basketball court twice, looking for Jerry, but he couldn't find them—or anybody else he knew, for that matter.

Suddenly, he noticed a handsome couple dressed like court magicians: black-hooded cloaks and strange fedoras with raven wings where the feathers would typically be. They were walking with a little girl who couldn't have been more than six, dressed in the same golden leotard as all the younglings set to perform that evening.

As Theo moved closer to them, he was nearly sure they must be Shivansh's parents; he could pick out his friend's features in each of their faces: The mom had Shiv's same sharp nose, and the dad had gifted him his thick black eyebrows. Moreover, their eyes all carried the same forceful intensity, making them seem like they glowed.

Theo stammered as he approached: "H-hello . . . Mr. and Mrs. . . ." Theo froze, realizing he had forgotten his own friend's last name. He pivoted: "Are you Shivansh's parents?"

They stopped and glared at him for a moment, making Theo think he'd gotten it wrong.

"Yes, we are . . . and who might you be?" said Shivansh's father suspiciously.

"I'm Theo. I wanted to see how he was doing; he hasn't been at school lately."

"So . . ." glared Shivansh's mother. "You're Theo."

She turned to her husband, and the two whispered in Punjabi, which resulted in Shiv's dad leaning in close to Theo. "You are not to have further contact with our son, understood?"

"But, is he okay?"

"He will be. If he stays away from you . . . ."

They pushed past Theo and headed toward the makeshift backstage of rollaway whiteboards to drop off Shiv's sister with the kindergarten teacher. The little girl turned and flashed a cute gap-tooth smile at him. "Byyyyyee."

The lights dimmed as a tender melody came on, a deep cut from the Motown catalog. Theo had heard the song before but was too rattled to remember the name. What had he done to be banned from seeing Shiv again? And where was he? What happened?

The soulful jam inspired a massive run on the snack table.

Specks of light from a disco ball scattered across Theo's face, drawing his attention to center court, where Anita and Fernando were slow dancing on top of the Crucible High Knights logo.

Anita resembled Athena in her braided goddess dress and glitter eyeshadow, and Fernando looked like Alexander the Great in his deep purple robe. They really did make an attractive couple, but they didn't seem to generate the same heat he noticed when he'd first met them. Resolved to let them be, Theo went to look for his mother.

"Theo!"

Before he could turn around, he felt Anita wrap her arms around him and spin him into a hug so big and warm it smothered his thoughts of Jerry and his concerns over Fernando. Then, after several seconds of bliss, she broke her embrace and smiled at him.

All his mirror neurons fired, and he smiled back—it was quite possibly the first genuine smile he'd had since he arrived in town.

Anita smoothed the bedsheet around his chest. "I dig the toga on you."

"Thanks," said Theo, too stunned by her beauty to remember to return the compliment. Instead, he stumbled to recover, "I-I . . . I mean, you . . . look stunning."

"Bible length apart, you two."

Theo turned to see Fernando behind them. He adjusted his robe to expose a sheath around his waist with the hilt of a plastic sword sticking out. "Or heads will roll."

Anita pursed her lips, "Ignore him. He's been following me around all day." She focused back on Theo, "Are you feeling better? Didn't you have a bad fever or something?"

Theo tilted his head, thrown by her question. He looked to Fernando for answers. But, instead, he shrugged and threw his hands in the air as if to say, *your guess is as good as mine.*

"You got your memory back?" Theo said timidly, not wanting to upset her if she hadn't.

She smoothed Theo's hair out of his face and smiled. "Why would you ask a silly question like that?"

"Hey fire boy, where's your mom?" said Fernando, not-so-subtly changing the subject. He had drawn his plastic sword and wiggled it in the air, to not much effect.

"Oh . . . she should totally meet my dad!" exclaimed Anita. "Lemme go get him."

Fernando and Theo stood there as they watched Anita get absorbed into the crowd.

"She doesn't remember as much as she thinks she does," said Fernando.

Theo didn't know what to say. He half expected Fernando to jab him with his prop sword for the hug she gave him, but remembering his goal for the evening, he searched his mind for a way to make things right. An apology didn't feel appropriate, but neither did the silence. Finally, after much deliberation, he settled on: "So . . . your parents here or what?"

Fernando nodded to the snack table where Mrs. Diamond was directing traffic with the head of school, enforcing the one bag of chips limit while fighting off his advances.

"Mrs. Diamond is your mom!?" exclaimed Theo.

"She's also the CrossFit instructor and runs the farmer's market on Sunday. Small town." Fernando waved to Mrs. Diamond, who smiled and indicated she'd be over in a minute.

"Theo," said Alice, grabbing onto his shoulder. She held a frantic look in her eye. "Who were those people you were just with?"

"What people?" Theo said, confused.

"The ones in the raven hats? Who were they?"

"Is this your mom!?" shouted Anita, pulling her father toward the group. "It's so great to meet you finally!" Anita's dad was a broad-shouldered man of about fifty with movie star good looks, dressed in a bespoke, blue-and-white suit made out of the Greek flag. "Dad, this is Theo."

"Don Keaton. Pleased to meet you." Don stopped briefly to shake Theo's hand before turning to walk away. As Mr. Keaton faded into the crowd, Theo noticed the side of his head and was taken aback by a massive, bronze-colored plate fused to his skull.

What sort of trauma could have caused such a horrible injury? Theo wondered.

Things were happening too quickly, and this was supposed to be a cakewalk; an easy meet-and-greet with the parents before slipping away for a kumbaya moment with his friends. But now his mom was flipping out over raven hats, and the most attractive girl in town had Frankenstein for a father. He couldn't imagine how it could get any worse.

"Well, well, well . . . look who we have here," said Mrs. Diamond in her slow Southern drawl as she sauntered up to their small group. Her eyes were fixed squarely on Alice. "I heard you were teaching here."

"Do you know each other, Mom?" asked Fernando.

Mrs. Diamond responded with a loaded: "We've met before . . . once or twice."

Theo was sure the band was still playing, but all he could hear was dead silence. He watched his mom as she sized up Fernando's mother. Two panthers on the prowl, circling each other while looking for the right moment to strike.

"How have you been, Constance?" In using Alice's former name, Mrs. Diamond drew first blood.

While Fernando struggled to follow, Theo's synapses were firing in overdrive. Their secret was out in the open, and no amount of pruning was enough to put this genie back in the bottle. Theo was panicked over how his mom might react. The only upside to an all-out brawl would be an event powerful enough to make people forget about his behavior in the library a couple of weeks back.

Alice hung on Mrs. Diamond's words for what seemed like an eternity. She offered no response. Instead, Theo watched as her eyes narrowed and her jaw clenched. Whoever these people were to her, it was bad, really bad.

"Come on, Theo. We're leaving."

CHAPTER 26

"Mom? Will you slow down! What's going on?" said Theo, racing to catch up to his mother.

Alice had abruptly left the gala without saying a word.

She now stomped through Town Square Park with arched eyebrows and clenched fists—visibly distraught. Theo pulled up his toga to jog across the wet grass, slipping and sliding in his leather sandals.

"I don't understand," he said, finally reaching her side. "How did she know your real name?"

Theo had never cared much for Mrs. Diamond. She always set off a creepy vibe, but he thought it was mostly a schoolteacher thing. Nevertheless, it racketed his anxiety to a whole new level to believe his fears might be real. He needed to know what was going on, and it didn't look like he would get answers.

Alice still wasn't talking. Her eyes darted around as if coping with an intense bout of claustrophobia, clearly arguing with herself inside her head.

Theo turned his gaze to the heavens. It was another clear, cloudless night, offering front-row seats to the Milky Way. The moon looked cartoonishly big as it rose beyond the mountain peak.

Theo looked for Orion, still confused why he couldn't find the ubiquitous constellation.

The smell of freshly baked pizza from the parlor on Main Street brought his senses back to Earth. He calculated the odds of stopping for a slice, given his mom's manic state.

"How much do you know about The Pantheon?" said Alice, breaking the silence.

The sentence shook him. The Pantheon was always at the top of the *do not talk about* list. He carefully responded, half expecting he was being baited. "Only what you told me," he said, underselling how much he knew.

In researching his father the other day, he'd learned a lot about the terrorist organization. Scanning through decades of articles on microfiche had made him a bit of an armchair expert.

"Nothing more than that?" prodded Alice.

"Umm . . . I know they're a gang of criminals with Enhanced abilities."

"That's the simple answer." Alice stopped, allowing Theo to catch his breath.

"They started in the '40s. The war in Europe was over, but communism was on the rise. Our government found an answer to the threat, Enhanced soldiers fueled by a dangerous mix of patriotism and paranoia. They hoped to protect America by stopping any threats before they happened. Everyone in the government was happy until, they weren't. Instead of ending wars, the Enhanced warriors were creating new ones, and had to be recalled. Once back on American soil, they focused their attention on the supposed threats to our nation. These soldiers turned on their own country and had to be stopped."

Rest over. Mom was on the move again.

"I don't get it. What made them turn?" said Theo.

Alice picked up her pace, motioning for Theo to keep up as they walked in the direction of their neighborhood.

"They claimed they were forced to carry out war crimes and then were made scapegoats when the world found out what they did. They felt betrayed and said that the real threat to democracy was the government itself. The organization went underground and grew—evolved.

They became radical outlaws with their own definitions of right and wrong.

"This new group of Enhanced Humans wasn't just bred in a laboratory—they were being born. When they reemerged, they became so powerful that Congress reinstated the EH program to create other Enhanced Humans to fight them."

"Dad," Theo said, nearly tripping in the slick grass.

"Your father was everything they weren't," said Alice. "He made it his mission to dismantle The Pantheon, one member at a time."

Theo stared at her, waiting for the other shoe to drop. He appreciated the history lesson but feared why she felt one was warranted. "Okay . . . so . . . what about them?"

Alice took a deep breath and looked over her shoulder. "I saw several members here tonight," she said in hushed tones.

"What? Who?"

"That family I asked you about . . . the one with the raven hats—"

"You mean, Shivansh's parents?!"

"You know them?"

"I'm friends with their son."

Alice sighed and rubbed her temples, even more profound concern growing in her eyes.

“They’re part of The Pantheon?” said Theo, feeling like he had been gut-punched.

“His parents call themselves The Magic Masters.”

Theo combed through his memory banks, searching for clues he may have missed that would indicate Shivansh had criminal anarchists for parents—sure, they were rude to him at the gala, but Shiv and his little sister seemed so nice.

Alice continued: “They’re descendants of a powerful ancient tradition out of Northern India of invisible warriors . . . somehow, they got mixed up with The Pantheon and lost their way. Your dad locked them up after they transformed all the senators into vipers during a televised session of congress.”

“I remember that! That was Shiv’s parents?! What are they doing here?” said Theo.

“I don’t know,” said Alice with a grave tone. “That guy with the metal plate in his head is also part of The Pantheon. The press nicknamed him Powerhouse.”

“Holy shit,” said Theo. Then, realizing he cursed, he added, “Sorry . . . .”

“No. Holy shit is right . . . . Do you remember all those rolling blackouts when you were in eighth grade? It was that guy trying to take down the power grid, and your dad had the hardest time bringing him in. He’s like an energy parasite. He absorbs *everything*.”

Like Anita, Theo thought, remembering how she'd handled herself in the forest.

Theo's mind went to Mrs. Diamond, Fernando's mother. *Could this proper, Southern teacher with a passion for Russian literature be part of The Pantheon, too?* He hesitated to ask: "What about my English teacher?"

Alice chortled in disgust. "You mean Countess Blood? I wouldn't be surprised if she were the devil's only daughter. That woman is pure evil."

Theo recognized the name from his mom's meet-cute story with his dad. Countess Blood had been the one keeping Odysseus's powers contained via some ray gun in a van parked in Times Square while her colleagues attacked the city.

"People believed she was the leader of The Pantheon. Your father spent almost fifteen years tracking her down . . . ." Alice trailed off. Her eyes fixed on some distant point on the horizon. The color had drained from her face. "She's responsible for a lot of bloodshed and needless suffering."

Overwhelmed by what he was being told, Theo felt his body tense. Anxiety squeezed his chest and flushed his cheeks. For the second time in a week, his whole understanding of how the world worked had been erased and redefined.

"It doesn't make sense," Theo muttered to himself. "If Dad captured all these people, then . . . what are they doing here?"

"I don't know," said Alice.

They reached the edge of the park and waited on the sidewalk for the light to change, even though there was no traffic. Still, Alice looked up and down the street like she was expecting a crash.

Theo caught his reflection in the storefront across the street—the same office Wilding Judge had taken them on their first day in town.

"They told me Crucible would protect us from The Pantheon," said Alice. She shook her head. Her brow wrinkled over her eyes. "This place must be filled with people your dad put away . . . and their families."

The light changed, and Alice stalked across the street. Theo followed, momentarily getting lost in a surveillance sphere watching them from its traffic light perch.

They were decidedly not sticking to the script, and it would only be a matter of time before Judge showed up. The thought caused Theo's temper to flare. The hours of memory programming and fear he had been made to endure at the hands of that bearded old man were barbaric.

"Wasn't it Dad's idea to bring us here?" said Theo. He could feel the trickle of sweat in his pores as his blood pulsed with heat. "Isn't that what you told me?" His voice was forceful and accusatory. All the lies his mother had fed him bubbled to the surface, jabbing his brain like barbed wire. He wanted the truth.

He stopped, forcing his mother to face him. Mannequins clad in rugged outdoor wear watched them from their display case inside the closed American BullShirt store.

"It's what *they* told me," said Alice, sensing her son's ire. "They said we'd be safe here."

"Who's they? Judge?"

"Your dad was part of the program. He was here with Wilding and a group of others sensitive to the needs of Enhanced Humans. He helped build this town. Your father trusted Wilding, that's why I trusted him too."

Theo tried to connect the dots: Wilding must've turned or secretly worked with The Pantheon the entire time. Either that or his dad wasn't the hero everyone thought, and instead of putting criminals away, he took them to Crucible. Theo shrugged off both theories; they simply didn't answer the most critical question: Why were he and his mother taken here? If The Pantheon's greatest enemy was Odysseus, with him gone, why not just kill his family in Queens? Why take the trouble to abduct them?

Theo glared at his mother, he still felt lied to about his father and why she allowed them to be taken to Crucible. His voice quivered, unable to conceal his anger: "How could you let this happen?"

"I didn't know," said Alice. Tears were forming in the corners of her eyes, but she wouldn't allow herself to cry. She hated being vulnerable, especially in front of her son.

"You lied to me my whole life," said Theo through clenched teeth. "And now we're trapped here with these monsters!" His voice echoed down Main Street.

"I know you're upset," said Alice, backing away from him, "but you have to trust me—"

"*I am long done trusting you*!" exclaimed Theo.

Yelling released more adrenaline, which brought more heat. His skin began to steam. He stalked toward his mother, rage burning like flames in his eyes. His mind convulsed with images of the hell he'd been through—fake memories, demonic creatures, and constant surveillance. He thought of how the entire town was in on the conspiracy and how his new friends kept their family identities concealed from him.

It felt like the entire world was against him, and it pissed him off.

His skin began to glow like white-hot embers. His toga smoldered, and his sandals melted into pleather goo under his feet as black smoke rose from around him.

"I know you're upset . . . ." said Alice, still backing away. She stepped off the curb, putting a parked car between them, unsure what her son was capable of in this state.

"I need you to breathe, Theo."

"My name is *Nick*—!!!"

His body exploded with pure energy before he could finish his thought.

An intense white light lit up Main Street, visible from anywhere in town, followed by a powerful blast wave that felt like an earthquake.

The explosion obliterated half of the street in a massive fireball of devastation that rattled windows five blocks away and sent two-ton vehicles into the air like leaves riding a gust of wind. It left a crater the size of a house under his feet on the sidewalk.

The last thing Theo remembered seeing was a look of pure terror on his mother's face.

CHAPTER 27

A soft, rhythmic beeping nudged Theo from his slumber. His eyes fluttered open. Morning sun danced across a bland pastoral painting hanging by its lonesome on freshly painted drywall, lending it an almost ethereal shimmer.

Somehow, he had ended up back in his bedroom. Unfortunately, this was all too familiar. Waking up in bed after trauma was starting to become a nasty habit.

Nightmare images came crashing back into his mind: shattered glass, sublimated buildings. Cars flipping into the air on clouds of fire and, most of all, his mother's eyes frozen in fear.

Theo bolted up with staccato breaths, but his movement was restricted.

He looked down to find his wrists bound to a hospital bed in strange plastic cuffs. His bare chest was covered in cords and taped-down wires. He traced the beeping to a nearby cardiograph machine. Other strange monitors stood next to it, tracking his vitals.

"Hello! Is anyone there?! Mom?" Theo cried out.

Theo looked at his arms and body, realizing he should be disfigured by the energy he'd produced on Main Street. But there was nothing. He fought against his restraints, thrashing around wildly. How long had he been out? And how the hell did he survive?

"Haven't you caused enough destruction, Mr. Alexander?" said Wilding, appearing with the tap of his cane and click of his Oxfords across the wood floor.

"What the hell is this?" Theo said, panicked.

Wilding Judge pulled a chair to Theo's bed and rested his chin in his hands in an unsettlingly child-like pose. "We couldn't very well keep you in the hospital, could we? You might turn it into a burn ward . . . ."

"Where's my mom?"

"We'll get to that."

"Is she alive?" Theo asked, afraid of the answer that would follow.

"Why should that matter to you?" Wilding said. He studied Theo's eyes, enjoying the rollercoaster of fear and relief he was seeing reflected back to him like a conductor of emotions.

"Where is she?" exclaimed Theo.

Wilding ignored the question. He stood from his chair with the push of his cane as he cleared his throat, speaking as he paced about the room. "Now that it's just you and me, I thought we could have a little heart-to-heart about what this town truly is and how you can become a better citizen—"

"I already know everything. My father trusted you, and you screwed him over—"

Wilding stamped his cane on the floor. "It must be hard growing so strong physically without the mental capacity to match."

Theo fell back into the bed, trying to decipher the insult. "Dad meant for Crucible to be a safe haven for people with Enhanced powers—to protect them from people like you. And you filled it up with your Pantheon friends—"

"Wrong. But valiant effort. Crucible was always meant to be home to heroes and villains whose powers needed to be . . . contained," said Wilding.

"All I see is villains."

"That's your father talking. It's not so black-and-white, my boy. It's about choices, both good and bad."

The bearded man stalked toward Theo's dresser, where Theo's teddy bear was propped up. Theo tugged on his restraints, rattling the plastic cuffs against the steel frame of the hospital bed. But, oddly, he was more interested in his teddy bear. Someone had saved it from the trash.

"Don't worry, your bracelets are fireproof," mused Wilding.

"If this is about our parents, you're keeping all the kids here against their will."

"I'm sure you've noticed your friend group is a little . . . *special.* It's important we keep an eye on younglings who might develop Enhancements. You never know which way the apple will fall from the tree. More often than not, it's been our experience that kids follow closely in their parents' footsteps."

Wilding pointed to Theo with his cane: "Exhibit A."

"Tell me where my mom is!" demanded Theo.

Wilding collected the teddy bear from the dresser and straightened its little bow tie. "You did quite a number on mommie dearest. She had to be placed in ICU, where her human functions are currently being carried out by machine."

Theo felt the rush of panic and the urge to free himself as Wilding walked over to him and placed the teddy bear on his lap, looking him in the eye.

"You're lying! That's all any of you ever do is lie!" said Theo, seething.

"Careful, Theo . . . you are getting a little heated."

"Untie me. Now!"

"No-no-no. There are rules on my watch."

Theo cocked his head, confused by Wilding's phrasing.

"Oh, didn't I tell you? I will be your guardian until your mom recovers . . . or should I *say if* she recovers. I've watched over you your whole life. So I suppose this shouldn't be too different, just closer than I usually like to get."

"Go to hell," shouted Theo.

"You will have to be housebroken, I suppose."

Theo's body started to turn red at the thought of this man in the room next to him as he slept, watching over his every move, monitoring his every breath. Theo let out a scream, feeling himself getting hotter and hotter, his arms pulling at the restraints.

"I'm going to kill you for what you've done to my family!"

"Me? I'm not the one who put your mother in such a state. That's all you and that little temper of yours."

"I'm getting her, and I'm getting out of this prison."

"And how do you suppose you will do that? Don't you realize I will do everything in my power to stop you from leaving Crucible? And even if you did manage, you met the Mirror Men. They are always waiting on the outskirts of town. They are there specifically to keep thoughts like yours in check."

Theo stared at Wilding, adrenaline and body heat rising. Uncontrollable rage burned like flames in his eyes once again.

"No-no-no. You are going to stay right here. And you know how I know that? Because it's not just your poor mother who's under my care; there's another family member near and dear to you here in Crucible. And I'd hate for anything bad to happen to him—he's been through so much already."

Theo's vision of his father being alive in that bizarre tank flashed through his mind.

"Where is he?! Where are you holding my father!?" Theo shouted, furious.

Wilding leaned over and, wiping away the sweat from Theo's brow, said, "Your father always said you liked to play hide-and-seek . . . . It's almost like we're engaged in the game right now. But I imagine it's a little hard to play while strapped to a bed."

Suddenly someone attacked the downstairs door in a frenzy of side fist knocks, destroying Wilding's moment of malicious revelry.

Judge peered through the window to see who it might be. His expression shifted to one of unease. He buttoned his coat jacket. "You must excuse me for a moment . . . . Let's not start the newest phase of our relationship on the wrong foot."

Downstairs Theo heard Wilding argue with someone. Unfortunately, the conversation was too muffled to listen to details. At times, the voice sounded male, but it could've easily been female. Theo had a hard time focusing past the sweat stinging his eyes. His skin was glowing again. Steam began to rise.

The door slammed shut, Judge had left the house, and Theo could hear the low rumble of a large engine turning over. He recognized it as Wilding's armored SUV. He listened as it pulled out of the driveway. It was followed by silence. Part of him couldn't believe that Wilding had gone—that Theo had just been left alone, tied to the bed.

He could hear warblers sing and a lawnmower giving grass hell somewhere down the block. In the distance, sirens wailed. Theo tried to break free of his restraints, pulling so hard they cut into his flesh. Tears formed in his eyes, and his sheets became wet with sweat that began to sizzle under his skin. He thought of his parents. His mom was in an intensive care unit somewhere because of him and his dad was being held in some science experiment.

Theo screamed at the top of his lungs and ignited into a ball of flames.

His bedsheets and pajamas combusted, filling the room with thick, black smoke. He watched helplessly as his teddy bear melted in his lap, the only keepsake he kept from his father and the last remaining relic from his life as Nick.

Just as Wilding foretold, Theo's wrist restraints remained intact, impervious to his body's powerful heat.

However, the steel bed was not.

The metal softened in the maelstrom of energy radiating off Theo, and he was able to use his handcuffs to cut through the frame.

Glycerin bulbs shattered overhead, and emergency fire sprinklers embedded in the ceiling sprang to life, bathing the room in musky-rose scented water.

With his hands free, Theo grabbed his teddy bear and threw it to the ground in a vain attempt to save it. Instead, it clanged with the hollow sound of a hard frisbee on asphalt. As the flames receded and the smoke cleared, a streak of sunlight hit the bear's charred innards, revealing a brilliant gleam of gold.

Theo walked over to it carefully; it was a golden mask with ghastly features. Theo recognized it from his visions in the cave.

He lifted the strange mask closer to inspect it. Something inside coaxed him to put it on, but as he drew it closer to his face, he stopped himself. It somehow felt dangerous.

He wondered if the mask had been hidden inside the bear this entire time. He thought to himself, surely he would have noticed it at some point in the many years it sat in his room, all of the hugs he'd given it as a child.

He shrugged on some clothes and tossed the mask in his backpack. Wilding might be back any minute, and he had to get out of there.

He took one last look at his room, knowing he would never be back. His eyes fell on the sphere mounted inside his shattered mirror. Theo's outburst had scorched the surveillance device; blisters had formed on its blackened plastic shell, yet it was still able to track him, rotating as he moved across the room.

Theo stood in front of the orb. In one move, he ripped it out of the wall and threw it to the ground hard enough for the case to smash open. He then stomped on its electronic guts until he was sure they would never record again. He considered it his warning shot.

Theo was determined to find his mother and unravel the secrets of Crucible, knowing it would take everything they had to stop him.

CHAPTER 28

Mist rose from the depths of the canyon. Sunlight refracted off the droplets, creating thousands of tiny rainbows that flickered in and out of Theo's view. Finally, he had made the long trek back to the one place he could think of out of Wilding's reach: the cave.

He'd done his best to stay off the streets and out of the gaze of surveillance cameras on the way, cutting through people's yards and bypassing the town by taking the long way around through the woods. But, of course, it helped that something big was going down in town.

The entire way here, Theo had heard sirens and caught glimpses of armored SUVs with pulsating lights screaming down backroads. After the little stunt he'd pulled at the house, he knew Judge would be pulling out all the stops to find him.

It was probably why Judge had left so abruptly. Whatever was happening in town was allowing Theo the chance to escape. Now all that stood between him and safety was a wobbly rope bridge.

More concerned about the consequences of being caught than slipping on wood planks, he pulled his backpack straps tight and made it across the bridge without incident.

Crawling through the claustrophobic rabbit hole alone, he could almost hear the spiders moving in the dank cloak of darkness and feel their webs on his face. Without candles lighting the way, he became convinced he would get lost.

Somehow, he made it to the antechamber and felt around his bag for matches, congratulating himself for having the wherewithal to remember them under the circumstances. In the warm glow of altered light, Theo took inventory: there were bedrolls, books, and five and a half bottles of water. Rodents had eaten the junk food they left behind; luckily, he'd brought a case of Power Bars. They would have to last.

As he ripped open his first protein-packed piece of chocolate, Theo thought back over the last twenty-four hours and the shambles that had become his life.

After escaping from his home, he'd desperately needed to see his mother. The hospital was less than two miles from his house, and he could easily make it there by foot. Theo sped through the streets under cover of night, only hiding briefly in some overbrush at the park, when two fire engines wailed by to answer the call set off by his home's alarm system. Theo was running on pure adrenaline and was at the hospital entrance by the time the firefighters broke down his slightly scorched front door. He had to move quickly; as soon as they found him missing, the chase would be on, and there'd be no way for him to evade Wilding's troops for too long while in town.

Theo knew this was a mistake to be piled on all his other mistakes, but he quickly pushed those thoughts away and made his way inside. But, of course, Theo knew there would be time for recriminations later; Wilding Judge had played some serious mind games on him earlier, and all that mattered now was knowing his mom was okay.

The easiest way to make it through a place you don't belong is to act as if you do belong—that helpful piece of advice he'd learned from Dante back when they attended parties as uninvited guests—led Theo to stride through the hospital halls with the confidence of a chief surgeon, stopping only once to ask for directions to the ICU. Then, weaving his way through gurneys and disinterested orderlies, he stole peeks in each hospital room, hoping to catch a glimpse of his mother.

Theo wasn't sure what he'd find once he entered the hospital; all he wished was for it to happen faster. Time was against him, and every minute it took to find his mom was a minute closer to being caught. He refused to think the worst but was nearly ready to give up. Just one more room . . . .

His heart jumped when he saw a familiar face. It was Nurse Ratched, who, despite her unfortunate name, was quite nice to him the one time he made a voluntary visit to the school's medical office to deal with his persistent fever. She was standing over his mother with a sippy cup in hand, straw bent and ready. Theo was awash with emotion as he observed his mother pull herself up for a drink. He was joyed to see she wasn't tied to machines, as Judge said. There were bandages on her hands and face, and one eye was covered, but she was alive and able to sit up. Theo's eyes welled up with tears, and he could not hold them back. Only a lump in his throat could suppress his urge to call her name.

For the moment, knowing she was alive was good enough. Luck seemed finally on his side. He just wasn't sure how long it would last.

He had to get out of town; that was obvious. But he also needed to gain control of the power that burned inside him. His body was an Enhanced nuclear reactor capable of untold destruction. He had more than enough power to free himself of this place. He just had no idea how to use it.

Theo reasoned that even if he could teach himself the basics, escape from Crucible wouldn't be easy. The Mirror Men surrounded the town, and fully armed agents were on patrol everywhere. Theo had to get to the one place where he could secretly test out his powers.

In the cave, Theo wrung his hands, suddenly feeling overwhelmed. Judge's words echoed in his mind. The bearded old man implied he would kill Theo's family if he tried to escape, but the thought of another minute as a prisoner here was too much to bear.

Feeling like his power was somehow tied to his anger, he tried to use the emotional turbulence of the moment to summon the fire within, but it wouldn't come.

He took it further, racking his brain for moments in his life he had been enraged.

He recalled when he was seven, and his dad told him he'd pick him up early from school to go to the traveling carnival, and he never showed up. No fire came. He thought about when his mother spilled red Kool-Aid on his new baseball card collection and how Dante told Christina that he liked her when they were in seventh grade, and her response was to yell "*Theo reeks!*" loud enough for the entire class to hear. But that didn't work either.

Theo poured the contents of his backpack onto the ground. It occurred to him he was still hungry. Maybe he just needed a Power Bar, and fresh ideas would blossom.

The mask toppled out with the bars, hitting the ground like a blacksmith hammer hitting an anvil. Theo picked it up. The inside shimmered in the candlelight. He had thrown the strange object in his bag on impulse without really understanding why.

He thought about his vision of himself wearing the mask in this cave and took it into his hands. He was suddenly overcome with an impulse to put it on, almost as if the mask was beckoning him. He slowly raised it to his forehead.

The metal grabbed his skin when it touched his face and melted into his flesh. The sensation wasn't painful, so much as it was odd. It reminded Theo of putting his arm inside a blood pressure machine at the drug store. He clenched his fist as the pressure squeezed his temple. The fire throughout his body was channeled into the mask, holding it, controlling it.

With a single thought, flame exploded from the mask in a concentrated burst.

Changing tactic, Theo refocused and put forth a short staccato blast—similar to a laser cannon—strong enough to leave a basketball-sized crater in the cave wall. Theo pulled off the mask and stared at it. It was still smoking from the discharge. *How the hell did that happen?*

Theo picked a new spot on the wall and nervously placed the mask on again. Another thought, another concentrated burst of energy, igniting the air as it bored out another chunk of the cave wall. Theo nodded in approval as debris rained down.

Theo squinted as if squeezing his eyes to narrow the blasts. He fired again. And again. And again. Letting the energy flow for longer, more powerful bursts every time. He spent the next twenty minutes playing with his new toy, allowing pure, concentrated heat to flow from him—his own personal volcanic laser. Focused starlight. Fire beams sliced the cave rock like a hot knife through butter.

The mask somehow knew his intentions. If the thought occurred to him that he wanted to emit a small beam, the mask accommodated. If he wanted to make a fireball, it would make it happen. But always, the physical activity was the same. The mask was a conduit of fire.

"What's that you're wearing? Practicing for the school play?"

Theo turned, startled to see Jerry standing behind him. They brushed the mud off themselves they had picked up on the way through the rabbit hole.

"Or are you secretly into latex?" Jerry added coyly.

Theo's stomach immediately filled with butterflies as he watched Jerry take in the eviscerated cave wall, parts of it still glowing cherry red. Jerry coughed on the thick steam hanging in the air. "Whatever you're doing, you'll roast yourself alive in here."

Feeling self-conscious and a little embarrassed, Theo peeled off the mask and stuffed it in his back pocket, rubbing his face where it had been. "Long story. How'd you know I was here?"

"This is *our* secret hideout, remember?" snapped Jerry.

Theo kicked smoldering rubble and Power Bar wrappers out of the way in a half-hearted attempt to straighten up, realizing the damage he had caused. He stammered nervously, "I-I'm sorry, I didn't know where else to go."

"Sure . . . I guess it's tough to find good places to melt in town," deadpanned Jerry.

An awkward silence filled the air. Theo wanted to make things right with them. He wished to confess he stole the library keys and apologize for being a selfish jerk but didn't know how. Jerry beat him to the punch. "I need to talk to you about the library—"

"I'm sorry," said Theo. "I wanted to tell you I took the keys, but every time I tried to talk to you, you'd disappear and leave me with Jenna and James."

"I know . . . ." Jerry said. They trailed off and looked away, making it impossible for Theo to guess what they were thinking. "I'm the one that should be apologizing."

"For what?" said Theo.

Jerry hesitated for a moment, then looked Theo in the eyes. "I kinda set you up."

"I . . . don't understand," said Theo as he wiped a hand through his sweaty hair.

"Father made us do it," said Jerry. "He knew you were trying to contact the outside . . . he made me lure you into the workroom. He knew if you saw YouTube on the screen and where I hid the keys, you wouldn't be able to resist and you'd come back."

A knot formed in Theo's stomach and squeezed the Power Bars he'd eaten.

"You weren't talking to your friend online," said Jerry.

Theo's mind spun, trying to put the puzzle pieces together. He thought back to the night in the library. No alarm on the library door. No password protection on the computer. Dante being online so late. It was too easy, by design.

"Wait! You catfished me?!" said Theo.

Jerry nodded and shrugged. "In a manner of speaking."

"What the hell?" said Theo.

"I didn't want to . . . but my father can be very persuasive."

Theo saw the fear in their eyes when they mentioned "father." It was the first sign of vulnerability Theo had ever seen in Jerry. But then another piece of the puzzle snapped together in his mind. "Your dad is Judge's boss . . . Isn't he? The one you warned me about."

Jerry nodded. "The Eternal Brain."

The color drained from Theo's face. "That's your dad???"

As famous as Odysseus had been for fighting crime, The Eternal Brain had been for being a criminal. His name was constantly in the headlines—or it had been, before he was put away.

He had been given twelve life sentences without parole for his atrocities. The idea that he was Jerry's father was almost too shocking to believe. It was like finding out Genghis Khan was your next-door neighbor.

"Isn't he supposed to be in some sort of supermax prison?"

"He is. He's the architect behind Crucible. He built *this* prison. He's the reason you're here. He's the reason we're all here . . . ." Jerry trailed off.

Memories were stirred of the panic Theo felt the day he left New York. The bitter smell of smoke over Manhattan. His childhood home being vaporized in an airstrike. The entire city was in hysteria. It had all been because of one man.

"He caused the midtown explosion, didn't he?"

Jerry nodded.

Theo felt the anger burn inside of him. The pain The Eternal Brain had inflicted on not only his family, but the entire world, was impossible to comprehend, and he'd hidden his tracks well. The common wisdom had been that Countess Blood was the leader of The Pantheon, but it became apparent to Theo at that moment who the real leader was and had always been.

"I guess that's why I kept my distance," said Jerry. "I felt too much guilt."

Theo's thoughts drifted to his parents being held against their will somewhere in Crucible. He wondered how many other families were suffering the same fate as he stared at his mask, his rescue mission quickly evolving into a plan for revenge. He wanted to put an end to this monster, to make him pay for all the misery he'd unleashed on the world, and make sure it never happened again.

"I don't give a crap how you feel. I want you to take me to your father," said Theo, fighting back the anger with a level of resolve. "I'm going to force him to release my family."

"Don't be stupid. I know my father. Confronting The Eternal Brain is not the way out of town! Listen to me. We have a plan."

"I've had enough of your plans. I have plans of my own," Theo stated with an unmistakable dose of false bravado. His only plan had been to get to the cave, and that's as far as it went.

"Yeah, we know you have your way of doing things, but ours is actually working."

Theo stopped pacing, confused by Jerry's comment.

"Who do you think distracted Judge so you could escape your room?"

"That was you?"

"It was all of us. Jenna and James banged on your door, and Anita and Fernando set off alarms on opposite ends of town."

"*That's* what all the sirens were for . . . ." said Theo.

"And why it took so long for the fire engines to arrive at your house."

Jerry craned their neck and whistled. A moment later, Anita and Fernando crawled into the antechamber from the rabbit hole.

"We know what our families did to yours. They share a long history of hate. But that's them, not us," said Fernando. "And we want nothing to do with Crucible, either."

"I'm not even a fan of my dad; he's a bit of a dick," said Anita, taking in the pockmarked cave.

"So, you ready to get out of this place?" called a fourth voice.

Theo turned to find Shivansh crawling out the rabbit hole. Theo's face lit up. "*Shiv!!*"

He ran over to his friend and tackled him in a big bear hug, completely ignoring the multiple times his parents had tried to kill his father. Shivansh was touched by Theo's affection and, simultaneously, was panicked. He was excited to see his friend again, and Shivansh seemed happy to see him too. But Theo could tell something was on Shivansh's mind, something troubling, something he had to keep to himself.

"Where have you been!? I've been worried sick!" exclaimed Theo.

"I've been gathering my strength for tonight."

"Tonight? What happens tonight?"

"We're busting out of Crucible," said Jerry.

CHAPTER 29

It was great seeing all his friends together again, but for Theo, reality once again reared its ugly head. He was in a cave with the children of his father's greatest enemies, including the one responsible for Odysseus's death. This betrayal of his father's memory, coupled with his mother lying in a hospital, made him question why he was even standing here, pretending things were fine.

The only reason he didn't bolt from the cave or roast them all alive was because of his uncertainty about who they really were or what they knew. Yeah, their parents were supervillains; that was the easy part. But since arriving in Crucible, he was given a false identity and memory and had been pruned twice. They'd been there even longer. God knows what they'd been through or what their names genuinely were.

Theo's hardest part was that he liked them—even Fernando. He considered Shiv a true friend and found himself flip-flopping his hormonal interest between

Anita and Jerry. As for the twins, he was still getting used to them. So, for the moment, Theo decided to compartmentalize his friendships from his fears and join the group as they plotted the downfall of Crucible.

Theo walked over to the others and sidled up to Fernando. Now that they were all together, Fernando gave a slight nod; he was ready to begin.

"Alright," announced Fernando. "This is Crucible." In a single motion, he pulled out a folded piece of butcher paper and smoothed it on the cave floor, revealing a map the size of a small desk.

Anita placed rocks on the corners to keep them flat. Thanks to Theo's practice session, the stones looked more like abstract sculptures made of melted chocolate than limestone.

Jerry stationed herself slightly behind Anita, looking at the map from a distance. Shivansh brought a candle over and set it down on the ground, illuminating the bewildering strange marks and lines.

"This is Main Street . . . that's Town Square Park . . . the library's here," said Fernando. He moved his finger over the map as if it explained the pigeon scratch. Jerry and Theo glanced at each other, neither impressed by Fernando's amateur cartography skills.

"If you say so, Fernando," said Jerry.

Fernando raised a warning eyebrow. He pointed to a long, blue, squiggly line: "That's the river . . . which puts the cave here. The entire city sits in a steep valley, with only one road in and out." He traced his finger along a thick black line representing the road, culminating in a giant red X.

Theo squinted, trying to decipher the meaning. "Is that supposed to be the guard gate?"

"Yes, it is," said Fernando, smitten by the beauty of his creation.

"But that's just what we see on the surface," said Shivansh. He unrolled a film of plastic transparency from a thick cardboard tube and laid a professional-grade vector blueprint over Fernando's map.

"Now that's what I'm talking about. *That's* a map," said Jerry.

Fernando threw up his arms in protest, his feelings hurt. "C'mon! No need for shade. My map is more than fine and serves its purpose."

Theo laughed. "Yeah. You keep thinking that."

"I've been working on mine for quite a while," said Shivansh, "The map's incomplete, but it was the best I could do."

"What's this a map of?" asked Theo.

"This is what's underneath Crucible," said Shivansh.

Theo studied the transparency, trying to visualize the elaborate network of tunnels and hidden annexes under his feet. Utility lines and sophisticated urban infrastructure mixed with underground storage silos and residential compounds. It was all very impressive.

“It’s like a whole other city,” said Theo. “I knew some buildings had sub-basements, but this is unbelievable.”

“Look at the overlay. Fernando and I did our two maps to scale,” said Shivansh. A laser dot traveled along the edge of the town on Fernando’s map. But on the transparency, the underground city continued past the woods and town borders.

“The best way out of Crucible isn’t through the woods,” said Fernando. “But under them.”

“Once we have access to the sub-basements, we can make our way past the guard stations and Mirror Men by going beneath them,” said Shivansh. But then he looked around the group. “That’s if, of course, they don’t have an equal number of guards and Mirror Men underground.”

“Why would they? I’ve seen the badges, and all entrances are password protected,” said Theo.

“And all the troublemakers are above ground,” Anita added, shooting him a coy look.

Shivansh concentrated his laser pointer back on the transparency, identifying the best points of entry. The light trailed across the meticulously drawn map and across to a spot labeled "restrooms."

Restrooms? Theo thought as he stared at Shivansh incredulously. *How did he know all this?* "Hey Shiv, I have to ask: Where'd you get the info to make a map this detailed?"

The question struck a chord with the others; Anita and Jerry cast their inquisitive looks and nodded softly in agreement. "He must have had help," Fernando said. Not precisely to challenge Shivansh, but more to defend his map and work.

Shivansh sighed and put his pointer down. Theo's entire body clenched, and he prayed this wasn't another revelation or moment of truth. He'd had his fair share and doubted he could take much more. In times like this, Theo wished his deepfake dog, Riot, was here so he could give him a friendly, big hug.

"This map was built from images I gleaned from other people's minds. Teachers, guards, students, even our own," Shivansh admitted.

"Wait. How can that be? I've never been to the lower level in my life," said Fernando with absolute certainty.

"Yes, you have. We all have. We just don't remember. It was pruned."

Everyone was aware their minds had been tampered with, but to what extent, they would never fully know.

Yet, strangely, this was one revelation that didn't have the anticipated effect on Theo. "My vision quest! I saw the basement and laboratory! Is that part of your map?"

Shivansh smiled, "You know it."

Just bringing up the vision quest lightened the mood. Theo reminded himself and the others of the laugh everyone had had at his expense.

"All roads lead to this section," Shivansh continued. "It's a command center where they monitor and control the city."

"I'm sure that's where my dad keeps his office," Jerry deadpanned.

"You're right. And that is exactly where we don't want to go," said Shivansh, matter-of-factly. "But have to."

"So that's the plan?" Anita said, standing to a stretch. "We pick one of these access points, storm the tunnels, grab Jerry's dad, and force him to show us the way out?"

"The Eternal Brain?" said Jerry. "I know my father. He'd see us coming a mile away."

"Then why do we even need to go to the control room?" asked Theo. "Can't you use the green pixie dust and teleport us past all this?"

"No. I wish I could, but I can't," said Shivansh.

His tone caught the attention of the group. It was laced with a heavy wistfulness. Anita, Fernando, and Theo turned to see if he was okay. Jerry continued to pace behind them, apparently being railroaded by their own train of thought within their head.

"Why not?" asked Theo. "It's our best weapon."

Shivansh stared at the cave wall, getting lost in some divot. His electric blue eyes were burdened with sadness. "Magic comes at a cost, and I'm not willing to pay that price ever again."

Once again, the group was wrapped in silence. This time it was Anita's turn to break the ice. "We were having such a nice moment," she said. "Let's not ruin it."

"The question remains," said Jerry, also desperate to change the subject, "how do we get into the control room if we can't even gain access to the underground?"

"Well . . . that's where I come in," said Fernando, jumping in, desperate to take charge. Pulling Shivansh's laser pointer from his hands, Fernando used it like a king with a scepter addressing his subjects. The thin red beam pointed out their school near the center of town. "While Shivansh was playing with maps, I came up with a plan." Fernando glanced over at Shivansh as if to remind him who was in charge of their little group. "You know, you're not the only one who can perform a little magic. I have the ability to make things, like my mother's teacher badge, disappear . . ." said Fernando, slowly reaching into his pocket, "and reappear exactly when we need it most." Then, with a magician's flair, Fernando's hand flashed over his head, revealing the stolen item. "I have our golden ticket."

Theo tried to stifle a moment of jealousy. He had made several attempts at stealing this coveted badge, always coming up short. Theo tried to rationalize his emotions, theorizing that he would never stoop to robbing his mother to accomplish his goal. But then he remembered it was his fault his mom was in the hospital, so that argument quickly went out the window. Still, Theo couldn't help but be annoyed as Fernando looped the badge's lanyard around his neck like he was awarding himself a gold medal on national television.

Feeling pleased with himself, Fernando handed the laser pointer back to Shivansh, allowing Shiv to continue.

"Now that we have a hall pass, we have underground access. But I don't expect we can just walk up to the elevator entrance. To make this plan work, we must draw attention away from the school. Any panic or confusion we create will help provide cover. "

"I can cut the power again," said Anita. "Piece of cake."

"They fell for that trick once," added Theo. "They'll be ready for it if we try again."

Theo made his way to the map and pushed his finger down on the center of town. "Leave this to me. I'll give them a light show they'll never forget." Theo instinctively tapped the mask stuffed in his pocket, knowing it contained the firepower to back up his statement.

Happy to see Theo wanting to participate, Shivansh continued, "With the town's attention away from the school, we can make our way underground to the control center."

Shivansh snapped off his laser pointer. "Cut the power there, and the entire complex goes blind. Once we're back on the surface, we will split up and hike to the main road or the next town over."

"Is that wishful thinking or first-hand knowledge?" said Theo.

Shiv smiled. "A little of both."

Anita let out a little laugh. "Easy breezy." Wrapping her arm around Shivansh's neck in a rough but loving way, she said, "I love this plan. Let's get to it."

Theo caught Fernando staring at Anita like there was no one else around. Anita was behaving like the Anita of old, and the love Fernando felt for her was back in full force. Theo was happy for their future together, supposing they would survive the next twenty-four hours.

The group spent a bit more time clarifying everyone's roles, but they were all past talking. Each knew the monumental task before them and the danger it entailed.

More mentally exhausted than physically, it was time to go home and get a little rest. If that was even possible.

"We'll need to leave here one at a time . . . can't attract too much attention," said Jerry.

"Agreed," said Fernando, scanning the group's worried faces and feeling their mission's weight. "Guys, have faith. We can do this. Where there's a will, there's always a way."

Wrapped deep in thought over the mission that lay before them, one by one they started to leave until it only Shiv and Theo were left. As Shivansh turned to go, Theo grabbed his shoulder to stop him. "I wanted to keep this between us, but I have to ask. Are you holding back any more surprises we should know about?"

Shiv cocked his head slightly, unsure what Theo was asking.

"You know, mind-reading for maps, dark occult rituals. Is that all of it?"

Shiv thought for a moment and sheepishly added, "Well, I mystically backed up all our memories, just in case we get erased or pruned again."

Theo was stunned, unsure what to say next.

Shiv smiled, "Don't worry, I didn't look—too much . . . ." And with that, he was gone.

CHAPTER 30

Night settled over Crucible, and, once again, the three stars of Orion's Belt seemed slightly out of line. This was the least exciting but probably the most telling of all the mysteries surrounding this town. People tend to see meaning in the patterns and shapes around them, so Theo took this as a warning and omen for the challenges ahead. Despite its Americana façade, nothing about Crucible was expected, and the stars reflected that.

Having nowhere else to go, Theo stayed behind as the others went home to prepare. Once again, while alone with his thoughts, the loneliness brought on a suffocating cavalcade of doubt and concern.

Theo began to pace; he was a tiger trapped in a cage searching for an exit that didn't exist. He wanted to stay with his friends—after all, in unity, there was strength. Together they had the best chance to escape this small-town prison. But he kept remembering his vision quest. So much of it had come to pass—the underground city, the mystery mask; why wouldn't seeing his father alive be true, too? Theo couldn't get past the nagging doubt that his friends were playing him again. How many times did they leave him hanging or turn on him? Between prunings and supervillain parents, it would be hard for anyone to tell the difference between right and wrong. Truth in Crucible wasn't only optional, but outright discouraged.

Then there was the mask, adding a new dynamic to the equation. It brought a sense of control to the rampant powers raging through his body. This was something Theo desperately craved. It also brought a strength he never believed he ever possessed, powerful enough to be free of his need to count on others. His parents, the kids in Crucible, had been lifelines, enabling him to cope with situations he couldn't manage. But now, he commanded the power to stand on his own two feet and, more importantly, make a difference. Emboldened at the moment, he decided to go to the school with a different plan.

Up ahead, a trail cut off the side of the road. Theo was making his way through the woods and could see the map in his head, not that he needed it. He had been through these woods enough times and knew every path and pitfall. Yet, regardless of his familiarity, there was danger all around him, passing almost the exact point he first encountered the Mirror Men.

As he sped down the trail, he felt his strength and speed increasing with every step, another unseen benefit of his manifesting powers. The physical exertion helped displace some of the adrenaline he felt. Nevertheless, he was still conscious of the town's defenses and kept looking back, glancing between the trees for signs of that sickening shimmer.

Theo's breath frosted in the cool evening air as the trail emptied into a small clearing. This seemed like a good moment to stop and reset his bearings. He had been pushing himself to his limit and momentarily lost his sense of direction.

While the clearing gave him an unblemished view of the forest edge, it also exposed him woefully. Theo took off his backpack to retrieve his mask.

As he raised it to his face and it began to grab hold of him, he glimpsed something from the corner of his eye. The trees at the base of the trail he'd taken here bowed and shook under the weight of some invisible force. Theo tensed.

Was it the Mirror Men? Or had Judge gotten wise to their plan and sent his goons?

It was neither. A loud displacement of foliage revealed the beast boy taking form in the darkness. The elusive kid stalked toward Theo, who instinctively backed away.

"H-hey . . . It's you . . . ." stammered Theo.

The kid said nothing as he strolled toward Theo, one menacing footstep at a time.

Seeing him out of the trees made Theo realize how big he was. He had long arms, long hair, and the athletic physique of an Olympic gymnast. *I bet he could tear a phone book in half with those forearms*, thought Theo.

"I never got to thank you for the other night," Theo said. "You saved my life." Theo rationalized the best way to connect with this wild child was through playing nice.

Silent, the beast boy just stared Theo up and down. Not exactly the reaction he hoped for. Theo looked toward the mask in his hand, deciding it might be time for Plan B.

"Come with me," said the boy, extending his hand.

Theo looked into his dark brown eyes, trying to discern his intention. The boy was guarded but earnest. Theo nodded in agreement and slid the mask back into his backpack. He took the boy's hand; the boy latched onto it with a careful but commanding force and tossed Theo on his back. He leaped onto the nearest tree, climbing its trunk with complete ease, as if he were taking a Sunday afternoon stroll. Theo held on for dear life as they swung through the canopy, dodging limbs before coming to rest at an impossibly dense part of forest anchored on a steep hillside.

The beast boy set Theo down and motioned for him to follow as he crept under a collection of branches and military netting. Theo was surprised to find a veritable fortress built into the tree canopies and filled with items found in the forest. Under the protection of a camouflaged tarp used as a roof was a thatched branch floor that held a bed, radio, and storage locker filled with hand-forged spears—it even had a rainwater cistern fashioned out of a blue plastic barrel. It was like something out of Swiss Family Robinson.

Theo marveled at the craftsmanship it took to construct the place.

The boy lit a lantern, illuminating the pièce de résistance of the tree house: a dozen or so pencil drawings impaled on makeshift branch walls: brutally realistic portraits and still-lifes of people and places from another time.

"This is a pretty amazing place you have here."

"Serves its purpose. Keeps things private." Nature Boy spoke in a gruff, yet measured tone.

Theo looked at the hulking man-child standing before him—his tattered clothes and bare feet belied the intellect and humanity he held inside.

"I'm Theo."

"I know who you are."

"But I don't know your name?

The boy paused before answering, "People call me Nature Boy. Don't mind. Who cares what people think?"

"I think it's pretty offensive. What's the name your parents gave you?"

"My parents are dead."

Wow, this got dark really fast, Theo thought.

Nature Boy reached over to the branch wall and pulled off a pencil drawing of a strong-jawed man wrestling a bear. The shadowing was so natural it looked like it might jump off the page. "My father was a hero, just like yours."

Theo was taken off guard by the comment. "How do you know about my father?"

"You hear a lot in the forest. Voices carry."

Nature Boy sat down at a makeshift table and went back to work on a wooden pike he'd been carving into a deadly-looking spear. Theo grew anxious, knowing the others would start arriving at the school soon.

"Why'd you bring me here?"

"I was hoping to talk you out of what you're planning to do."

"What makes you think I'm planning anything?" said Theo, feeling exposed.

"I know everything that happens here . . . I know about the cave . . . I know about the map, and I know about your plan. So don't do it."

Theo fidgeted with the straps on his backpack, wondering if he would be able to get his mask on in time to fight back against this hulking kid if he had to.

"I tried what you're about to do . . . . I was with my father. When we tried to escape, we were betrayed. It ended with him dead and me living in a tree."

Theo felt a pang of guilt for getting defensive. "I'm sorry."

"You want my advice? Stay here and forget all about tonight." Nature Boy moved over to his latest picture, grabbing a pencil to tighten a couple of lines of art.

"I can't, this might be my only chance to escape—"

"Villains don't change, and neither do their children. Your so-called friends will turn on you—"

"You don't know them—"

"I don't need to. You don't get it. You can never trust anybody. The only point of this town is to screw with your head!"

"I can't give up. We have to expose Crucible for what it is! Bring back help for everyone living here against their will."

"You sure about that? Stay. You'll be safe," said Nature Boy.

Theo's mental clock alarm started to ring. He knew everyone would be reaching the rendezvous spot in the next few minutes, and his plan to arrive early became showing up late and possibly missing the only chance to discover what exists under the city.

"There's too much at stake, and I have to believe in something, trust someone. I can't hide forever, like you," said Theo, surprised to find how much truth was in his words.

Nature Boy hung his head. "I'm not here to hold you, only offer advice."

Taking Theo from the tree, Nature Boy placed him softly on the ground. "I'll leave you with one last thought. Ever wonder who gave you that fiery mask?"

Theo watched Nature Boy recede into his home. For all his power, intellect, and skill, he seemed to be a prisoner of his bitterness, a fate that Theo wouldn't allow himself to fall victim to. There were too many unanswered questions to be resolved in one night. So he waved goodbye, looked for a path, and found a way back to his friends.

"Hey! There he is!" Shivansh called out in a hushed yell as he rushed to Theo with Jerry. The pale light of the moon made them all look like vampires.

The three met in a group hug, relieved to have found each other. Jerry immediately picked up on Theo's energy, sensing something was amiss.

"Where were you?" said Jerry, embarrassed by the amount of emotion in their voice.

Theo glanced back up the hill, then back to Jerry as he took their hand.

"Just taking a moment to get my thoughts together," said Theo, convincing himself it wasn't a lie. He decided at that moment to put aside his own plan and stick with theirs.

"I know what you mean. Are we really doing this?" Jerry said, squeezing Theo's hand for assurance.

"We'd be crazier doing nothing," said Theo.

CHAPTER 31

Dusk was settling in, casting a charcoal gray across the sky. Fernando struggled to read his map as he and the others huddled behind a shadow of trees at the edge of the town's park. He twisted the parchment sideways, then held it away from his body in a vain attempt to catch a mix of moon and street light.

"Hey, Fearless Duke. We're only a hundred yards from the school; I don't think we need your chicken scratch map anymore." At some point, they'd decided they would use code names for the mission. They were steeped in espionage, ready to take on the dark forces of town, so, naturally, it only seemed fitting.

"Let's go over the plan one more time," said The Duke, ignoring Gemini Gold's sarcastic remark about his cartography skills. "Time is short, and everyone has to be in position." The Duke returned to his map, pointing out where each was to be positioned.

"Grim Karma. You and Gemini Gold stay here with me until we're ready to move. Anita Dynamite. Get close to the school and wait for us." Theo looked over at Shivansh, now Grim Karma, a little concerned. Karma wore dark clothes similar to his parents' from the toga party. *The apple never falls far from the tree*, Wilding Judge's warning reverberated in Theo's mind.

"*Theo*." The Duke—hating that he hadn't picked a code name—stabbed the center of the map, ripping a hole around his finger and the center of town. "This is where you put on your show." The Duke crumpled his map and tossed it at Theo. "Make it a good one."

Theo reached into his knapsack and dug past his Power Bar stash to retrieve the gold mask. It caught the moonlight and twinkled as he pulled it out of his bag. Theo put the mask to his face and allowed it to grab onto his skin as they watched in awe. It had fused into place within a second, wrapping around his eyes and temples. No one knew what to make of Theo's accessorizing, but it was clear from Shivansh's and Jerry's expressions that they both approved.

Theo turned his attention to a somewhat confused Fearless Duke. "Look for my signal. You'll know it when you see it." Theo turned to walk away, looking back for only a second. "And my name is . . . the Fiery Mask!" Theo strode from the group and walked to the town center as if he didn't have a single care. Fernando asked them to create a distraction and draw some attention. Theo had to laugh; in all the time he'd spent in Crucible, that was the one thing he had no trouble doing.

As Theo, The Fiery Mask, walked off in one direction, Anita Dynamite appeared to be doing a drunken sprint the opposite way. Bouncing off a series of trees before launching herself into the side of a building, she might have looked masochistic to the casual observer, but to those in the know, she was building a reservoir of power for the tasks that lay ahead.

Jerry watched Theo with obvious concern; his slow, deliberate walk drew the desired attention. The first to spot him was a pair of older women out for an evening stroll. They cautiously crossed the street, turning their heads to avoid eye contact. Next came the older man assigned to sweep imaginary dirt in front of the protection program's staging office. To Theo, he was coming full circle, ending the lies at the place where they'd started. Theo smiled and nodded, and before he was completely past the storefront, the older man was already on a headset, calling for backup.

On cue, a couple of armed guards burst out of the school. They never even noticed Anita standing by the side of the building. The plan was beginning to work, and things were about to get interesting.

All eyes were on Theo, waiting to see what he had planned. They didn't have to wait long. By the time he reached the center of town, a band of guards was closing in. Theo was a fan of westerns and loved any movie that climaxed with a high-noon showdown. Clint Eastwood was his particular favorite. As the guards surrounded Theo, he took a gunslinger stand worthy of The Outlaw Josey Wales. With his head down, Theo could sense the guards were in arm's reach.

"Get back, little lady. Hell is coming for breakfast!" Theo growled in an overreaching attempt at an Eastwood drawl, and while the impression might not have had the desired effect, the fiery glow from his body certainly did.

Theo concentrated on the ground beneath his feet, visualizing the fire within him, feeling the energy coursing through his body. He radiated enough heat to force his pursuers to take several steps back. Pressure mounted in his veins. He closed his eyes in deep focus.

Clenching his fists, Theo opened his eyes, and a beam of white-hot energy burst from them, vaporizing the earth before him and lighting up the night sky.

"Whoa!" marveled Jerry.

"Okay, now that's a signal," said Fernando, setting the team in motion. "Grim Karma, Gemini Gold! You're with me."

Shivansh and Fernando broke from the trees and began a mad dash to the school. Fernando kept waving for Jerry to join, but their concern for Theo held them in place. "You go! I'll get Theo and catch up."

"His name is The Fiery Mask!" The Fearless Duke yelled, enjoying this probably more than he should.

Anita Dynamite smiled as the two boys rushed toward her. *Guess that's my cue*, she thought. From the moment she threw herself against the school wall, she'd been struggling to contain the kinetic energy built inside her. With one explosive punch, she cleared an opening three times the size of the doorway while taking out a piece of a small retaining wall inside. Fernando and Shivansh ran past her; neither said a word about her Herculean feat. Slightly miffed, Anita added, "You better have that damn swipe card."

Back in the town center, Theo burned out of control. The beam he emitted continued to flame, creating an ever-widening crater that had the potential to swallow him whole. Realizing the danger, Theo redirected the flames to the sky, only to watch it rain down and singe some neighboring roofs. He had the potential to burn down the entire town, but thought better of it. The flames served their purpose; everyone—including the guards—had run for cover, and now he wanted to join his friends.

Theo ripped the mask from his face, ending his vicious display of fire and light. Exhaustion grabbed hold of his body, pushing him to the verge of collapse. He could barely stand, let alone make his way to the school. Once the guards regained their nerve, he wouldn't have the strength to stop them. Theo tried to move, but his body refused to respond to his commands. The muscles in his legs seized, throwing off his balance and forcing Theo to one knee. His mind was swimming through a sea of fire-roasted molasses, and he struggled to focus. He felt like he was falling forward and being lifted simultaneously. The combined sensations made little sense until his mind cleared long enough to recognize Jenna on his left arm and James on his right, pulling him back away from the wreckage.

"Jerry sent us to get you, bro," said James.

"Thought you might need a pair of helping hands," added Jenna.

Theo, throat parched and raw, tried to thank them but could only manage a dry, hoarse croak.

"Save your strength, bro. Gonna need it."

"We'll get to where the others are waiting. Even if we have to drag you there."

Back inside the school, Fernando impatiently tapped his mother's teacher ID against the elevator door. "We can't keep waiting. We lost sight of them. Don't even know they're still alive."

Shivansh refused to believe anything Fernando was saying. "They'll be here. Give them another minute."

"I'll wait, but this is the one time your little mind game could be wrong."

"You sure of that?" Shivansh said with a smile, as he watched Jenna and James turn the corner of the hall with Theo trailing close behind.

It was less than a minute from the town center to the elevator, and Theo was feeling better already. His healing power had kicked into overdrive, if this was another one of his Enhanced changes to his body, it couldn't have come at a better time.

Shivansh, happy to see his friend, stepped up to give him a big hug. Then, realizing he was still not 100 percent, Theo collapsed in his arms.

"That was some amazing show," Shivansh said. "Was that the mask from your dreams?"

"It was," Theo said, standing up on his own again. "And if the mask is real, so is my father being alive."

The ding of the elevator door accentuated the word "alive." Fernando, ever impatient, swiped the card when everyone was talking. But now that the elevator was here, they all hesitated to take the first step.

"Floor, please." The elevator was the first to speak.

"C'mon. Get on," Theo whispered to Fernando, almost afraid the elevator would hear him.

"It's voice-activated," Fernando whispered back. "Does that mean it has voice recognition, too?"

"You only thought of that now?" said Theo, raising his voice.

They all froze in place with analysis paralysis, and the elevator grew impatient. "Floor, please."

"Oh, for God's sake." Jenna and James were now Jerry, and they wanted no part of this. Pushing past Theo and Fernando, Jerry stepped on the elevator. "The basement."

The elevator took a beat, "Watch the closing doors," before returning to its function.

For the others, that was their cue. They dove through the doors before they shut, not wanting to be left behind.

Except for that moment of indecision, their plan was running as scheduled, Theo looked over at Fernando, and he seemed quite pleased with himself. Theo knew that Fernando, as the only member without power, felt the constant need to prove himself as leader, if only to justify his own self-worth.

"I'm surprised it's taking this long." Shivansh's map of the underground facility captured the length and width, but not its depth.

"Either this is a very slow elevator, or we're a mile underground." Theo had another thought, a more frightening one. "What if the elevator is purposely slow? Delaying us."

Fernando knew that made the most sense, and began barking orders, "Theo, get your mask on and be ready. Anita, Up front, and run block. Shiv, if you have any magic, use it. I'll get your next sacrifice myself."

As Anita moved into position, the elevator picked up speed. It was listening to them the entire time. Theo reached in his pocket to pull out his mask. Every time he put it on it seemed to meld with his skin and didn't like the way it felt. Not that it mattered, they needed his powers. The elevator had reached its destination, and the doors were set to open.

Ding. "Have a nice day."

Outside the elevator, the guards also stood ready, yet unsure what was the imminent threat. They looked to each other for insight, their walkies squelching with words like "intruder alert" and "possible perimeter breach." Every gun was cocked and loaded, and the muscles in the soldiers' trigger fingers were attuned to the sound of the elevator bell.

Three of the guards didn't even wait for the doors to open before shooting. The rest quickly followed. Within seconds, the elevator doors were riddled with bullet holes, courtesy of their overzealousness. By the time the elevator finally opened, all their weapons were spent.

HIDE OR SEEK

While the elevator cab appeared to be a trap, it was also well-fortified. Reinforced with the finest titanium steel, not a single bullet penetrated the car. The group arrived in the sub-basement safe and sound, and now it was their turn to strike.

As the guards reloaded, their focus was off the elevator and on their weapons. They heard the doors open but never saw Anita Dynamite as she tore into their perimeter. Some rushed their shot, others used the guns as clubs, but none of it mattered; Anita absorbed all their energy and began tossing them around like rag dolls.

"About time I got to hit something," she cackled. "Is this the best you got!?"

If Anita had any weak spot, it was stamina; she could only keep absorbing energy in bursts, and overextending burned her out. She was holding them off but would need help. Quickly.

A fountain of fire roared from the elevator, igniting the ceiling over the guards' heads and setting off every sprinkler on the floor. Anita was starting to falter. It was time for Theo to take over. The mask gave him renewed strength, and he was ready to use it. The guns in the guards' hands exploded in short bursts of flames, and a long-sustained wash of flames cleared a path to a long, empty hallway. The only thing blocking the way were a couple of dead, burning bodies.

Theo stood there a moment, stunned at what he had just done. But, until now, the fact they would have to take lives to reach their goal hadn't really registered.

Theo felt a barrel against his back; it snapped him out of his state. *So this is it*, he thought.

Then, suddenly—Anita appeared and grabbed the barrel away. The guard squeezed the trigger, lighting Anita up with a spray of automatic fire into her chest. Theo gasped as she stumbled back.

But Anita lifted her head and grinned as she absorbed the energy of the bullets and sent the force back at the guard with ten times the strength. The guard's body turned to paste before spreading itself across the floor.

Shivansh came running up behind her. "Come on guys, I'm sensing something big. We need to get moving."

Fernando was already making his way down the hall, checking to see if they were heading in the right direction, not that it mattered. It was the only clear path out.

Shivansh looked around, his senses going wild, "That was too easy . . . ."

"Speak for yourself," said Fernando. "I figure we have a mile to go before we're in the clear."

"Don't you see? There weren't supposed to be any guards underground," said Shivansh, alarmed. "And if they're guards . . . ."

Theo noticed the shimmers as they began appearing all around, moving off the walls, rising from the floor.

"Mirror Men." There had to be a half-dozen of them moving toward them.

"Guys! Look out! The Mirrors are here!" Theo screamed to the group.

Any guards that were following backed away. They wanted no part of what was about to happen.

Fernando and Jerry tried to reverse field and head back from where they came, thinking they stood a better chance against the guards than they did against the mirrors. It was too late; more Mirror Men appeared and blocked every exit. They were trapped in a killing zone.

Anita, who had been leading the assault on the guards, stood frozen, fear limiting her ability to move. Conscious of her plight, Theo took the lead and rushed to them, firing volley after volley of flames, shocked at his accuracy and skill. Seeing his friends with their backs against the wall sent him into a blind rage.

He melted everything in his path, flames ripping through the halls, melting the walls, hoping for a chance to burn their way out. Instead, concrete walls dissolved to reveal reinforced steel, impervious to his heat. Any hopes he had were completed dashed.

As Theo turned, a Mirror Man was on a collision course with him. Theo raised his fists, unloading a stream of white-hot fire, stopping the Mirror.

More shimmers appeared; the Mirror Men kept coming and coming, swarming him and the others. Their numbers were too great to stop.

Theo gasped as he looked out to his friends amid battle, Anita and Fernando holding onto one another's hands as they were dragged apart by Mirror Men and disappeared into their cloaks.

Another Mirror grabbed Shivansh from behind, enveloping him in its cloak as he fought with everything he had. Theo watched him scream as he was torn apart, photon by photon, sucked into its swirling, galactic belly.

"Theo, hold on!" Jerry cried out with desperation—a Mirror swooping in front of them, spiriting them away before Theo's eyes.

And then, like the flip of a switch, Theo's world went black.

CHAPTER 32

The sound of trickling water gently nudged Theo awake. He could make out the clean smell of ozone and decided it was raining. But he kept his eyes shut; he wanted to continue his dream.

He and his mother had been reunited and allowed to return home, where a brand new, chromed-out Mercedes sat in the driveway in a custom candy-apple wrap, a gift for finally passing his road test. He delighted in the soft feel and oaky smell of the white leather interior and couldn't wait to drive over to Dante's to show it off. He laughed as Riot grabbed his tennis ball and begged to go with him into town. They were all heading over to Main Street. Today was the day Odysseus received the key to Poughkeepsie as the town's favorite son. It was the best day of Theo's life.

No. That's not right. None of this is right.

"Save your strength, Mr. Alexander," commanded a sharp, wheezing voice.

Theo's eyes bolted open. He tried to sit up, only to discover he was strapped into a coffin-sized isolation tank quickly filling up with milky-colored salt water. Oppressive light blinded his retinas from a porthole in the lid above his head.

"You've been through a rather traumatic event."

A breathing regulator was strapped into his mouth, pumping condensed oxygen into his lungs, making them feel like they had been lacerated. He still wore his gold mask, but it was jagged and cracked.

He clenched his fists. But no fire came out. His arms were intubated, and he wore a catheter; blood from several flesh wounds diffused into the water in tiny red plumes.

"The Mirror Men have been known to empty one's mind and erase their immortal soul."

The water stopped, and there was a metal CHA-CHUNK as the lid of the tank creaked open. Theo's eyes adjusted to the harsh overhead lights and a terrifying silhouette came into focus. A slender figure with an elongated skull draped in a long black tunic.

He hovered over Theo, watching him with the unnerving focus of a surgeon. His eyes were inky saucers with no detectable white. His face was scarred, his features sunken. His eggplant-colored flesh was wrinkled like an old, battle-worn elephant and sagged around his cheeks like a bulldog's. Lesions along his shaved head oozed a clear jelly-like secretion that he mopped up every so often with a dedicated towel.

"And yet, you seem no worse for wear," said the figure. He smiled, revealing a mouth of sharp, discolored, butter-bean teeth. "Tell me, are you still able to dream?"

Theo froze. *How did he know I was dreaming?* The thought terrorized him.

"We've never met, but I imagine you know who I am."

Theo nodded, unable to speak with the regulator stuffed in his mouth, but the figure was unmistakable: *It was The Eternal Brain.*

"I thought so," said The Brain. He patted his lesions with his towel and ripped the regulator from Theo's mouth in one violent yank. Theo spit blood where it cut his gums. "Now, explain why you have been so resistant to Crucible and all I have done for you?" he demanded with a harsh rasp.

Theo was too stunned to answer. His mind was frantic, hopping between the horror he woke up to and thoughts of what happened to his friends.

The Brain lunged toward him, reaching for the pod lid. "Maybe Mirror Men did more damage than I thought."

"You have my father!" exclaimed Theo. "Keeping him here as a prisoner!"

"No one is a prisoner in my town or beneath it," said the Brain, laboring to breathe. "As for your father . . . let's just say his death was a necessity."

"You lie! Judge told me he was here and alive!"

"You're confused, child. Wilding said no such thing. You heard what you wanted to hear. Believed what you want to believe."

"I had a vision! And all of it came true! I saw him. My father is here!"

"I'd say come and look for yourself, but I prefer you stay in the tank until you show some measure of control."

The figure punched a button embedded in the isolation pod, and the pod rotated to give Theo the impression he was sitting up. The milky liquids and gels that floated around his neck and chest ran down to his waist, filling up the lower half of the tube. This new position gave him a view of the pristine medical facility lined with rows of white, cylindrical tanks. He could tell there were people trapped within. They all beeped with the steady rhythm of cardiograph machines. It was exactly what Theo saw in his vision in the cave. His heart began to race.

"I knew your father and his father before him. I'd say he'd be missed, but now, I have you." The Brain wobbled over to the row of tanks and approached them with all the care of a midwife in a maternity ward, gently stroking each as he passed. "Look around; these tanks are filled with foolish people. Your father was not a foolish man."

Theo's vitals spiked, causing the sensors monitoring him to beep with alarm. People in lab coats came rushing toward him, but The Brain waved them off.

"You sick bastard, I'm going to kill you!"

"I don't think so, Mr. Alexander," The Brain said with a phlegmy cackle.

Overhead, Theo caught movement and saw Judge looking down at him from a loft, precisely the way he had in his vision. Theo's breath turned shallow, and his chest heaved. The sound in the room became deafening. He was having a panic attack.

How could everything in his vision come true? The gold mask. The medical facility. Wilding Judge looking down from the loft. Everything except his dad being alive.

The Brain wiped a particularly gummy lesion, digging into it with his towel. He stared at Theo with mock sympathy. "Poor boy . . . you've been constantly surrounded by lies and deceit. Afraid to trust anyone." He smiled, flashing his stained nubbin teeth. "Well, you can trust me. I have no reason to lie."

Theo stared at him, unable to process what he was saying.

"Good and evil. Heroes and villains. You misunderstand the role I must play. I am here to maintain the balance, to keep both sides engaged in an endless struggle so the rest of the world can move on unaffected, living in ignorant bliss." The strange man hissed with a shrill, hoarse cackle that rattled again with the phlegm in his chest and sent black saliva into the air. "I ensure that the combatants are so evenly matched, neither side could ever win." He coughed, spitting black blood into his towel. "If one side gets stronger, or the other gets weakened, I correct the paradigm."

Theo was stunned. This lunatic talked about the most powerful beings on Earth as weights on a scale. He was finally getting some answers, just not to any questions he asked. He had to fix that. "What's my family have to do with any of this?"

The Brain coughed, hacking and gasping for breath. He spit more black blood into his towel, then folded it to wipe the slime off his head lesions in a sickening spectacle. "Your father was so powerful; he kept throwing off the scales, forcing me to readjust. He truly believed good could triumph over evil. He was a menace," said The Brain, spitting the word out with complete disdain.

Theo felt himself heating up. He clenched his fists again, his thoughts focused on blasting this vile creature to hell with concentrated hellfire, but nothing came out.

"Even worse. He was stubborn, just like you."

Though it didn't show, Theo took enormous pleasure in hearing that, and his eyes welled up uncontrollably.

The Brain moved close to the tank. "I'm so glad you found my mask." He caressed Theo's gold mask with his long, yellow fingernails. "I made it special, just for you. It allows me to control your budding enhancements." He dug into his tunic to retrieve a pipe. As he stoked the charred tobacco inside, he continued, "We tried to do the same thing with Odysseus, but he was just too powerful . . . . So, we had to take a different approach . . . ."

He sucked on his pipe as he held a lighter to it, taking in a deep lungful of smoke and coughing it back out into the room. "I assigned him a handler, someone to keep him in check. Little did I know they would fall in love. But no matter, it accomplished the same result. It made him less reckless, more cautious. It made him a family man."

What the hell!?! Mom was part of this? A handler?

"Poor Theo. Your father tried his best to keep you from all this. Of course, the great irony is, if he just would've listened to me and left The Pantheon alone, you and I would've never met. The world would've been perfectly balanced."

"Let me go," demanded Theo.

"I'm sorry, but you know I can't do that."

"What about my friends?"

"I have tanks waiting for them all, even one for my own child, if they ever step out of line again."

Theo ignored the threats of that statement and embraced the fact that they were still alive. "You'll never get the chance to hurt them. Ever! When I break free, I'm burning you and this whole place to the ground!" Theo couldn't believe what he had just said, but he meant every word.

"I am starting to believe this has been a fruitless conversation." The Brain sighed, shoved the regulator back into Theo's mouth, and slammed him back into the water. The pod lid crashed shut, and water came rushing in. Theo thrashed around, trying to float on top of it, but his restraints kept him in place.

"You are going to feel weak, Theo," shouted The Brain on the other side of the door. "We're putting you into chemical stasis while I clean up the mess you made . . . . Rebellion runs in your family, and now I have to decide if you are to be contained or dead."

As the tank filled, Theo began to struggle, all the while noting The Eternal Brain's look of sadistic satisfaction.

Theo's panic gave way to rage as his head went underwater. He thought about the pain this man had inflicted on his family and the world. He had killed his father, imprisoned him, his mother, and his friends, and subjected them to fake memories and authoritarian terror. And he was going to erase their minds and do it all over again!

Theo felt the chemical cocktail being dumped into his body start to make him drowsy, but he fought it. Instead of getting weaker, Theo's fury intensified. His body got hotter and hotter. Alarms blared as the milky white liquid he was submerged in started to boil.

Through the porthole window, he caught glimpses of The Eternal Brain and Wilding Judge with concerned expressions, frantically motioning for someone to do something.

People in lab coats scurried around, punching buttons and adjusting settings on his pod. They even tried to up his dose of medicine and contain his rage. But it was too late. Golden strings spiraled from his face to the top of the tank.

Theo had melted his mask. His eyes danced with flames.

CHAPTER 33

Alarms bombarded the medical facility as frantic men and women in lab coats worked to secure Theo's isolation tank. One attendant tried to lock the lid, only to have the skin of his fingertips seared to the metal. The pod rattled and moaned under the intense steam pressure his body heat created, and slowly, began to force itself open.

Lab coats gathered at the base attempted to drain the pod, but boiling water melted the pipes, causing them to burst. They screamed as flesh peeled off their faces.

Theo was lying in the center of the maelstrom. With his senses heightened, he was fully aware of every sight and sound around him. Through the portal, his eyes locked with his jailer's, as he watched a sickening black liquid frothed around the corners of his mouth. He heard The Brain wheeze in disbelief.

Behind them appeared Wilding, clicking his cane on the polished epoxy flooring. “Agents are on the way to transport you to safety, sir,” said Judge.

“If you had done your job properly, this would not have happened!” barked The Brain.

“I remind you, sir . . . I recommended that we shut him down.”

The Brain grabbed hold of Wilding with force, digging his boney fingers into his arm. “And I said I wanted to manage it. My way.”

The two stood there for a tense moment. Wilding felt emboldened as the façade of The Eternal Brain’s power was rife with fissures at his inability to stop Theo.

“But perhaps, in this instance, you were right.” It was the first time The Eternal Brain ever relented, and Wilding took immense pleasure in it.

Nonessential equipment abruptly shut off. Monitors and every other light overhead went black. The alarms stopped, and the facility’s air conditioner powered down, leaving a sound void in its absence.

Theo’s pod continued to bulge under the intense heat and spiderweb cracks formed in the porthole glass. “We don’t have much time,” said Wilding.

“These pods withstood the power of Agamemnon,” said The Brain in an almost reverent tone, clearly contemplating the implications. "I am sure they can hold his grandson."

The hydraulic whir of huge bay doors at the far end of the facility echoed through the space, followed by the piercing headlights of the SUVs speeding inside.

Agents filed out, ready to open fire, setting the stage for battle, while drivers corralled high-ranking lab coats into the vehicles to haul them to safety.

"Handle this," seethed The Brain, toweling a gooey sore on his head. He hobbled toward one of the SUVs. As he sat down, he called out the window. "And Wilding? I trust you will use proper judgment."

Wilding nodded to the driver, and the SUVs peeled off from the facility, spiriting The Eternal Brain away. The massive bay doors whirred shut. They were intent on keeping Theo inside this building at all costs.

Unable to withstand the pressure, Theo's pod exploded open with the force of a car bomb. The shock wave floored all the agents and sent the isolation tanks around him careening into the walls in an expansion of steam and fire. Drywall crumbled, and steel rafters boughed. The halogen lights overhead shattered and swayed, leaving the windowless facility in absolute darkness.

Theo rose from the tank, possessed with his own power and fueled by the anger that was trapped inside him. His entire body glowed from within like burning steel.

He levitated in the air above the pods, focused on the agents below, who were fumbling for their weapons. Theo's heat intensified. The air around him caught fire.

"Think about what you're doing, Theo," Judge shouted behind a toppled pod. "Your friends. Your family. I can take you to them."

But Theo wasn't listening as he glided past the mess of cylindrical tanks. The light from his glow highlighted the men and women trapped inside.

One face stopped him cold. Theo came back to himself for a moment, hovering over a tank, trying to make out the familiar face inside. He put his hand to the glass. *Could it be my father? Why does he look older? Is it all some kind of trick to keep him here?*

Footsteps took his attention—he turned to find every agent had encircled him with their M4 assault rifles cocked and ready to shoot. Theo looked at them, considering his power against theirs. It scared him. He was a boy trying to control the power of a god.

"It doesn't have to end like this," Judge said as he pushed his way through the agents. "Your father died putting family first; don't make the same mistake!"

The comment sent emotion through Theo's body he couldn't contain. The sensation caused him pain with nowhere to direct his fury.

Theo looked at Judge, then to the faces of the agents, his eyes dancing with the power of a thousand suns—he could kill every single one of them. The agents' faces were bathed in the light of his flames like they were sitting around a campfire. They reflected back the fear in Theo's eyes, neither of them wanting this.

Theo raised his head and—with a resounding *scream*—all of the rage and energy trapped inside him channeled into a single beam of fire light, followed by a percussive blast that blew Judge and the agents back into the walls.

As the dust settled, Judge looked up from the rubble and saw the moon and stars. A hole had been ripped through the center of the facility, exposing the night sky.

"Find him!" screamed Wilding as he wiped blood from his forehead.

As steam wafted from his body, Theo walked alone in the cool night air. The fire in his eyes was gone, but his eyes were still sharp with focus.

Behind him, smoke billowed from a hole in the mountain that danced in the moonlight. The medical facility was built inside it, in the forest just outside town.

His eyes locked on something ahead. On one side of him were the twinkling lights of Crucible, and on the other side was the road he had taken to get here.

He was on the other side of the guard gate. On the other side of the Mirror Men. On the other side of hell. He was staring at a road that led to the outside world. That led to help.

Without a second thought, he turned away from Crucible and set off into the unknown.

CHAPTER 34

Nine-year-old Nick pulled the sheets over his head and clutched his teddy bear tight. A car door had slammed shut, causing the German shepherd three houses over to bark himself into a frenzy, rattling the chain-link fence as he jumped on his hind legs.

Nick hadn't fallen asleep yet, but he wasn't really awake either. The dog had startled him, taking him from the fleeting moment in between the two states, when a man is said to be touched by genius. He was trying to find an answer to where his dad had gone.

After a perfect day of playing hooky and going to the ballpark, Paul had disappeared during a game of hide-and-seek. His mother had used all the familiar lines to justify his sudden departure: *There was an emergency at work. He had to fill in for someone who got sick .... He won't be long.*

But Nick didn't buy it. It felt different this time. Paul had just gotten home after weeks on the road, and there were still people in the house when he ducked out. The mood of the party shifted without his dad there. It was as if he left a trail of apprehension in his wake. Constance Pappas seemed anxious, and the neighbors couldn't help but gossip. Not that it mattered; she was concerned over something else.

Constance sent Nick off to play video games with Dante, but he wasn't interested. He wanted to know what was troubling his mother. Standing in the hallway, he could hear the news playing on the TV in the family room.

An anonymous man calling himself The Eternal Brain had hacked the New York Stock Exchange. He threatened to destroy the world's economy unless Odysseus ceased his unlawful brand of justice. He demanded the famous Enhanced Human stop his campaign against The Pantheon immediately. A distorted audio clip, allegedly sent from the man, said, "Why do the people reward this zealot for his excessive vigilantism? Don't they understand the damage he is creating? Balance must be restored."

"What are you doing, Nick?" called Constance. She surreptitiously wiped tears from her eyes as she picked up her son. "Why aren't you playing with your friends?"

Later that night, after the din of company faded into memory, and Constance read him two entire Golden

Books at tuck-in time, Nick was left alone with his thoughts. And they all lead to the same place: *Where did Dad go?*

He overheard his mom on the phone. Their rooms had a shared wall that did not allow for secrets. She was crying, something she rarely did but had done twice that evening. He listened closely as his mom said things like "I don't know how much more I can take of this" and "It's too hard on Nick, and this is no way for a boy to grow up" and "He needs his father."

Downstairs the front door creaked open, and his mother hung up abruptly. Nick could tell who it was by the footsteps on the stairs and pulled the sheets off his head.

As his doorknob turned, he closed his eyes and pretended to be asleep.

He felt his dad lean over and kiss his forehead. His sandpaper stubble tickled Nick's skin. He smelled musky, like he had been at the gym. "I love you, pal," whispered Paul.

Nick's eyes sprung open. His father's shoulders hung low; he looked beaten and worn.

"Where'd you go?" whispered Nick. "Why'd you leave the party?"

Paul hesitated, his eyes holding the weight of the world inside of them. He brushed his son's cheek and smiled. "I was looking for a safe place to hide." Then he picked up his son and kissed him gently. "And hoping you'd come to find me."

The memory warmed Theo as the night air grew colder. It pained him that he had misunderstood his father for most of his life. Paul hadn't been the aloof, absentee man Theo had thought he was. He had just been busy ridding the world of some of the vilest people ever known. Everything he'd done was to keep Theo and his mother safe and help make the world a safer, happier place. Theo wished he had known. He wished he would have appreciated his father more. He would give anything to talk to him one more time and tell him how much he loved him and how proud he was to have him as a dad.

The stars were beginning to fade into a sea of cobalt blue.

The sun would be rising soon. It felt like he had been following the same winding road for miles. Mountains gave way to rolling hills. The bottoms of his bare feet were coated in blood and dirt, his lips and mouth were cracked with dryness, and his entire body ached with every step. But he couldn't stop. He had to find help for his mother.

He remained hyper-vigilant with his head on a swivel, expecting Mirrors to materialize out of the bushes or agents to open fire at any second. His Enhanced senses were on high alert to such a degree that the sound of a blade of grass bending would be enough to earn a fireball hurtling in its direction.

Headlights crested on the horizon behind him, lighting up the eyes of deer hidden in the woods in front of him. Theo fell to the ground to blend in with the brush.

As the headlights approached, Theo watched a bus come into view. A big, boxy, white charter with double axles in the rear and dark tinted windows. It was unlike anything he had seen in Crucible. And that was a good thing.

Theo pushed himself to a stand and walked to the middle of the street. He held his arm with his palm out, and five fingers splayed, commanding the enormous vehicle to stop. The air brakes screamed, and the bus lumbered to a stop, inches from Theo's face.

The door hissed open, and Theo stepped to peer inside.

A terrified bus driver stared back at him with his mouth agape.

"Are you okay, son?"

"I've been better," said Theo, smacking his lips to try and moisten his mouth.

"What happened to you?"

Theo wore enough charred clothing to avoid embarrassment, but his body was covered in bruises, cuts, and clotted blood. Theo saw the two plastic cuffs around his wrists that Wilding Judge had used to tie him to the hospital bed in his bedroom. He hadn't even noticed they were still on until now. "You mean these?" said Theo, lifting his arms to show the driver the cuffs. "I don't know how to get them off. They don't melt."

The bus driver just stared at Theo, confusion spreading across his face.

"Do you mind?" said Theo as he stepped onto the bus. People gasped as he got on, but he could care less. He looked over the crowd, assessing potential threats.

Satisfied, he sat next to a white-haired woman with thick glasses and a floral blouse who reminded him of Betty White. The woman smiled politely at him and then stared straight ahead, trying not to show how horrified she was by what was happening.

Theo felt the vibration change in his feet as the bus shifted into gear and drove off. He took in a deep, cleansing breath. He finally made it out.

"Excuse me?" said Theo to the woman next to him. "Where's this bus going?"

"Atlantic City."

"Atlantic City, New Jersey!?" Theo asked, incredulous.

He squinted behind him at the passengers. A gaggle of wrinkled faces stared back at him. Most had lanyards around their necks with a "777 Senior VIP Tour" logo.

"Crucible's in Jersey?" Theo said to nobody in particular. He laughed to himself.

Conversations swirled around him. No one seemed particularly interested he was there. Topics ranged from which slots were luckiest to when was best to attack the buffet.

One Atlantic City regular seemed to take pity on his plight and offered him a juice box. It was beyond delicious.

As rolling hills gave way to bluffs, Theo watched the sun rise over flat-top rock ridges. He was exhausted by the week he had been through. Finally, he laid his head back.

The next time he opened his eyes, he was in the back of an ambulance with two mustachioed medical attendants staring at him with a knowing smile.

"What happened? Where am I?" asked Theo.

The attendants didn't acknowledge Theo, and he began to wonder if he had even spoken the words aloud. He tried again, "This isn't the bus to Atlantic City?"

He checked himself over. Same clothes. Same bruises. Same wrist cuffs. Yet the bus and kindly old ladies ceased to exist. He felt an epic migraine coming on as every bruise on his body screamed to life.

"I could really use some aspirin," Theo said, already knowing there would be no response. From then on, he decided to keep all his thoughts and opinions to himself.

As they drove in silence, Theo admired the ambulance's neatly organized drawers and hidden compartments. *I wonder if that's where they're keeping all those lovely old ladies.*

Finally, the ambulance stopped. An attendant with thinning hair opened the back door, bathing the cabin in golden sunlight. Theo had a perfectly framed view of Town Square Park, with the ancient ponderosa glowing front and center. Another attendant, with blue nitrate gloves, helped Theo out of the gurney and onto the sidewalk. Beyond any rational explanation, he was back in Crucible.

Theo's first reaction was to scream, but he couldn't find his voice. He thought of running, but his body wouldn't move. A day ago, this stress level would have him burst into flames. Now there was only calm. He felt like he was a guest in his own body, resigning himself to be an observer rather than a participant in the events unfolding before him.

It was a beautiful day on Main Street; robins were singing, and squirrels were chasing each other around trees. Young couples were out with their babies and walking their dogs. A group of kids pedaled by on their bicycles as they rode toward the library. One bike looked more than familiar.

The cute salesclerk at the American BullShirt Shop was bobbing along to music in her earbuds as she changed the window display. Theo remembered the store burning, but there it stood, pristine and polished.

Somewhere, jingle bells jangled.

"Hi, honey!"

Theo turned to see Dr. Limley wheeling his mother Alice out of a single-story office building. The jingling bells were coming from the office door.

Alice was in a hospital gown with bandages covering her left arm and face.

"Mom!" exclaimed Theo.

He ran toward her and threw himself into her arms.

She held him tight and stroked his hair. "You ready to go home?"

EPILOGUE

Theo laid his foot on the pedal—not expecting the car to take off with such oomph as it rocketed forward with the force of a precision V8 performance sport package.

"Theo, watch out!" Alice shouted.

Theo slammed the brakes as his front tire hopped into a parking block. He and his mom both jolted forward against the seatbelts.

"Sorry . . . I don't know what happened." Lost in his thoughts, Theo stared out the windshield and watched heat waves rise off the asphalt of Main Street. It had a just-pressed sheen, as if it had been recently repaved.

"You're doing fine . . . ." Alice said, "just, please try to watch the road." She smiled with a tinge of pain as she touched the fresh bandage on her left cheek. "And dividers."

"The doc said you should get plenty of rest; I could have driven to the store myself," Theo stated defensively.

Arguing in a car felt very familiar and brought a wistful sense of déjà vu.

"Sorry, honey. You only have a provincial license issued by the town. A licensed driver must always be present," she said as she leaned over and kissed her son.

Dr. Limley had told them that Alice would be shaky for a while following the accident—she had been under his observation since they were t-boned near Town Square Park heading back from the Gala. Limley reminded Theo that he was lucky his injuries weren't as severe. What Limley didn't explain was how they could have been in a car accident while never owning a car—until now—in Crucible.

"Just take it slow on the way back home." And Theo drove, just as his mother asked.

At the edge of the park, waiting for the light to change, Theo glanced at the school. He kept playing over the chain of events from the night starting at the school to the point where he woke up in the back of an ambulance. The more time passed, though, the more everything became jumbled and stopped making sense.

At the school, Theo noticed a group of kids sitting on a patch of grass near the flagpole. His eyes sparked with recognition: It was Shivansh, Fernando, and Anita.

As Theo drove past, the newly waxed gleam of the Jeep caught their attention. Anita and Shivansh made brief eye contact before returning to their conversation. Only Fernando kept on glaring as if to send a warning.

"Do you know those kids?" asked Alice.

"I used to."

"We're here," announced Theo as they pulled into the driveway of their tract home. "Let me get you in the house, Mom. Then I'll bring the groceries in." He noticed someone on the front porch with their back turned to him. Although he couldn't see their face, he'd recognize those gold sweatpants anywhere. "Jerry?" said Theo. His hands trembled as he unbuckled himself. He couldn't account for why he felt such a surge of emotions—he was both excited and nervous to see them.

"Who's that?" said Alice. "I feel like I've met her—"

"They, Mom. It's Jerry. You introduced them to me at school, remember?"

"Oh, right. Yes, of course," said Alice. But she didn't remember; she felt embarrassed and was doing a clumsy job of trying to cover.

Jerry appeared at his mother's door. "Hi, Ms. Alexander . . . let me help you out."

"So good to see you again, Jerry," said Alice.

"Same here," replied Jerry. "Theo and I have a lot of catching up to do."

✘

The evening was settling in, and the sky glowed in rich hues of orange and pink. Jerry and Theo sat in the backyard near a row of withered planters under a once-proud oak tree now infested with wilt. Alice was back inside, falling fast asleep almost as soon as they'd arrived home.

Theo stared at Jerry with a puzzled look as the shadows of leaves danced on their face with the dying light of a summer day.

Something wasn't adding up in his mind. He felt like there was a piece of him someplace else, but he couldn't put his finger on why. "So what's it been? About a month?"

"Try longer. I didn't know if you were alive or dead until a week ago," said Jerry.

Theo was taken aback at Jerry's show of emotion; he felt terrible about how good it felt to be missed on such a deep level.

"Sorry about that. I've been trying to keep a low profile" Theo replied. "How much do you remember?"

"I don't recall anything after the Mirror Men."

"But you still have some memories? You still remember me, you still remember us. That's more than I can say about the rest of the group."

Jerry paused for a second, searching for the correct answer, "I guess my dad raised me to be resilient."

"I see you remember things, too," Jerry continued, defensively.

Theo's pause to this question was more protracted than Jerry's. Then, in a confessional tone: "I made it out," Theo stated. "I survived a meeting your father and made it out of Crucible."

"What? You made it out?" Jerry jumped up, both surprised and annoyed. "Why did you come back?"

"I didn't . . . . I mean, I didn't want to. I was in a tank, broke free, and made it to the surface. There was a bus, and I was on my way to Atlantic City, then I was in an ambulance. Next thing I know, I'm back in Crucible. I know it sounds ridiculous," said Theo, shaking his head. "You believe me, don't you?"

"I believe you believe," Jerry sincerely answered.

Their hands touched; Theo fought his nerves and softly lifted Jerry's chin, looking them in the eye as they fell into a kiss. It sent shock waves through his body. His heart pounded and his skin tingled from beads of sweat.

"Come to my room, I want to show you something."

Jerry pulled back and shot Theo an incredulous look. "I was wrong. I think your mind is still a little scrambled."

"No! Not like that!" Theo, wildly uncomfortable, flushed with embarrassment. "Please, just follow me."

Theo led Jerry up the stairs into his room, and Jerry was surprised how much Theo had settled in. Theo had been fighting Crucible since he arrived; he wondered, by inviting Jerry to his room, was this a sign he had given up and was resigned to making this place his home.

Theo immediately corrected that assumption. “Crucible kept stealing my memories, so I’m surrounding myself with nothing but memories—things I love and treasure most.”

On the wall, he’d made a collage, a cornucopia of images and memories no one would ever steal from him again. There were photos, taken from a distance, of all his friends, hoping they would one day remember and make new ones together. They were mixed in with pictures of his mother and articles on his father he’d sneaked out of the library.

And in the center of it all was Jerry.

“Because you matter most, and I never want to forget you ever again.”

Jerry took it all in; Theo’s heart and emotions were on the wall for everyone to see. Then, without saying a word, they turned and moved to the bedroom door. Not to leave, but to close it.

It was Jerry’s turn to kiss Theo. A kiss so deep and sensual it took his breath away.

“So, where do we go from here?” Theo said, looking longingly into Jerry’s eyes.

"Anywhere we want," they paused to answer before kissing him again.

For Theo, and for this moment, that was good enough.

THE END, for now.

ABOUT THE AUTHOR

Photo by Mitch Haddad

For nearly twenty years, Dan DiDio served DC Comics in several roles, during which, his innovation and energy made him synonymous with the characters and publishing line.

Dan DiDio joined DC in January 2002 as Vice President of Editorial and quickly ascended into the role of Senior Vice President/Executive Editor of DC Comics one year later. In that position, he directed the creative development and helped contemporize the superhero line of titles to bring increased relevancy and diversity to the line. He was also responsible for attracting some of comics' top talent to DC and locking them into exclusive contracts to ensure quality books for years to come.

DiDio was also an accomplished writer at DC Comics, having created and redeveloped several comic series at DC, including Sideways, OMAC, Phantom Stranger, and, Metal Men.

In 2010, DiDio was named Publisher of DC Entertainment alongside Jim Lee. As Publisher, he directed and oversaw DC Entertainment's entire publishing business under its key three imprint—DC, Vertigo, and MAD. Currently, Dan is partnered with comic and media legend, Frank Miller, and together they started their own publishing line, Frank Miller Presents, for which he created and writes the new series, Ancient Enemies.